The Geriatric Vigilante

By David Nesbitt

This book is dedicated to the woman who is my unfailing support in all that I do. Her comments and criticisms have improved this story immeasurably. So thank you to my wonderful wife Sue – for everything.

Preface

Mr Spurgeon is a very old fashioned man. Brought up in a close knit family by loving parents, their black and white views on life still govern his behaviour, although he is now in his seventies. He inherited their strict moral code and deplores more or less everything in the modern world, with the possible exception of radio four extra. He lives alone with his cat in a small terraced house and leads a dull and somewhat lonely life.

Dull, that is, until the bank he trusted with his life savings did something he considered dishonest. The bank, of course, would admit no wrongdoing and steadfastly refused to credit his account with the interest he should have received. Outraged by their cavalier attitude towards a loyal customer of many years standing, Mr Spurgeon takes his revenge, on the person he considered responsible, the bank manager. He does this in a terrible and permanent fashion that baffles the police. His first successful murder triggers a killing spree that sees the less savoury denizens of the town falling like saplings in a gale.

Due to his frailty and advanced years, each murder has to be meticulously planned and executed in a way that demands original thinking but doesn't demand too much in the way of strength or stamina. Mr Spurgeon is very much up to meeting this challenge and has the police scratching their heads in a combination of bemused admiration for his cunning and frustration at their inability to apprehend the Geriatric Vigilante.

Chapter 1

Mr Spurgeon sat patiently waiting for the security guards to evict him from the bank. He had made sure that he was smartly dressed for his visit, his shoes gleamed, the creases in his trousers crisply defined, his sports jacket carried a Royal British Legion enamel poppy badge in its lapel. His small, neatly trimmed moustache that had once been brown was now the same silver colour as his hair. On his head he wore a smart Harris tweed cap. Under the cap he wore a determined look on his slightly weather-beaten face. As he waited he read a poster that advertised incredibly high interest rates on loans and correspondingly low rates for mortgages, all provided with customer service of the highest order. He wondered how a huge multinational organisation such as his bank, which he had considered to be highly respectable, could get away with such blatant deceit.

That was the trouble with the country these days, no standards, not like the old days. They thought because they were big they could get away with anything, and up until a few days ago Mr Spurgeon had trusted them implicitly. He had opened his account at the bank with a single pound note that had comprised almost his entire first week's wage packet and now he was seventy-five years old. His loyalty to the organisation though seemed to count for nothing. All the staff wanted to do was sell him things he didn't need so that they could earn bonuses and commission. That was why he was constantly pestered by fast talking idiots on the telephone who wanted him to claim back PPI or some such set of initials. They were almost as bad as the automatic messages asking him if he had had an accident that he could claim for and telling him he could be paid thousands of pounds. Legalised vampires, leeching off naïve people who weren't bright enough to tell them to go away and pester someone else.

This was Mr Spurgeon's fifth visit to the bank since he had discovered that his ISA savings account was attracting a measly 0.1 per cent interest and not the 4.5 per cent it had promised when he had bundled all his ISA's into one on the advice of a lovely, friendly girl who had chatted to him about financial planning. All he wanted was for the manager to acknowledge that there had been a mistake and to credit his account with the missing interest. Surely that wasn't too much to ask?

Unfortunately, the manager refused to see him and had sent an underling to explain to Mr Spurgeon that the change of rate had been advertised in the Guardian so he had no excuse for not knowing that the bank had exercised its prerogative to alter rates without notice. It was his account and his responsibility to make himself aware of any rate changes. *The Guardian*, he thought with contempt. The Guardian wasn't Mr Spurgeon's favourite newspaper, he considered it an amateurish left wing rag, only fit for wrapping up fish and chips. Mr Spurgeon could have thought of another use for it but he liked to consider himself a gentleman of the old school and although such a thought might cross his mind it would never pass his lips. He read the Daily Telegraph and prided himself on completing the cryptic crossword puzzle on most days of the week. He religiously sent off his completed prize crossword first thing on Monday mornings but had yet to win the prize pen he coveted.

On entering the foyer of the bank he had once again politely requested an interview with the manager and been turned down flat. He had taken a seat and informed the young lady who had told him of the manager's decision not to grant him an interview that he would sit in the bank until the manager came out to go home and he would speak to him then. He hadn't raised his voice or used inflammatory language when he told her of his decision to remain, that was not his way of conducting himself. He was studiously courteous, despite his feelings of anger at the way the bank was treating him. He had standards.

She was a sweet girl and after he had sat calmly in the small reception area for an hour or so, she had returned and told him that if he didn't leave within the next few minutes he would be removed by security. She was obviously unhappy at having to tell him the news and he politely told her not to worry about him but informed her that he was intent on remaining exactly where he was until he saw the bank manager.

When they arrived a few minutes later and saw the slight figure sitting quietly in the waiting area the two guards seemed to be a little uncomfortable with their mission and spoke to Mr Spurgeon quite civilly when they told him he had to leave. Mr Spurgeon was just as polite when he explained that he simply wanted the money that the bank had swindled from him and he wasn't going to leave until he had a promise that his account would be credited with the appropriate sum.

Without a further word the security men each took Mr Spurgeon by an elbow and escorted him briskly from the premises. Mr Spurgeon while not exactly in his dotage was frail and slightly built with only the strength of an average septuagenarian. All was going smoothly with his eviction until the guard on Mr Spurgeon's left slipped on a burger box that a thoughtless consumer had thrown down in the doorway of the bank. The hapless security man fell backwards and dragged Mr Spurgeon down with him. Mr Spurgeon in turn pulled the other guard to the pavement and the three of them sprawled in an untidy heap. Mr Spurgeon's folder containing all his notes was taken by the wind and his precious papers were dispersed the length of the High Street.

Mr Spurgeon's hip hurt where he had landed on it and his elbow was giving him gyp. The headache that had been plaguing him on and off for weeks had returned and his vision was a little blurred. The younger of the security men looked down at him as he struggled to regain his breath.

"You OK Granddad?" He enquired, concern evident from his tone.

Granddad! Granddad! I'm not his bloody granddad. Mr Spurgeon was badly shaken by his fall or he would never have allowed an expletive to enter his head. No standards anymore. They obviously didn't even know his name. They knew him well enough to lay hands on his person and forcefully remove him from the bank but they hadn't been told his name. He wasn't a person, he was just a nuisance, not important to the bank or its employees in any way. They had the money they had conned out of him and they were going to keep it.

That was when Mr Spurgeon decided he had been pushed as far as he would go. The bank had to be punished and made to regret its uncaring attitude. If they wouldn't give him the money they owed him he would have to emulate Shylock and have his pound of flesh. There was only one thing for it, he would kill the bank manager. That would make them regret exploiting people who didn't read the Guardian!

Chapter 2

The nice girl who had dealt with him had rushed from the bank and helped Mr Spurgeon to his feet. She had wanted to send him home in a taxi or to send him to the hospital to be checked over but he had refused her offers of assistance politely but firmly and walked, with as much dignity as he could muster, to the bus stop where he caught the number sixteen home. He was a little shaky and the bus driver had asked him if he was alright when he had paid his fare. He had thanked him for his concern but assured him that he was fine. It appeared that not everyone had embraced the modern way of not caring about anyone other than number one and that cheered Mr Spurgeon as the bus trundled away from the town centre and towards his stop.

He was glad it was late morning as that meant the bus was only carrying shoppers returning home after visiting the shopping centre. He dreaded having to catch the bus when schoolchildren from the local comprehensive were travelling. The language that they used so casually would have brought a blush to the cheeks of his old sergeant major when he was in the territorials. And the way they behaved! Lounging around, putting their feet onto the seats where other people would have to sit, eating burgers or chips and throwing their litter onto the floor of the bus. And they were so rude if you mentioned their behaviour to them. No respect for their elders at all. One girl had even told him to f*** off and when he had seen her meet her mother when she alighted from the bus he had approached the parent and informed her of what had happened. He didn't get the response he had hoped for, she had told him to mind his own f***ing business and leave her girl alone and had then gone off into a rant about old men pestering schoolgirls. Mr Spurgeon had made a rapid departure before the mother started using the dreaded paedophile word. What a world he was living in, he sometimes felt like a stranger in his own land.

It wasn't that immigrants that bothered him although foreigners in general were to be treated with deep suspicion. Especially the French. No, he had some neighbours who hailed from the sub-continent and they were always pleasant to him and their children were unfailingly polite. Bindhi and Prem at the local post office cum general stores were always cheerful and passed the time of day and it was a pleasure to enter their crammed to the rafters store. It was his fellow countrymen and women with whom he had a problem.

It seemed to him that the country was in a total mess. The people with the money made it by unscrupulous methods, exploiting the less financially astute people like him to line their pockets. There was a huge underbelly of people who would not work and sponged off the state so that they could go to the pub and buy cigarettes instead of getting a job and standing on their own two feet. Politicians were worse, the scandal over their expenses had finally disillusioned Mr Spurgeon to the extent that he now refused to vote at all on the grounds that it might encourage them. He was not a religious man but he considered that the moral collapse of the country was largely to do with the Church of England employing vicars with beards who played the guitar instead of preaching the ten commandments to their ever diminishing flocks.

Mr Spurgeon was roused from his thoughts when Mrs Dalrymple from over the way spoke to him. "Come on Mr Spurgeon, you can't sit there dreaming, this is our stop."

He thanked her and hurriedly rose from his seat to leave the bus, remembering to say thank you to the driver as he alighted from the vehicle. Good manners cost nothing his father used to say but you'd think they cost the earth the way there were used so sparingly these days.

*****

He let himself into his little two bedroomed terraced house that was located in what had once been a respectable neighbourhood. The area was still just about alright but parts of it were decidedly run down and a couple of houses hadn't seen a lick of paint in years. Mr Spurgeon shook his head as he filled the kettle for a nice cup of tea. His cat, Lady Mae, so named because she was too snooty to eat canned or dried cat food and had to be fed a diet of fish or chicken, occasionally supplemented with a premium pouch of something in jelly, wrapped herself around his legs and meowed piteously to remind him it was time for her to be fed.

He reached down and scratched her behind her ears before opening the fridge to get her some chicken left over from his Sunday lunch. He talked to the cat as he chopped up the slightly dry breast. "You are a lucky cat you know. It's only lonely old bachelors like me with no family to speak of other than a nephew that I only see once in a blue moon who would treat you like this. I feed you better than I do myself." He added untruthfully for Mr Spurgeon as a lifelong bachelor was an adept in the kitchen, he had had to learn to cook if he wanted a decent meal to come home to after a hard day at the office. Mr Spurgeon wasn't a confirmed bachelor in the sense that he was not homosexual but he had never been terribly interested in women either. He had enjoyed (if that is the right word) sexual congress with one or two young ladies when he was a young man but had not particularly enjoyed the experience and had resorted to very occasional self-abuse when his urges became too much for him to bear. He was glad those urges had disappeared many years ago and he no longer felt the need to sully himself.

He sometimes wished that he had a companion when he wanted to talk about something that was in the paper or if the television programme he was watching was interesting or funny. That didn't happen often these days either. There was so much swearing in the so called comedy shows that he couldn't bring himself to watch them. Not that they were particularly funny anyway, it seemed that modern comedy was about being unnecessarily cruel to people in the news or it was a lad who looked about twelve years of age, (although he usually needed a shave), lecturing people about how he thought the world should be run. No life experience and too stupid to realise that he was making an idiot of himself by trying to tell people like Mr Spurgeon that all things left wing were perfect and Mrs Thatcher (whom Mr Spurgeon adored) had been an evil witch who had deserved to die in agony.

As for the police shows, the English ones were OK but the American ones were utter rubbish. Hundreds of formulaic episodes churned out to be viewed by uneducated and gullible Americans and bought by British TV companies because they were cheap. As for the so called celebrity programmes Mr Spurgeon was at a loss to understand their attraction, perhaps if he had ever heard of one of the celebrities that featured in them he might have made a connection to the show but he had no idea who any of these people were. Worst of all was a programme he had heard one of his neighbour's mention. The Jeremy Kyle Show. Mr Spurgeon had watched it in horrified amazement for almost ten minutes before firmly clicking the off button and vowing never to look at it again. Those awful people!

As Mr Spurgeon made himself a cheese and chutney (and what had happened to PanYan pickle?) sandwich he thought over the morning's events and his resentment at his treatment. As he mused his determination to teach those evil so-and-sos at the bank a lesson grew exponentially. He took his sandwich and cup of tea into the sitting room, his mother had called it the parlour and most people would have called it a lounge but to Mr Spurgeon it was, and always would be, the sitting room. His mother would have been pleased to see that he kept it as clean and tidy as she had, a place for everything and everything in its place had been another of her sayings that he had heard a thousand times. The small china cabinet that had been her pride and joy still sat against the wall and still contained the same pieces of china that she had purchased over the years as treasured souvenirs of seaside holidays taken every August in Skegness. There was an easy chair that matched the sofa and a small side table upon which he placed his cup and saucer, no mugs in this house he thought smugly, I have standards. A television sat in the corner of the room and a Roberts digital radio which he habitually referred to as the wireless, sat on a bookshelf in the alcove at the side of the fireplace. It suited him perfectly. He mused that this room had been his mother's territory and he had always felt at home in it but his father's workshop had been the place that he had loved best as a child. Located at the bottom of the small back garden it was a sturdy brick construction with a tiled roof. Inside there was a pot-bellied wood burning stove, a workbench set before the window and shelves containing all the paraphernalia that a watch repairer and inveterate tinkerer could ever want. Even now, twenty years after his father had passed into the great beyond he could still find a screw to replace a missing one from a household gadget. As a child he had loved to sit by the stove watching his father work on clocks and watches that needed repair and listening to his wise words about the world and people in general.

    He sat on an overstuffed old fashioned sofa holding his plate beneath his chin to catch any crumbs as he munched on his sandwiches. His hip ached and he thought he would probably have a large bruise in the morning. His elbow was much better though and he thought the pain there would have disappeared altogether by morning. His thumping headache had receded but he was used to the constant dull pain that occasionally erupted into lightning bolts of pain that incapacitated him for a few minutes. He had considered going to the doctor but had decided that going to the surgery for something as minor as a headache would be verging on hypochondria. Besides the new fellow who had taken over Doctor Bland's practice was foreign and he struggled to understand what he said. All in all, better just to swallow a couple of painkillers and put his feet up with a cup of tea for a few minutes. That usually did the trick. Lady Mae had followed him into the room and sat curled up next to him purring gently. He spoke to her softly between bites, telling her all about the bank and its very rude manager. She snuggled against him as though in empathetic understanding of his situation.

"What I have to do now Lady Mae, is find out more about the swine. I can't kill him at the bank unless I want to spend the few years I have left on this earth locked up in prison and I'd sooner not do that. How can I find out where he lives?"

Lady Mae meowed and he gazed at her benignly as he thought about his plan to kill the bank manager. He decided that he needed a list of things that would help to solve his problem. An action plan the twelve year olds who ran the country would have called it.

The bank manager's name.

Where he lived.

If he had a family.

How did he travel to and from the bank?

Did he go out in the evenings?

He looked over the list. That seemed to be about it. Once he had got that information he could move on with his plan by deciding on the method of execution. Not murder. Murder was a nasty crime committed by criminals or drug addicts. He wasn't a murderer, he was an executioner, a nemesis, a bringer of justice, a righter of wrongs.

Mr Spurgeon did not own a computer, so to do some research on the internet he needed to pay a visit to the local library. It was running on reduced opening hours and was under the threat of closure but they had computers that the public could use and he had used a computer for stock control before he retired so he thought he would have no problem in getting the information that he needed.

The following day Mr Spurgeon entered his local library and greeted Mrs Dacre the librarian with a friendly hello.

"Hello Mr Spurgeon, this isn't your regular day to visit us, have you got through that Margery Allingham already?"

"No, Mrs Dacre. I am really enjoying re-reading the Albert Campion novels but I haven't finished the current one yet. I am here to use one of your computers to find some information on the world wide web thingy."

"You know where to find them don't you, we've had a little change around and they are in the side room that used to be the children's library."

Mr Spurgeon thanked her gracefully and walked in the direction indicated. He looked at the rows of shiny boxes full of technological wizardry of which he had not the remotest understanding and wondered why the county council saw fit to supply these expensive gadgets when the book stock was seldom refreshed and the opening hours cut. This was supposed to be a *library* not a branch of PC World. The council were useless, the men and women who had stood for election years ago had largely done it as a means of public service but nowadays it was a paid position and local councillors just seemed to want to have their snouts in the trough of public money and all thought of community service had disappeared. They spent his rates on subsidising lesbian workshops and gay encounter groups (whatever they were, anyway they didn't sound very wholesome), instead of supporting this wonderful library. Perhaps when he had seen to the bank manager he would turn his attention to a councillor or two?

Mr Spurgeon drew up a seat and accessed the internet. He went immediately to the bank's web site and clicked on the "All about us" button. He entered the address of his branch and gazed in admiration at new technology in action as the screen immediately filled with a photograph of the bank's employees. His target was standing in the middle of his staff wearing an expression of smug self-satisfaction that Mr Spurgeon instantly wanted to remove, possibly with the judicious application of a house brick.

Below the photograph were the names and job titles of all those pictured. So, his target was called Darren Bentley. Bent more like, he mumbled as he memorised the name, and *Darren*! What sort of a name is *Darren* for a bank manager? It was a very common name, people who lived in the council flats were called Darren or Jason or some-such. Bank Manager's should be called George or John or Tom, something properly English and reassuring. They could even once have been called Horace, as he was, without being mocked.

He thought of checking the electoral role but swiftly discounted that idea. People were listed by their address and he would have had to peruse all of the registers to be sure of locating his man. Mr Spurgeon was not about to give up at the first hurdle and thought a little more. Know your enemy, isn't that what they say, and Mr Spurgeon thought he knew how a jumped-up, pompous, patronising so and so like Darren Bentley would perceive himself. He looked up the local Rotary Club and sure enough Bentley was listed as Vice President and President Elect for the coming year. The Rotary Club met fortnightly at the Camform Arms Hotel and their next scheduled meeting was for that night.

Chapter 3

That evening Mr Surgeon wrapped up warmly, making sure that his cardigan was fully buttoned under his jacket before donning his coat. It might well be early summer but June nights could turn cold and he might have some waiting to do as he watched for his target to arrive. He put a packet of extra strong mints, a notebook and a pencil into his coat pocket, double checked that everywhere was secure, poured a saucer of milk for Lady Mae and set out to walk to the Camford Arms.

The walk would normally have only taken him about thirty minutes but his hip was sore and it took him almost twice that length of time before he saw the hostelry as he exited the side road. It was sitting in all its Victorian gothic splendour at one side of a large car park, lights were shining through the bay windows of its frontage and twin towers pointed skywards. A chalkboard was propped near the entrance of the hotel advertising "Tonight's Specials" and a distinct odour of frying fish permeated the air as he strolled casually across to the solid wooden door that led into the reception area.

He stopped and looked down at the chalkboard, trying to look as if he were a potential customer who was torn between the choices of "Fish in Beer Batter" or "Cumberland Sausages with Mash and Onion Gravy." He shifted his glance towards a brass plate that was fixed to the wall next to the door and read the engraved words.

Clingford Norton Rotary Club meet here in the Imperial Room at 6.45pm on the second and fourth Monday of every month.

He looked down at his watch. It was 7.30pm. It was a good watch, his parents had given it to him for his twenty-first birthday and it still kept perfect time. He gave it a clean every now and then to maintain it in good order and was proud that his father had passed on the knowledge that had enabled him to clean and repair a watch while he was scarcely tall enough to see onto the workbench. He hadn't followed his father into the trade though. By the time he had finished grammar school it was fairly obvious that cheap throwaway watches made by the likes of Timex were the future and watch repairing was a dying trade. Nowadays, of course, watches were digital and covered in extra little dials that told you that you were fifty feet below sea level or what the time was on the moon or some-such useless nonsense. If you were fifty feet beneath the sea you would be dead and have absolutely no interest in what the time was on the moon or anywhere else for that matter he thought, as he once more despaired of the modern world.

He shuffled about, trying to give the impression to any casual observers that he couldn't make up his mind before turning on his heel and strolling slowly down the road in the direction from which he had arrived. This time he looked at the cars that almost filled the large car park. Almost all were new or nearly new and tended towards the solid and respectable end of the market. Jaguars, BMW's and Mercedes Benz were in the ascendency with the odd Lexus or Prius intermingled. He wondered which one belonged to Bentley. He found a spot at the edge of the car park which was almost completely screened by shrubs and small trees and sat down on the low wall that separated the pub from the adjacent house.

Satisfied that he was invisible to all but the most perceptive observer he waited patiently for Bentley to leave the hotel. If he was noticed and challenged to explain himself, he would simply say that he was getting on in years, had walked further than was sensible and was merely resting before he returned to his home. He stared at the exit door that led into the car park with fierce intensity, determined that his quarry would not escape his notice. He was certain that Bentley would have arrived by car and just hoped that no-one had given the swine a lift to the meeting.

Around an hour after he had installed himself in his observation post there was a general exodus from the hotel. Groups of overly cheerful men, who probably shouldn't have been driving in Mr Spurgeon's opinion, entered the car park wishing each other loud good nights before climbing into their vehicles.

Mr Spurgeon waited with bated breath as he observed the Rotarians leaving but of Bentley there was no sign. Just as he was about to give up and plod his weary way home he spotted his target exiting the hotel. He walked over to a brand new Lexus that was parked at the rear of the car park under overhanging trees, evidently in an attempt to keep the car out of the warm evening sunshine, and drove rapidly away. But Mr Spurgeon now had his car registration number entered in his notebook and had noticed that his direction of travel was towards the outskirts of the town. If he lived in Clingford Norton there was only one area that would be upmarket enough to satisfy that man's social ambitions. The Friars Lodge Estate. The up-market estate consisted of individually built four and five bedroom houses that were way beyond the means of the vast majority of the residents of the town. An amble around the estate should enable him to locate Bentley's address. Of course, he could live further out in one of the villages but Mr Spurgeon considered that was unlikely. A pompous swine like Bentley would want to live amongst those he perceived as his own kind, not amongst the homogenous social mix to be found in a village.

More than content with his evening's work Mr Spurgeon rose from his seat and stretched his tired muscles before commencing the long journey home.

When he eventually arrived at the house his feet hurt and his hip was quite painful. The return journey had taken twice as long as the outward trip and his feet ached terribly. He slipped off his shoes, pulled on his comfy old carpet slippers and removed his coat and jacket, hanging them neatly on the hallway hooks, before walking through to the kitchen. Lady Mae followed him, purring as she rubbed herself against his legs.

"Careful, you silly girl, you'll trip me up and then where would you be then? Who would wait on you hand and foot if I broke my ankle?" That should be hand and paw he thought and chuckled to himself as he put the last of the leftover chicken into her dish. He filled the kettle and switched it on for a nice cup of tea before almost immediately switching it off again. Tonight was a special occasion and he would have a wee glass of whisky both to celebrate his discoveries and to revive him after his long walk.

He took his small glass of Famous Grouse into the sitting room and retrieved his notebook and pencil from his coat pocket. He took his habitual place on the sofa and began to think.

He wrote MUST NOT GET CAUGHT across the top of a fresh page. He had used capital letters to underline the seriousness of his intent. He did not intend to go to prison for what he considered to be a completely justifiable homicide. Below that he wrote possible methods of execution and followed it with all the different ways he could think of to kill a man. Next to each item on his list he wrote either "No", and the reason why not or "Possible" and no other remarks because these were the methods to which he would have to give deeper consideration.

Strangulation: NO. Not strong enough.

A blow to the head: NO. Couldn't be sure to knock him down with the first blow.

Shooting: NO. No gun and have only ever fired a rifle.

Stabbing: NO. Couldn't be sure to kill with the first strike.

Poison: Possible.

Sabotage his car: Possible.

An accident: Possible

Drowning: NO. Can't swim and he perhaps can.

Running him down with a car: Possible.

Electrocution: Possible

Bomb: NO. Could make one but have no access to high explosives.

Fire: Possible

He found himself jotting down 'push him off a cliff' before scoring it out and telling himself he was getting carried away and descending into the realms of fantasy. He scored through each of the items he had ruled out and wrote each possible method at the top of a new page. He had five pages, five possible methods to inflict the punishment that Bentley and his kind deserved.

POISON

Mr Spurgeon was an avid reader and a great fan of detective fiction. As well as Margery Allingham he had read all the works of; Agatha Christie, Dorothy L Sayers, John Dixon Carr, Gladys Mitchell and many more, including his favourite modern author P D James. He had read all of her works and was particularly taken with her genuine knowledge of pathology. He knew that undetectable poisons were complete fiction and simply did not exist. Any poison he used would have to be easy to obtain like weed killer and preferably tasteless or having so small a flavour that it could be disguised by a strongly flavoured drink or meal. Curry would be good. He remembered from an Agatha Christie novel that eye drops that contained belladonna were poisonous if ingested but that didn't help at all. He knew that the common name for belladonna was deadly nightshade but he had no idea where he could find it growing or which parts of the plant were poisonous.

Then there was the difficulty of working out what would be a deadly dose and how he would get it into something that Bentley would ingest. Mr Spurgeon wrote down:

Which poison?

How to obtain it?

Dosage?

How to administer it?

Below that he wrote NO in capital letters and turned the page.

CAR SABOTAGE

Mr Spurgeon still maintained his own vehicle. He had bought his Morris Minor in the late sixties and had serviced and repaired it himself until he had decided at the age of seventy-two that driving in modern traffic was not something he wished to do any longer. He had been reluctant to part with his faithful old companion and kept it stored in a lock up garage located in the next street. He washed it every Sunday morning and kept it in sound running order against the day when he once more decided to take to the road. Mr Spurgeon knew about cars. The obvious thing to do would be to sabotage the brakes or steering, both of which he was fully capable of doing. He could carry out that operation in The Camford Arms car park while Bentley was inside with his jumped up friends from the Rotary Club. With a just a little bit of luck he would crash on the way home and the accident would be blamed on the drink he would undoubtedly have consumed during a convivial evening with his cronies. The problem was that modern vehicles had seat belts and airbags that inflated upon impact, so Bentley's chances of survival were probably quite high. Then there was the awful thought that the ghastly man might crash into another car or even pedestrians. He couldn't have the deaths of innocent people on his conscience, it was Bentley and Bentley alone who must suffer the consequences of his actions. He wrote NO once more at the bottom of the page.

ACCIDENT

He wondered what he had meant when he wrote that. Staging an accident was always easy in the books he read but pushing Bentley down a flight of stairs or under the wheels of a train or bus was simply not something he could imagine happening. He would be happy to do it, but how he was to orchestrate the circumstances that would give him the opportunity to carry out the execution defeated him. Again he appended NO to the bottom of the page.

RUNNING HIM DOWN WITH A CAR

He could certainly do that. Any damage to the Morris could be repaired or he could just leave the vehicle in storage where no-one would ever see it. There were problems though.

Would he be able to get up enough speed to kill Bentley? The Morris wasn't the fastest car on the road and would take some time to reach a speed which would guarantee success.

Would he be injured in the crash? Quite possible, Bentley was a big man and might be thrown on to the windscreen, finishing up on his lap.

Would the car be drivable afterwards?

The car was unusual these days and easily identifiable.

If it was damaged when he ran Bentley down he wouldn't be able to wash it on Sunday and that would draw attention to it.

If he couldn't use the Morris perhaps he could steal a car. Mr Spurgeon dismissed that thought immediately. He wasn't a thief, he had standards.

NO.

ELECTROCUTION

Mr Spurgeon certainly had the necessary skills to use electricity as a method of electrocution but that would only work in Bentley's home or office and Mr Spurgeon could not work out how he could gain access to either of those places. NO.

FIRE

Mr Spurgeon was down to his last possible way of executing Bentley and determined to give this one deep thought. He had been trained as a Fire Marshall when he had been working and now gave thanks to the Fire Officer who had taught him about how fire starts and spreads. Mr Spurgeon was a meticulous man who took his duties seriously and had paid great attention in the class room and had thoroughly enjoyed being able to use a fire extinguisher during the practical element of his course. There was something primeval about fire that sent a thrill of almost sexual excitement through his body.

Of course he could never set fire to Bentley's house or to the bank. There would be innocent people at the bank and even the reptilian Bentley was likely to have a family. He determined that he would construct an incendiary device and blow up Bentley's car when he entered it after the next Rotary Club meeting. If anyone else was injured in the ensuing explosion it would only be Rotarians and they were cut from the same cloth as Bentley and thus wouldn't count as innocent casualties.

Chapter 4

Mr Spurgeon retired to bed with his detective novel and a cup of cocoa. He read a few pages of his book, drank his cocoa and switched off the bedside lamp. He slept the sleep of the just, content that he was now moving his plan forward.

After breakfast Mr Spurgeon sat and thought about exactly how he would construct his incendiary device. He knew that modern cars had sophisticated locks and alarms to deter thieves so he would be unable to gain access to the interior of the vehicle. That left him with only one option. The device had to be placed beneath the vehicle and modern cars were low slung so putting a five gallon jerry can under it was out of the question. He needed something soft that would slide under the car and could be filled in situ. He decided that he needed to conduct a little experiment to test the materials he had in mind.

He left the house locking the back door behind him, you couldn't be too careful with all the criminals there were about these days, and walked down to his workshop. He carefully tipped a small quantity of petrol from the can he kept there to top his car up from time to time into a small metal container. He placed a metal tray onto his bench and positioned an empty plastic drink bottle, a plastic cup and a plastic wrapper that had contained his breakfast rashers and he had rescued from the waste bin onto it. He dribbled the petrol over the plastic items and stood back to watch the results of his experiment.

The plastic wrapper instantly began to dissolve. Dissolve not melt, Mr Spurgeon thought, pleased that his school science should come in useful after all these years. The other two items also dissolved but more slowly, but still far too quickly for his purposes. He discarded his first idea of using a child's inflatable paddling pool to hold the petrol and began to think anew.

He thought while he dusted and vacuumed, he thought as he prepared his lunch and he thought while he ate it. The paddling pool would have been ideal if it had been made of another material. At last an idea emerged from the recesses of his brain. Rubber!

Now, what sort of things were made out of rubber that would hold at least five gallons of petrol and were similar in shape to a paddling pool? An inflatable boat! The idea came to him in a flash of inspiration. It would have to be a small one but it should be possible to find one of the correct size. The detonating device would be child's play to construct with his handyman's knowledge. All he needed to create an explosion that would send Mr Bentley to meet his ancestors was a big enough spark. At last he had a plan.

Mr Spurgeon's knowledge of fictional crime now came to the fore. He knew that whatever he did, however fierce the fire that ensued there was likely to be forensic evidence that proved the explosion was deliberate. His task was now twofold, to commit the execution and to get away with it without leaving any evidence for the police to find.

He decided that his first task would be to take the train to the coast and purchase a suitable boat there. The police would be able to identify the type of boat he used, he was sure of that, but tracking down the many that were in private hands and locating the purchaser of one amongst many in a busy seaside resort should prove too much for the constabulary. Getting it home would be the hardest part. His neighbours would probably notice him entering his house carrying a bulky parcel and might remember this unusual event if questioned by the police. He would think about that later. More than content Mr Spurgeon hummed softly to himself as he rang the railway station to check on the times of trains to the coast. He was disconcerted to find that the voice that answered his call was a robot telling him he needed to press the buttons on his phone to take him through various options. Mr Spurgeon replaced the receiver in its cradle, he was too damned old for this world of science fiction and he was blessed if he would talk to some sort of automaton. He resolved to simply walk to the railway station and wait for the first train that would take him to his destination. He would probably have to wait for a good while but at least he would interact with human beings.

*****

The following morning, he alighted nimbly from the rather dirty train and was soon strolling casually around the harbour. He stopped occasionally to peer into the windows of shops selling cheap, and sometimes not so cheap, tourist tat. The town was very different from when his mother had brought him here as child when the lure of Skegness had palled. Now it was full of amusement arcades and cheap shops selling rubbish to gullible holidaymakers and day trippers. A funfair had been built where the Jubilee Gardens had once been located and a huge rollercoaster dominated the seafront. Extremely loud music already bellowed out of loudspeakers, the sound distorted by being over-amplified. The resort was a travesty of what it had once been and Mr Spurgeon decided to make haste to conclude his business and leave the resort as quickly as he could. Seaside resort he thought, more like the last resort.

Before long he found what he was looking for – an old fashioned ship's chandlers. He entered the shop and was stunned at the variety of goods they had managed to pack into a relatively small space. An assistant, seeing that he looked a little lost, approached him and asked if he could help.

"I'm looking for a small inflatable boat for my grandchildren. Nothing too fancy or expensive. It doesn't have to be seaworthy, just something they can take on the river for a paddle."

"Very good sir, we have a range of inflatables that would suit you, I think, would you step this way."

Mr Spurgeon was guided through the shop to the rear of the premises. He walked through an arch into a large selling area and saw a number of boats mounted on a side wall. Most were obviously far too big but there were two or three that would serve his purposes.

He allowed the sales assistant to explain the various features of the boats before selecting one that was low at the sides and just about big enough for a couple of teenagers to squeeze into. He paid for his purchase and asked if he could collect it a little later.

"No problem at all sir, we don't close until nine o'clock during the season."

Mr Spurgeon left the store and made his way to a branch of WH Smith where he purchased several sheets of wrapping paper that had pictures of birthday cakes and balloons printed on it and a sticky tape dispenser. He returned to the chandlers and collected his parcel, it was heavy but nothing he couldn't manage for a while. He carried his purchases to the seafront and took a seat in a shelter on the promenade so that the wind from the sea wouldn't interfere with his activities. He swiftly wrapped his package in the garish celebratory paper and gazed down to admire his work. Now if he was seen no-one would suspect a thing. Just an elderly man carrying a present for a young relative.

The journey home was uneventful apart from a young woman who talked constantly into her mobile telephone. The fixation that people had today with always being available to talk on the telephone amazed him. When he was young no-one had a telephone except business and professional people. If his mother had wanted to make a call she had walked to the telephone box in the next street but that was a very rare occasion indeed. Nowadays it appeared that people considered themselves so important that they couldn't be unobtainable even for a few minutes in case the world stopped revolving around them. Mr Spurgeon was glad that he didn't own one of those infernal devices. He was forced to listen to the girl's inane chatter about her boyfriend and what a wonderful fellow he was, apparently he could make love for hours but to Mr Spurgeon's horror that wasn't the way she described the act. She used the F word and went into graphic detail that Mr Spurgeon tried to blot out but failed, her piercing voice penetrating the mental wall that he tried in vain to erect between them. She ended the call by announcing that she was nearly at the train station and she would soon be home. Unbelievable! It was a railway station not a train station. These pernicious Americanisms were creeping in everywhere! Mr Spurgeon thought that was probably due to the startling number of dreadful American television programmes that filled the TV screens of the semi-educated morons that sat slack jawed night after night sucking in such rubbish. He blamed comprehensive schools for the decline in educational standards. The teachers were no example to the young people either, constantly striking for more money when they had the cushiest job in the world. The hours they worked made them more or less part timers. As for all their nonsense about lesson planning, that didn't fool him for an instant. All they had to do was write a lesson plan and they could simply use it again the following year. The laws of physics didn't change, Australia remained in the southern hemisphere and Henry the Eighth's six wives didn't suddenly increase to seven. As for marking, they were supposed to know all the answers and putting a tick or a cross at the bottom of a page wasn't his idea of work. Lazy, that's what teachers are, a good day's work would kill them. They had the life of Riley! Five hour working days, thirteen weeks holiday and days off for elections and so-called training days when they sat around drinking coffee and moaning about how hard done by they were. That's what happened when you went to school, then university and then teacher training college. Your entire life was spent grazing in the groves of academe. They had no experience of real life. His reverie was interrupted by the tinny voice of the train manager, or as Mr Spurgeon would say, guard, coming over the tannoy system. The journey seemed never ending and was made worse by the announcements that continually reminded customers that a buffet service was available or not to forget their personal items. To Mr Spurgeon's mind anyone who was daft enough to leave their belongings behind had only themselves to blame and deserved what they got, or in this case what they didn't get. As to the actual words that the guard used Mr Spurgeon despaired. *Customers!* We are *passengers,* not customers. These people really had absolutely no idea!

    At last his nightmare train journey was over and he slid gratefully into the back of a taxi, dumping the heavy parcel gratefully onto the seat beside him, glad to indulge in this unaccustomed luxury. He asked the taxi driver to drop him at the entrance to the block of garages where he kept the Morris Minor and took his package into his garage. He quickly stripped of the wrapping paper and removed the boat from its box. He tore the box into strips and, making sure that the blank sides were facing outwards, put them under his arm. He gathered up the wrapping paper, screwed it into a tight ball and placed it in his pocket. He carefully locked the up-and-over door behind him and made his way the short distance to his house. When he eventually reached and entered his little home it was with a sigh of relief, stage one had been completed.

✢✢✢✢✢

    For the next few days he did nothing but experiment with detonators until he was convinced that he had created one that would give off a strong enough spark to ignite the petrol vapour. It only required a nine-volt battery to give him the result he was looking for, in fact a smaller battery would probably have done the job just as well, but why take a chance on failure? He took the jerry can on his sack barrow to his usual filling station and filled it with unleaded petrol. He had toyed with opting for super unleaded, thinking that the higher octane would be more likely to ignite but decided against that idea as he was concerned that the attendant might notice the change in his routine. He returned to the lock up and decanted the contents into the Morris before visiting a different filling station to fill it up the jerry-can again. The car's petrol tank held six and a half gallons. He would need to leave sufficient fuel to get the Morris back to his garage and he would have to guess how much remained in the tank. Mr Spurgeon was not the kind of man who liked to guess at anything, so after a few moments thought, he inserted the rubber tube that he used to syphon petrol from the jerry-can into the car's tank when he needed to top up the fuel supply, into the jerry can. He transferred a measured gallon from the tank into a clean plastic bucket. Making sure he had exactly a gallon was a bit fiddly but he used a one pint measuring jug to ensure accuracy. He timed the operation at one minute twenty seconds. If he syphoned out five gallons it would take seven minutes and forty seconds. That was very acceptable. Mr Spurgeon looked forward to filling the rubber boat with ten gallons of highly inflammable unleaded petrol and blowing Bentley to kingdom come. The whole operation should take less than twenty minutes from when he arrived at the hotel to departing the car park and Bentley would make his departure from this world soon after that. Very satisfactory indeed.

*****

On the night of the Rotary club meeting Mr Spurgeon was fully prepared. He had picked up some disposable gloves from the Tesco Extra store along with his ordinary shopping. He had made certain that he was in the middle of a long queue to minimise the chances of being remembered by the checkout girl. Not that there was much chance she would have remembered him if he had tap danced down the aisle singing Lily of Laguna while juggling his shopping. She was totally uninterested in her work and was chewing gum in a slack jawed way his father would have abhorred. Mr Spurgeon Senior had disliked Americans with a vehemence that, when it surfaced, always surprised Mr Spurgeon Junior. His father had refused to allow chewing gum, coca cola or rock and roll music to cross the threshold of his home and when young Horace had once asked for some chewing gum he had been asked.

"What do you want that muck for? You're not a Yank."

And that was the end of that. Mr Spurgeon had sometimes wondered what had made his father so anti-American and if it had something to do with a woman. It wouldn't be his mother of course but perhaps one of his aunt's had become entangled with an American during the war and it had ended badly. The odd thing was his father had been addicted to all thing cowboy. He loved to read Zane Grey and if there was a western film on at the cinema he would always find time to see it. Cheyanne, Bronco Lane, Wagon Train and Rawhide were staple television viewing in the Spurgeon household. His father didn't seem to appreciate that cowboys were American.

He had burnt the cardboard box the boat had come in along with the instructions and wrapping paper at the bottom of his garden, ensuring that everything was totally consumed by the flames and the ashes well stirred to prevent forensics from discovering what had been burned.

Now he loaded the Morris with the boat, the jerry can, the length of hose and the detonator and promptly at seven o'clock he drove sedately to the Camford Arms.

Mr Spurgeon was in luck, Bentley had once more parked in the shade and there was a free space on either side of his vehicle. Mr Spurgeon drew the Morris up next to the car that he intended to blow up. He looked around for any signs of life but there was no-one in sight. He inspected the Lexus and felt a little sadness that he would be destroying such a beautiful car. Still you can't make an omelette without breaking eggs as his mother used to say.

He knelt on the tarmac and peered under the car. It was as he thought, there was enough room for the boat. His plan would definitely work. He clambered up from his kneeling position and gave a little groan. His knees weren't made for this sort of activity and were complaining at his unaccustomed position.

He pulled the already roughly flattened out boat from the back seat of the Morris and placed it on the ground next to the Lexus. He had taken the precaution of using the tyre inflator he used to keep the Morris's tyres fully inflated to partially inflate the boat in his garage so that the inside and outside of the boat didn't stick together and impede the efficient flow of petrol.

He pushed the boat beneath the vehicle until the small hole he had carefully cut adjacent to the air hole was just visible. It projected slightly from the passenger side but that did not concern Mr Spurgeon, he only had to deal with a driver. Mr Spurgeon inserted one end of his rubber hose into the petrol tank of the Morris and then sucked until the burning unpleasant taste of petrol filled his mouth. He clamped off the hose and spat the petrol on the ground as he fed the hose into the opening in the boat. He had made it a tight fit and he had reinforced it with a bicycle repair kit that he had found on one of the shelves in the workshop. Goodness knows how long the kit had been there but it had five shillings printed on the top, nevertheless the tin had been properly sealed and its contents were in perfect condition.

Now he looked around, checking that he was still unobserved. All was well and he decided to sit in his car and have a rest while the petrol flowed. He had carefully checked his watch as soon as the petrol began to flow and knew he could do nothing until the required quantity had been transferred. The minute hand moved remorselessly on and Mr Spurgeon checked every two minutes to ensure that the hose hadn't worked loose. When the time was right he transferred the hose to the jerry-can and once more waited but this time until the container was empty.

Now for the final part of his preparations. He had prepared a detonator by connecting a small motor that had once powered a toy car to a carton that he had filled with gunpowder. He had obtained the explosive by the simple means of carefully emptying out the contents of a box of fireworks that he had bought the previous year with the intention of giving them to his grand-nephews when his nephew Geoffrey brought his family to visit. On the morning of the proposed visit his nephew had phoned to say that something had come up and they wouldn't be able to come after all, but they would visit again soon, certainly before Christmas. It was now June and he hadn't seen or heard of them since the phone call, so the fireworks had still been under the stairs where he had put them for safe keeping.

The motor was attached to the nine-volt battery and two wires would connect when he sent a radio signal via the toy cars control panel. That would cause a spark igniting the gunpowder and thus the petrol vapour. Perhaps the gunpowder was unnecessary but it was best to be thorough he thought as he attached the detonator to the boat with some double sided sticky tape. Just like Blue Peter – here's one I prepared earlier, he thought and gave a grim chuckle of satisfaction as his deadly business was concluded.

He quickly entered his car and drove it to the side road he would be using to get home, then returned to sit on the wall that he had sat on two weeks before and waited for Bentley to leave the hotel. He thought he was far enough away to be safe when the car exploded and considered the slight risk of being injured by flying debris a chance worth taking if it meant he could watch Bentley being blown to perdition.

Just as before, the bank manager was late leaving the hotel and the car park was almost empty when he finally emerged. He strolled over to his vehicle as though he hadn't a care in the world. Another couple of minutes and you won't have, thought Mr Spurgeon as he watched his target walk up to the car and open the door. He stood for a moment and seemed to be sniffing the air. Perhaps he can smell the petrol Mr Spurgeon thought in a moment of apprehension. But he climbed into the Lexus, apparently dismissing any misgivings he might have had and turned on the ignition.

Mr Spurgeon pressed the red button on the control pad and watched the red light blink. For a long moment nothing happened. Mr Spurgeon held his breath, it had got to work. Suddenly an explosion boomed and a mass of flames shot into the air as the Lexus was lifted from the ground and turned into a fireball.

Mr Spurgeon smiled to himself and hopped down off the wall, suddenly feeling more sprightly than he had for years. He made his way across the road towards the Morris as a crowd of people rushed out of the Camford Arms to see what had happened. They were far too busy concentrating on the burning car to notice an old man making his way home.

Chapter 5

Detective Chief Inspector Cedric Miller was not having a good evening. He had been settled in front of the television watching Coronation Street when both his house phone and his mobile had rung simultaneously. He had just polished off a large portion of toad-in-the-hole and was sipping an after dinner brandy as he watched the goings on in Weatherfield when his mobile and house phone rang simultaneously. The twin calls could only mean one thing - trouble with a capital T. He cursed quietly to himself and felt the first signs of indigestion bubbling behind his over stretched waistband.

He heaved himself from the cushions that had moulded around his corpulent frame and waddled over to the house phone. He listened carefully to the message, told the caller to stop calling his mobile, instructed his long suffering wife that he had to go out and had left the house within seconds of putting down the phone.

Now he was looking down at the smoking remains of what had once been a nice car and thinking this was a complete bugger. He had donned the white overall, gloves and booties that were deemed essential apparel at a crime scene and looked like an overweight snowman. His retirement was only a few short weeks away and he had hoped that no major incident would disturb the tranquillity of his working life before he collected his clock or whatever retirement gift his colleagues intended to give him. He consoled himself that at least he wasn't an American cop. Any of those that were approaching retirement were inevitably shot and killed in the closing scenes of the film.

"So what do we know Sergeant?" He asked the thin figure hovering behind his left shoulder.

"A bit, enough to get the ball rolling." His long-time assistant Jimmy Mears responded. Down at the nick they were known as

Laurel and Hardy but not to their faces. DCI Miller had an odd sense of humour and might not have appreciated how appropriate that appellation was. Miller was below average height and stout with dark hair. Mears was taller, thin with spikey fair hair that would never respond to his efforts to make it lay flat. Put them in bowler hats and ask them to sing "The Trail of the Lonesome Pine" and they would have passed at a distance for their bowler hatted doppelgangers.

"By the time the fire service got here the vehicle was almost completely burnt out. One of the hotel staff tried to rescue the poor sod who was in the car but was beaten back by the heat. He's been taken off to the hospital to get his burns dressed but he lives in the staff quarters at the back so we'll have a chance to question him when he returns. It was a very brave but foolhardy thing to do. As far as I can make out the driver must have been killed instantly or as near as makes no difference. The fire service just damped down what was left of the vehicle. They knew there was nothing they could do and didn't want to destroy possible forensic evidence by pumping water everywhere."

"Do we know the identity of the victim?" Miller demanded impatiently.

"We believe it was Darren Bentley the manager of the Metropolitan Bank but, as no-one actually saw him get into the car we can't be certain. We know it was definitely his car because one of the few surviving pieces is the rear number plate and that has been checked out as definitely registered to Darren Bentley."

"Right, take yourself off to Bentley's house, have a word with his Mrs, if he has one, and break the bad news if he isn't sitting down watching telly like I ought to be. And where the hell are forensics?" He added savagely.

"On their way Guv, should be here any minute."

"Don't call me Guv, we ain't the bleedin' Sweeney and this is the supposedly peaceful town of Clingford Norton not the east end of London."

"Yes sir, sorry sir." Mears responded insincerely.

It wouldn't make a blind bit of difference. Miller told Mears several times a day not to call him Guv and had done every day since they were teamed up together long ago when the world was young.

"On your way then." He turned his attention to a young constable who was standing close by to ensure that non-existent press and by-standers didn't interfere with the crime scene.

"What's your name then sunshine?" He enquired in a honeyed tone that would have warned anyone who knew him that he was up to no good.

"PC Jordan sir."

"I know you're a bleedin' PC 'cos the uniform sort of gives it away."

"Yes sir"

"So, do you reckon that hotel serves coffee?"

"I would think so sir."

"Then why are you still here? Milk and three sugars in mine, and see if they've got any biscuits. This smell of cooked meat is making me peckish."

PC Jordan blanched at this reference to the smell of petrol combined with roast pork that hung over the area. He gulped, visibly holding back from vomiting and rushed away towards the hotel before he disgraced himself in front of the DCI.

Miller chuckled as he watched the retreating PC and wondered if he had ever been that green. He supposed he must have been but it was so long ago that it had slipped from his memory.

As he waited for his coffee to arrive the scene of crime officers arrived and began working on the wreck. Miller left them to it knowing that they would tell him nothing until they were certain of their information.

He doubted that there would be much they could tell him until they had taken samples from the wreck and had them analysed. Any fool could determine the cause of death just by looking at the smoking remains of the vehicle. He knew, almost certainly the cause of death. He knew, almost certainly the identity of the victim and he knew beyond a shadow of a doubt the time of death. What he needed to know was the composition of the device that had blown the Lexus sky high, so that he could get his team working on where the individual parts had come from and trying to trace any purchasers of suspect materials. He was puzzled though. The first thing that a suspicious explosion brought to mind was terrorism. How could a small town bank manager be linked to a terror group? One thing was certain, as soon as this hit the press every hole in the corner outfit with a grudge against the state would be claiming responsibility for the outrage. That meant that the regional crime squad and possibly the anti-terrorism unit would want to become involved. Oh God, it was all too much. Couldn't the bastards have done this later in the year when he was spending his time peacefully fishing in the canal?

He wearily phoned the station to get as many coppers as were available sent to the crime scene to begin the routine questioning of the staff, residents and customers of the Camford Arms. Once PC Jordan returned with his coffee he sent him over the road to canvass the houses opposite and then sat on the same wall that Mr Spurgeon had rested on to drink his coffee.

*****

Mr Spurgeon meanwhile had put the car away in his garage. He didn't bother to hide the jerry-can, rubber hose or his disposable gloves. They were clearly what he used for topping up the Morris and were quite innocently in his possession. He had walked home from the lock-up whistling softly under his breath. He petted Lady Mae on his way to the kitchen to prepare a late supper of ham sandwiches and a slice of cake. Now he was watching TV, sipping a celebratory whisky while he waited for the local news to come on. He felt content that his plan had worked well and that a useless parasite who preyed on the vulnerable had been removed and would take no more advantage of people who could ill afford to lose their hard earned cash. He felt no guilt over his actions, only satisfaction in what he had accomplished.

The explosion was the main item of news. There was little to say other than it had occurred but some enterprising soul had filmed the fire on his mobile telephone and downloaded it to the BBC. Mr Spurgeon didn't really care for the commercial channels, he considered them far too downmarket. The reporter didn't speculate as to the cause of the explosion but inferred that it was deliberate and said that no names would be released until the next of kin had been informed.

Mr Spurgeon smiled grimly and said to himself "One down, quite a few to go." Then he went upstairs to sleep soundly and without troubled dreams.

*****

Detective Sergeant Mears had been given the job that all policemen dread. He had to talk to the widow, or other next of kin. He had done it before, usually after a road traffic accident and only twice when it was a homicide. It was never an easy job and he felt a chill of apprehension pass through him as he rang the doorbell of the Bentley residence.

His ring was answered by an attractive woman in her late thirties. She was wearing a silk robe that clung invitingly to her and revealed that she had curves in all the right places. She smiled at him and said "Yes?" in a voice that would have boiled milk it was so hot.

"DS Mears ma'am, Clingford Norton CID." He flashed his ID." May I come in?"

"Of course Sergeant." She stepped back to allow him to enter. "Is there a problem? Is it my husband, he's rather late returning home?" She didn't sound unduly worried at the prospect of bad news Mears thought.

"Would you like to sit down Mrs Bentley? It is Mrs Bentley, isn't it?"

She agreed that indeed was who she was and sat down on a large settee indicating to the Sargent that he should sit opposite her in an armchair.

"I'm afraid that I have some bad news Mrs Bentley. A body has been discovered tonight that we have reason to believe may be your husband."

The new widow gasped and reached for a tissue to dab at an eye that contained no tears. "How, was it an accident? He was always driving too fast and he would always have too many when he went to his bloody Rotary Club meetings."

"I'm afraid not Mrs Bentley. It appears that your husband was murdered." He paused to let that bombshell sink in then continued. "Are you aware of anyone who might wish your husband any harm?" Like one of your lovers, he thought.

"It's unthinkable, Darren was a very popular man. I don't think he had an enemy in the world."

"What about his business dealings, anyone he might have crossed swords with there?"

"I don't know. Darren seldom mentioned business. He was happy enough to go on about the Rotary Club or golf but he only ever mentioned work in passing and never gave me any details. I think he was very aware of his duty of client confidentiality."

Mears was getting fed up with this dead-end line of enquiry. "Did he have any relationships outside of marriage?" He said in an attempt to shake her out of her complacency.

"No, certainly not! We were very happily married and *neither* of us needed to look elsewhere for fulfilment." She stressed the word neither rather more than was necessary and gulped back what seemed to be genuine emotion as she asked, "How was he killed?"

"There was an explosion and his car caught fire," Said Mears as tactfully as he could. Telling the widow that her husband could be buried in a match box rather than a coffin would be unduly blunt and she would find that little fact out soon enough.

The widow Bentley was silent for a long moment as she took in the awful news, then said, "And you're sure it wasn't an accident?" In a low voice.

"Quite sure Mrs Bentley, your husband was definitely murdered."

Mrs Bentley again went quiet and dabbed again at her eyes, but this time the tears were real as the loss of her husband finally hit home.

Mears gave her a few moments to pull herself together then said as kindly as he could, "Thank you for your time Mrs Bentley. We hope to be able to make a positive identification tomorrow but believe me I would not be here now if we did not believe that his was the body discovered this evening. Do you have a toothbrush or comb that I could take for DNA matching?"

"Certainly Sergeant," She said, having regained her poise, "But wouldn't it be easier for me to identify the body?"

"I'm afraid not ma'am, I'm sorry to tell you that your husband was very badly burned and the only way to make an identification will be forensically."

She blanched at that, "Did he suffer?" She asked haltingly.

"No Mrs Bentley, he wouldn't have known anything about it." Mears lied, happy to do his good deed for the day. "I will have to go now, is there anyone I can call to come and sit with you? Or would you like me to send one of our home support team members?"

She assured him that she was fine and wanted to be left alone with her memories.

More likely sorting out the insurance policies Mears thought cynically as he handed her his card. "If you think of anything that you think might help, call me day or night, all my numbers are on there. Someone will be round tomorrow to take a formal statement so if you have to go out please let me know."

He bade her good night and left the house, relieved that she hadn't reacted as freshly widowed women should and intrigued as to why she didn't.

*****

While Mr Spurgeon was peacefully sleeping DCI Miller was busily ensuring that none of his team were getting a moments rest.

He had taken over a side room in the hotel to serve as a temporary headquarters and when not dishing out orders to his team or listening to their reports of fruitless results from door to door enquiries he was pestering the hotel staff for constant cups of coffee and, of course, biscuits.

"I don't suppose you've got any custard creams in your kitchen? I'm getting a bit fed up with these plain ones."

The waitress who should have gone off duty two hours previously, gave a theatrical sigh and went off to make her own enquiries of the chef.

Miller had two detective constables interviewing potential witnesses in a corner of the bar, formal statements would be taken at a later date if there was any information worth recording, but so far nothing had emerged of any interest. They had interviewed a couple of Rotary Club members who had remained for a last drink before returning to their long suffering wives but their information amounted to a twink more than bugger all.

Bentley was not as popular as he had thought himself. Once his fellow members realised that the interview was informal, the gloves came off and the truth came out. He was considered arrogant, pompous and bumptious. He believed himself to be indispensable to the club while pretty much everyone else prayed for the day he would be promoted to a bigger branch of the Metropolitan Bank, as far away from Clingford Norton as possible. He was also a bore and delighted in regaling anyone he could corner with the minutiae of his day, going into excruciating detail until the poor listener was so desperate to escape that they would feign illness and have to be helped to a quiet place to recover.

Higgins, the owner of one of the few surviving independent book shops was the one who dropped the bombshell.

"His wife played around you know."

D C Atkins who was a young man in a hurry looked up sharply.

"And just how do you know that sir?" He asked with interest.

"Oh, everyone knows that Karen Bentley is easy. Most of Clingford Norton have been in her bed at one time or another. She's man mad. If you haven't slept with her you're one of the few she missed. Don't worry though," He leered, "She'll get around to you eventually."

Mr Higgins was not an attractive man. He had a large nose, batwing ears and a comb over hairstyle that was, frankly, ludicrously unconvincing. His complexion was blotchy and he had a pot-belly. DC Atkins wondered if the bile that Higgins was pouring forth was as a result of being turned down by Karen Bentley or if there was a germ of truth hidden amongst the vitriol.

He ended the interview with Higgins and hurried off to report to Miller. He knocked and entered DCI Miller's temporary office and found DS Mears reporting his interview with the widow.

He stood patiently to one side until Mears concluded with. "So all in all I reckon she's a bit of a man eater. It could well be worth taking a look at her private life for a motive, perhaps one of her lover boys decided to take out the husband?"

Atkins interrupted before Miller had a chance to comment. "Sorry to butt in sir but that is what I came in to tell you." Miller and Mears listened attentively until he had given the details of his interview plus his opinion of Higgins and his doubts about his veracity.

"Well done Atkins, that could be useful and we will certainly be looking further into Mrs Bentley's affairs. Now tootle off and get those interviews finished."

Once Atkins had left the room Miller briefed Mears on what had occurred in his absence.

"The Fire Service say unofficially that it was petrol but there was more there than would have been contained in the car's petrol tank. They can't say much more than that until they have finished examining the car and they can't do that until it has cooled down. The press have been sniffing round and I told them to sod off and get a statement from the press office tomorrow. I'll get them to ask the press to include a request for any witnesses who may have been passing by on foot in in a vehicle between the hours of six o'clock and nine o'clock last night to come forward. I've also got the attendance sheet for the Rotary Club meeting and we'll need to question them all, so organise a team to visit each of them at work or at home but I want them all interviewed today, and I want to know any names that might crop up in connection with the love lives of either Bentley or Mrs Bentley and no excuses."

Miller was startled when his mobile rang and interrupted his instructions. He answered it with a degree of acerbity in his voice. "Miller."

"Yes sir." His tone immediately assumed a less aggressive tone. "No sir, at this very early stage we think it is probably domestic"

He paused while his superior officer spoke.

"Petrol sir, and that's not usual in a terror bombing."

He paused again.

"Yes sir, we are on top of things. Yes, I'll report directly to you with any new developments."

He switched off his phone. "Bastard."

Mears raised an enquiring eyebrow and Miller, after taking another pull at his coffee, filled him in.

"That was the Assistant Chief Constable, the anti-terrorism squad have been on and want to know if it's their baby. He's going to hold them off until forensics have done their stuff. That's all I need, a nerk in a peaked cap looking over my shoulder."

Mears grinned. His boss's dislike of senior policemen in uniform was legendary and the ACC had the reputation of being a bean counter who was happier juggling the forces budget than he ever had been as a proper copper.

"You were saying sir.'

"You and me are going home to get a couple of hours sleep. Then we are going to visit the Metropolitan Bank as soon as they open and ask a few questions there about our victim. After that we are going to have another chat with the grieving widow. By the time we've done that forensics should have a preliminary report waiting for us. I want a full team meeting at two in the afternoon, and when I say full I mean full. No absences because the poor darlings have been up all night or I'll have their guts for garters."

*****

Mr Spurgeon was out of bed feeling as fresh as a daisy promptly at seven thirty, that was a little later than usual but he had had, for him, a late night. Coincidentally that was the same time as an extremely tired and irritable DCI Miller was entering the police station to start writing his report on the previous night's events.

He opened the back door to allow Lady Mae to take a morning constitutional and put the kettle on for tea. He dropped two slices of bread in the toaster and put the butter and marmite on the table. Even if it's only toast, breakfast should be eaten at the table. Maintaining standards was important. He fetched his radio from the sitting room and plugged it into a wall socket above the work surface. It took a moment to warm up, digitals were similar to valve wirelesses in that regard he thought. The radio only had two pre-set stations. Radio Four or the Home Service as he always thought of it, and Radio Four Extra. It was the latter station that had convinced him to spend quite a lot of money on a Robert's radio. He had hesitated to spend so much on a luxury item but the mixture of old comedy programmes and drama had convinced him to splash out. The final decision had been made easy when he read that the Queen had a Robert's radio on her breakfast table, although it was said that she always listened to the Today Programme while he preferred something a little lighter at the start of the day. He munched his toast as he waited for The Goon Show to begin.

Chapter 6

Mears was waiting outside the bank when Miller arrived on the dot of nine o'clock. Both men looked a little dishevelled and in need of some sleep but they greeted each other heartily before walking into the bank. They were greeted by a customer service assistant, although her job title was much more high flown that that, who asked them if she could help. Miller displayed his warrant card and asked to see the manager.

"Mr Bentley hasn't arrived yet, can anyone else help at all?" She enquired in a sickly sweet voice that failed to disguise her complete lack of interest in being helpful.

"Whoever else is in charge in his absence then."

"Would you just take a seat for a moment and I'll see if he is free."

"This is a police matter," Miller boomed so that everyone present could hear. "I think you'll find he'll see me."

"Yes, of course, I won't be a moment." She hurried from the area of the bank that was open to the public and disappeared through a door at the rear.

She was back in a very short time and escorted the two policemen to the assistant manager's office. She tapped on the door and said. "The policemen to see you Mr James." Then hastily returned to her duties of steering members of the public towards her colleagues who were selling products that were neither needed nor affordable.

Neil James looked up from his computer screen and said. "I hope this won't take long, I have a lot to do getting period end figures prepared for head office." He said impatiently.

He was a good looking man in his middle thirties and would have been quite handsome if a frown hadn't distorted his features.

Miller took a seat without being invited and gestured to Mears to do the same. He fixed James with an icy stare and said coldly. "I am Detective Chief Inspector Miller and this is Detective Sergeant Mears. This is a murder enquiry Mr James and I will take as long as I damn well need."

James looked startled both at the content and tone of Miller's statement. "But whoooo," he stammered.

"Your boss, Darren Bentley." Replied Miller, watching carefully for any sign that indicated that James had previous knowledge of his boss's death.

James slumped in his executive type, leather look vinyl chair. He looked shocked to the core. "How." He managed to gasp.

Miller was reasonably satisfied that, judging by his reaction, Mr James had no prior knowledge of events and visibly relaxed. Now he needed to play the good cop and encourage confidences.

"Why don't you organise us some coffee?" Swiftly adding, "And biscuits. I'm going to ask you a few questions and if I'm satisfied with your answers I'll tell you what I can."

James lifted the receiver of his desk telephone and asked that coffee and biscuits for three should be taken to the meeting room. He asked for his day's appointments to be cancelled and all phone called intercepted while he was with the police. He led the oddly matched couple down the corridor and sat them down around a board room table. They waited until the coffee had arrived and were once more alone before Miller commenced questioning the badly shaken man.

"How long have you known Darren Bentley?"

"As long as I've been at this branch, about six years."

"How did you get along?"

"Fine, he had my job when I came to work here and we were both promoted at the same time so we sort of had a fellow feeling, if you know what I mean."

"What did the other members of staff think to him?"

"He was the boss and sometimes had to do things that didn't meet universal approval." James replied diplomatically.

"Come along Mr James. I shouldn't have to remind you that this is a murder inquiry. So please don't beat around the bush. This is an informal interview and I need you to be completely honest with me. Trying to protect Darren Bentley's reputation will be of no help whatsoever in finding his killer."

James shifted in his seat, squirming uncomfortably at the DCI's directness. After a moment or two he came to a decision.

"OK Inspector. This is the truth. Bentley was a thoroughly unpleasant man. He bullied the staff, and me when he thought he could get away with it. He smarmed around our important clients and treated the others with contempt. He took credit for anything good that we did and blamed his staff when things went awry. He was a power mad bully without a single redeeming feature and this bank will be a happier place to work in without him in it."

"Can you give me any instances that might have been serious enough for someone to decide they wanted to murder him?"

"There isn't a soul in the building that didn't bear a grudge against Bentley but I don't think any of us would have gone to the extreme of murdering him. Most of the staff would have a whip round for the person who did though, and I'd have dropped a few quid in the hat myself" He added.

"Thank you for your honesty Mr James. Can we turn now to the bank's clients, are you aware of any of them who might feel ill will towards Mr Bentley?"

"There are a few, obviously. People who have been turned down for loans or have had their house repossessed. I could get one of the girls to make you a list if it would help."

"Thank you Mr James. If you could do that as soon as possible and have it sent around to me at the local nick I'd be most obliged."

Miller drained his coffee cup and looked for all the world as if he was preparing to leave. He half rose from his chair and then plonked his ample backside down again and fired a further question. "How well do you know Karen Bentley?"

James flushed and answered too quickly. "Not very well, I've met her a few times at bank social occasions but that's all."

"Mr James, I am going to remind you that this is a murder inquiry one last time. We are going to be questioning every employee in this building as well as Mrs Bentley, some of your clients and all of her neighbours. Do you want to begin again or would you prefer to make a formal statement at the police station?"

"Alright, if I don't tell you someone else will. I had an affair with Karen about six months ago. It only lasted a few weeks then she moved on to some other idiot." He said bitterly. "That, apparently, is a well established pattern of behaviour. Bentley was no good in bed and Karen has a high sex drive and a low boredom threshold. She slept around a lot."

"Was Bentley aware of your relationship with his wife?"

"I don't think so but he must have known that she had affairs. There would have been too many for him to be ignorant of what she got up to when he was out."

"Thank you Mr James, you have been very helpful. Just a couple of final points and we're done for now. How many people work here?"

"Nineteen, including a couple of part timers."

"We will need to talk to them all, can you arrange for us to have the use of a room here or will we have to entertain them at the nick?"

"I'll sort you out a room of course Inspector, anything the Metropolitan Bank can do to help, you have only to ask."

"Thank you I'll have a team down here this afternoon to make a start. I doubt we'll get through them all today so if you could organise for us to see the people that worked most closely with Mr Bentley first it would be most helpful."

Mears snapped his notebook shut and accompanied his rotund senior officer out of the bank and back to the police station.

*****

Mr Spurgeon had enjoyed listening to the Goons and had cleared the table and washed up his plate as he listened to Bluebottle being "deaded again". He had chuckled as Neddy Seagoon was swindled by the arch villain Grytpype Thynne and hummed along to the Ray Ellington Trio. When he switched off the radio and took his accustomed seat on his sofa he was in a very buoyant frame of mind. He switched on the television to see if there was any further news about Bentley. There wasn't, merely a rehash of last night's news with the addition of a short interview with the manager of the Camford Arms saying how shocked everyone was that such a thing could occur in Clingford Norton.

So far so good. This had been a very successful first outing but Mr Spurgeon was enjoying himself more that he had in years and was unwilling to stop after ridding the world of only one useless character. There were others like Bentley and he had all the time in the world to plan their downfall. That councillor who was responsible for closing the libraries might be a good starting point he mused. I'll have to look into that. Fortunately he knew just where to find the information he needed – his local library.

As he entered the library he saw Mrs Dacre sorting out books that were piled high on her desk. She greeted him with a warm smile and a cheery, "Good morning Mr Spurgeon."

"Good morning Mrs Dacre, how are you this bright and sunny morning?"

"I shall be happier when I've got these books back where they belong. The youngsters we have working here are sometimes not terribly efficient, you'd think they had never heard of the Dewey Decimal System the way they stick books into any odd space they can find. It's enough to drive me up the wall."

"No standards Mrs Dacre, that's the problem with young people nowadays. I think the expression they use is "near enough," the idea of completing a task properly just doesn't occur to them. Too busy playing with their ruddy mobile telephones." Ruddy was as strong a word as Mr Spurgeon would allow to pass his lips in the presence of a lady and that was a measure of the contempt he felt for "the younger generation".

They continued to pass the time of day until Mr Spurgeon made his excuses and made his way to the fiction section to see if the next Margery Allingham in the series was on the shelf. He perhaps suffered from a mild form of obsessive compulsive disorder as he found it impossible to read a series of novels out of the sequence in which they had been written. It was there, he gave a sigh of pleasure and relief and picking it up he carried it with him through to the public access computer section.

It didn't take long to get into the County Council web site. Finding the information about who was in charge of the library service was a different matter. The home page was just a puff for the council but after saying how wonderful the council was there was a small section that listed the committees. He clicked on Leisure and Libraries and found himself viewing a photograph of a country park. After clicking the mouse several times he eventually found a page that summarised the work of the library service in a single sparse paragraph. That demonstrates quite clearly what they think of reading books he thought, page after page of where you can go for a walk or have a picnic and a measly hundred words or so devoted to what was still one of the most popular leisure activities that people enjoyed. The trouble was that so many people had one of those Kindle contraptions that it was generally only the elderly and people on low incomes who borrowed books these days. Well they ruddy well should remember that it was the elderly who turned out to vote while younger people were too busy watching satellite television to bother to exercise their democratic rights and they might well get a nasty surprise on election night.

After half an hour of fruitless searching he eventually found what he was looking for, a list of Councillors and their responsibilities. Councillor Ms Janet Tomlinson was the Chairman of the Leisure and Libraries Committee. Ms? What sort of word was that? Either she was married and a Mrs or she was a spinster and a Miss. But the fact that she was a female, albeit an apparent member of the bra burning brigade, gave him cause to pause. Could he kill a woman? He would have to give this a great deal of thought, he had been brought up to respect women and to treat them with courtesy at all times. The idea of offering one violence was complete anathema to him. He determined to complete gathering the information he sought before coming to a conclusion about Ms Tomlinson's fate.

He scoured the site assiduously until he eventually found what he wanted on an obscure page that was reached by a link that did not appear to be a link, ironically entitled "Your Council and Democracy". All Councillors received a standard allowance of eight thousand pounds a year plus expenses. Committee Chairmen (Mr Spurgeon did not agree with political correctness and refused to use the term "chair") received an additional allowance of twenty-one thousand pounds per annum. With her expenses included, Ms Tomlinson was in receipt of well over thirty thousand pounds of public money every year for chairing a few committee meetings and overseeing the grass growing in country parks while she casually destroyed a library system that had once been an example of local government at its best.

That did it! The scales had been tipped irrevocably on the side of justice and Ms Tomlinson's fate had been sealed.

*****

DCI Miller called the team meeting to order. He was standing in front of a whiteboard that had photographs of the victim and the burnt out car fixed to it and looked like an owlish schoolmaster. They were gathered in a large open plan office that had been taken over by his murder squad for use as an incident room. He had a team of around thirty sergeants and constables who had been seconded from other duties. They were eager for information about the progress of the case and the excited buzz of conversation died down rapidly when Miller rapped on a desk.

"OK boys and girls, I'm going to bring you up to speed but first a couple of things need to be made ultra-clear. Number one. If any of you lot speak to the media you are not just off the case, you'll be off the force before your feet can touch the ground. Is that clear?"

There were mumbled responses in the affirmative.

Miller continued. "There would normally be an Inspector acting as my second in command on a murder case but with Jenkins on long term sick leave there isn't an Inspector to spare so Sergeant Mears has been promoted to acting Inspector for the foreseeable future. You will report to him and he will report to me. Is that clear?"

Again mumbled responses with a few cries of congratulations or "Well done Mearsy," intermingled with the general consensus.

Miller brought the meeting to order with a sharp. "That's enough of that." Before briefing his team on what was now known about the Darren Bentley killing. To ensure that everyone was given all relevant information he, like all good story tellers, began at the beginning, continued through the middle and finished by telling his captive audience about their interview with Mr James.

"Since we returned to the station we have heard from forensics and they have confirmed that the explosion was caused by petrol being ignited under the vehicle. No surprise there then. But they reckon that there were also traces of gunpowder that was probably used in a crude detonator. They say that the most likely source of the gunpowder is from fireworks and not many are sold in June so that could be a good lead. There is no information about the detonator as yet but they are hopeful that as they continue to search the vehicle wreckage that they may come up with something. They also know that the container was made of rubber and their preliminary thoughts are that it was some sort of inflatable, probably a boat that was filled with petrol after being placed beneath Bentley's car."

He paused to allow his team to take in this information before continuing.

"This looks like the work of an amateur. I have talked to the anti-terrorism squad and they concur with that view. They still want to be kept in touch with how inquiry progresses but will be hands off unless something develops that indicates they should take an interest. So at least we haven't got spooks crawling all over the place and getting in the way of us proper honest coppers.'

He walked over to the white board and wrote across the top "Who killed Darren Bentley?"

He turned back to the expectant policemen and women.

"So far our door to door enquiries have drawn a complete blank. No-one appears to have seen anything at all, let alone anything suspicious. At the time we are most interested in they were either eating their evening meal or watching the box. I'm hoping our appeal for witness will bring something out of the woodwork but in the meantime we have several lines of inquiry."

As he talked he wrote on the whiteboard.

Interview bank colleagues.

Interview Bentley's neighbours

Canvass places that sell fireworks

Canvass places that sell rubber inflatables

Canvass filling stations for suspicious sales of petrol

Re-interview Mrs Bentley – Me

Next team meeting 7am sharp Wednesday morning.

"Any questions, any points anyone wants to make?"

There was a brief silence before a constable found the nerve to ask if overtime was going to be available.

"Until further notice or until the ACC finds out what I've authorised, you are all on unlimited overtime. We want to crack this case fast and as you all know the first few days of an inquiry are the most important."

He quieted the hubbub that had broken out as he had finished by saying. "Acting Inspector Mears has your duty sheets. Collect them from him and get cracking. I don't want to see any of you until you have completed your tasks or until you have found some useful information. Off you go."

He watched as his team collected their paperwork and made their way out of the room to begin their investigations. They were buzzing with excitement. A murder in Clingford Norton was a rare event and the few that had occurred had been domestics that were easily solved. This was different, a chance to be involved in a real murder inquiry, probably the only one they would encounter in their entire careers. He knew though that their enthusiasm would soon diminish unless they brought in some concrete results. He had to report to the ACC in a little while but before he did that he had something else that needed his attention. He strolled back to his office and switched on the kettle that he kept there in flagrant breach of the health and safety regulations that were in force throughout the station and located a packet of garibaldi biscuits from his desk drawer. Lovely, he thought, squashed fly biscuits and a cup of coffee.

Chapter 7

Mr Spurgeon had continued to search for information on Ms Tomlinson and had been able to find her private address quite easily. What was eluding him was a photograph of the woman. He had managed to find photographs of most council members but Janet Tomlinson seemed to be unusually camera shy for a local politician. Finally, he found a picture of her making her victory speech after the results of the count had been announced by the Returning Officer.

He wasn't surprised she was camera shy. She would probably have caused any sensible camera to have a nervous breakdown. She had a face that would stop a clock at fifty paces. Grotesquely obese she had a fine collection of warts and a nose that looked as though it had been broken on several occasions, probably when she was attempting to kiss a baby to win a vote, and only just managed to divide her little piggy eyes. Her hair was untidy and looked as if it never saw a comb from one election to another and her skin tight top did not flatter to deceive. She hadn't just been hit with the ugly stick she had been battered senseless. None of that phased Mr Spurgeon at all. What made him catch his breath was the fact that his next victim was in a wheelchair.

Could he do it? Not just a woman but a woman who was confined to a wheelchair. He pondered the question as he stared vacantly into space hearing his father's voice in his head. "If women want equality, let them have it but they must be equal in all things. Let them go down the mines and join our brave boys in the front line, then they will be equal." Mr Spurgeon decided that his father, as always was correct. If Ms Tomlinson wanted equality she would have it. He smiled grimly as he silently passed a sentence of death on the unprepossessing councillor.

He was waiting for the bus to take him home when a disquieting thought occurred to him. If he was going to continue to despatch useless parasites that battened on the body of society shouldn't people be aware that they had a champion? Someone who was making a stand on behalf of the vast majority of the long suffering public. The answer came as soon as he had asked himself the question. Of course they should. Perhaps a few more right minded citizens would start their own personal crusades against the forces of darkness. He was old and wouldn't be able to continue in his self-appointed role forever.

How should he let people know? That was the question. Mr Spurgeon knew that it would expose him to increased risk of being caught but he thought that the inevitable publicity would be worth it. Mr Spurgeon continued to mull over his options as he journeyed home, fed the cat and ate his lunchtime ham sandwich and slice of coconut sponge cake. The coconut always became trapped in the gaps between his teeth but it had been a treat as a child and was still irresistible now he was in his eighth decade.

He had watched enough episodes of 'New Tricks' and 'Waking the Dead' to know that any amateurish efforts to disguise the source of an e-mail were inevitably doomed to failure. Telephone calls would be easy to trace and that really only left one way forward – the Royal Mail. Mr Spurgeon was reluctant to send a letter announcing his activities via Her Majesty's postal service, it seemed disrespectful. Then he remembered that the government has recently sold off yet another part of the public's property for a fraction of its worth simply to make a political point and to gain a short term injection of cash into the ailing economy. That was alright then, there would be no disrespect to his monarch.

That afternoon he visited Tesco Extra once more and purchased some cheap notepaper and envelopes. As he walked away from the stationery shelves he paused and quickly returned to add one blue and one red ball point pens to his basket. He didn't think that they would be able to prove that an individual pen had written a letter but it was better to be safe than sorry. He would keep his letter writing materials in a safe place and only use them when writing to the local paper.

For the remainder of the day he cogitated on what to write and how to sign his missive. He knew that the press would soon give him a nickname if he didn't supply one himself and he wanted one with a certain amount of gravitas. He certainly didn't want to be known as the bank bomber or some such nonsense.

Putting together the note proved to be the easy part and he was satisfied with the third and final draft. He had used his blue pen to write in block capital letters.

Darren Bentley was a nasty piece of work. He deserved to die. He was the first one to receive justice but there are more parasites and greedy, selfish people on my list and I will execute them too. I am aware that you probably think this letter is from some sort of crank so I will tell you something that is not public knowledge. Darren Bentley was blown up by a boat.

He hesitated then, unsure of how to complete his letter. Should he sign it yours truly or yours sincerely. He knew it definitely wasn't yours faithfully. In the end he opted for simply, sincerely.

Now he needed a pen name. Something memorable but not too flashy. He dismissed The Avenger and Nemesis as being too theatrical before finally making his choice and signing the letter,

Sincerely

The Vigilante

He addressed the envelope to the Editor of the Clingford Norton Star and attached a 64p first class stamp to the top right hand corner. Absolutely ridiculous he thought that's twelve shillings and nine pence in proper money and in the old days we had more than one post a day, and the postmen didn't lose letters. They didn't wander around the streets wearing shorts and strewing elastic bands in their wake either. They wore proper uniforms, a jacket, tie and peaked cap. And a badge. A proper brass badge not a cheap bit of plastic. The whole country's going to hell in a handcart.

Now he just had to work out where to post it. He wasn't sure if the post box he used could be identified but it would be sensible to take some elementary precautions. The General Post Office in the town centre would have been an automatic choice as it was so busy but there was a camera positioned on the building opposite and he might be identified if the CCTV was actually working. In fact, there were cameras dotted all around the town centre which pretty well meant that he had to use one the outskirts of town. He discounted those that he considered too close to his home and opted for a bus ride to the other side of town. He had to change buses to get there but that was only a mild inconvenience.

He had been careful to only handle the letter while he was wearing a pair of the disposable gloves he had bought from Tesco for the Bentley execution and it was now in an inside pocket of his jacket. He was wearing his disposable gloves under a pair of nice woolly gloves. Perhaps wearing two pairs of gloves was over cautious but when one's liberty was at stake one couldn't be too careful. He doubted that anyone would think it odd that an elderly gentleman was wearing gloves on a lovely summer's day, old folks were notorious for feeling the cold.

He got off the bus, pleased that his journey hadn't been ruined by rowdy schoolchildren and made his way towards a sub-post office. He sat on a convenient bench and checked the area for security cameras. Satisfied that there were none, he swiftly dropped the letter into the post box and made his way back to the bus stop on the other side of the road.

Mr Spurgeon felt very satisfied with his day's work. He would celebrate another successful day with some nice kipper fillets and bread and butter for his dinner. Lady Mae would also share in the meal and would no doubt spend the evening curled up in his lap while he read his book until it was time for bed.

*****

Miller handed Mears a cup of illicit coffee, slumped down behind his desk, shuffled his more than ample rump about until he was comfortable and said. "I don't know what to make of this Jimmy. I don't believe for a minute that there is any sort of terrorism angle. It's the method that's bothering me. There seems to be plenty of people with a motive, starting with his wife, her lovers and moving down the scale to remotely possible, we have more or less anyone he ever came into contact with. So far no-one has had a good word to say about the poor sod. I find it difficult to believe though that a woman would burn her husband alive however much she disliked him. And would she have the skills to construct a detonator? We need to look at her lovers, see if anyone had the technical knowledge to make that bomb."

"Yes Guv, I'm with you on that but what about a hidden motive, could he for example of had gambling debts that he couldn't pay and some nasty people made an example of him?"

"I can't see it Jimmy, those guys might break his legs or in an extreme case he might disappear under a load of junk cars in a scrap yard but they wouldn't go to the trouble of working out such an elaborate means of killing Bentley. There may be a reason behind this that we are unaware of but at the moment one of the lovers has got to be favourite. We'll have this coffee and then toddle off and give the grieving widow a harder time than when you first questioned her."

DCI Miller was just dunking his last biscuit when DC Atkins poked his head around the door. "Got a minute sir?"

"Be quick Atkins, we're just off to see Bentley's widow."

"I've been interviewing the bank staff and so far I'm getting the same story from everyone I've seen. Bentley was very unpopular and they're glad to see the back of him. Unfortunately, it appears that none of them hated their boss enough to blow him up. The last person I saw, a Miss Peters, did come up with some info that could be helpful. Bentley has really got on the wrong side of three customers in the past month or so. A George Smith who was turned down for an increased overdraft facility and had to close his business down. A Francis Danvers who had his house repossessed and a Horace Spurgeon who had to be removed from the bank by their security guards. I think the last guy is unlikely, he's an old man who got upset because he thought the bank had diddled him on his ISA interest rate – probably right too but I think it would be worth having a word."

"OK Atkins, James the Assistant Manager is putting together a list of disgruntled customers but as you've got some details you might as well chase them up, leave Spurgeon until last, the other two seem a better bet. Who else was at the bank with you?"

"DC Watkins sir, but the bank has closed now so he's getting a wad and a cuppa in the canteen."

Miller asked. "How many staff left to see tomorrow Terry?"

"Seven sir."

"OK, tell Watkins to continue the interviews in the morning while you go round and see your three possible suspects. Report back to me when you've done. You can both get yourselves home now and catch up on a bit of sleep. Well done Atkins, we'll make a decent copper out of you yet."

Atkins grinned. "Thank you sir, I'll be glad to get my head down." He whistled softly to himself as he walked down the corridor, praise from Miller was a rare thing indeed and he suddenly felt less tired.

*****

Karen Bentley opened the front door and ushered the two policemen into her kitchen. "I'm sorry to bring you in here but I've got a quiche in the oven and I need to keep an eye on it. Please take a seat." She spoke in a business like way and displayed no emotion at the unexpected visit as she gestured towards the table and four chairs that occupied a corner of the room.

Miller was a little surprised that a woman who had been so recently widowed and in such terrible circumstances should be so obviously in control of her emotions.

"Thank you for seeing us Mrs Bentley at what must be a difficult time. I'm sure you appreciate how important it is that we don't lose any time in interviewing anyone who we feel could be helpful to our inquiries, and I'm afraid that includes you. You knew your husband better than anyone else and you could possess knowledge, perhaps unknowingly, that could be vital to our investigation. You've met my colleague, DI Mears last night Mrs Bentley, I am Detective Chief Inspector Miller."

"I quite understand Inspector. Please ask me anything you wish but before we start can I offer you a drink?"

Miller glanced at the almost empty bottle of chardonnay that stood on the kitchen table. "A cup of coffee and a biscuit would be very welcome Mrs Bentley. Thank you."

As Karen Bentley pressed a button or two on a coffee making machine that looked like a cross between a juke box and a Wurlitzer organ, Miller looked around the room. It was overflowing with top of the range stainless steel equipment that made his humble kitchen look like something from the ark. The stainless steel theme included the work surfaces, cupboards and refrigerators. I bet she has a cleaner to polish this lot he thought uncharitably.

Once they were sitting around the table Miller began. "I know that you have spoken to my colleague but as we talk to other people that knew him we are getting a very different picture of your late husband from the one you have given us. I must stress to you that this is a murder inquiry and you must tell us the complete truth. Trying to spare Mr Bentley's reputation or your own feelings will not do at all. Now, what exactly was the state of your relationship with Mr Bentley?"

Karen Bentley topped up her glass before answering. She gazed defiantly at Miller and said. "My husband was a bullying control freak who couldn't get it up. I hated the sod and I'm glad he's dead."

"Thank you Mrs Bentley," Miller said dryly, "That chimes with what everyone else has told us. Thank you for your honesty. I understand that you have had relationships outside your marriage, would you tell us about that please." He continued.

She took a deep breath and said. "I am a normal woman with the normal needs of a woman. Darren couldn't or wouldn't satisfy me and after it became clear that he had no interest in having sex with me I looked elsewhere for satisfaction."

Mears was watching Karen Bentley as she responded to Miller's questions and wondered how Bentley had been unable to get it up. She was a very attractive piece of goods and he knew that if it had been him she was married to he would have been chasing her around the bedroom morning, noon and night.

"Was there one particular lover or……..?" Miller let the question hang in the air.

"I suppose there have been quite a few over the years but nothing serious. I just wanted sex and if any of them started to want to take things further I got rid of them pretty quickly. What you really want to know is would one of my lovers have killed

Darren? The answer to that is, I don't know, but I think it is extremely unlikely. Most of the guys I went with were married and just looking for a bit of fun."

"We'll need names and addresses, phone numbers too so that we can contact them. We will be discreet, I promise you. We wouldn't want to cause undue embarrassment to anyone involved."

"How far back do you want me to go? Do you want one night stands or affairs that lasted a little while?"

"I think we can discount a one night stand as a motive for murder so the affairs will do nicely thank you. Rough dates would be helpful too so that we can chase up the most recent first."

He turned to Mears. "Anything? Or shall I move on?"

"Nothing at the moment sir."

Miller turned his attention back to the woman. "What about your husband's sex life? Was he doing his own thing too?"

She paused before answering and then the words came tumbling out. "I don't think he really liked women. I think he liked men or boys and that's why he couldn't function with me."

"Do you have any evidence of that Mrs Bentley?"

"Only that I've seen desire on his face when he saw an attractive young man on the street or in a bar and he used to record that young diver every time he was on TV and watch him over and over again."

"Tom Daley you mean?"

"Yes, that's the one. He was quite obsessed with him. I tried to talk to him about it once. I thought that if he came out he would be happier and make my life less of a misery but he just refused to talk about it. He was so far back in the closet he was living in bloody Narnia."

"Did he know about your affairs?"

"He must have done, I tried to be discreet but he couldn't have been unaware of what was going on."

"What was his reaction to that?"

"He pretended that it wasn't happening. We always put on a good show for the Rotary and the golf club and tried to give the impression that everything was OK. As long as he could act like the "great I am" and show me off, he was content."

Miller glanced at Mears and raised an eyebrow in a silent question. Mears shook his head.

"I think that's all for today Mrs Bentley. In view of what you have said I think we need to take your husband's computer away for forensic examination. You wouldn't object to that?"

"Whatever you like Inspector. Despite the fact that I despised my husband he didn't deserve to die in quite such a horrible, vicious way and I'll do whatever I can to help you find his killer."

"Thank you Mrs Bentley. If you could show me where the computer is located, I'll load it into the car while you compile that list for Inspector Mears."

"Inspector! I thought you said you were a Sergeant."

"Rapid promotion ma'am and well deserved." Said Miller before Mears could reply.

Karen Bentley showed Miller through to her late husband's study. An extremely expensive looking desk top computer sat in the middle of a solid looking desk. A filing cabinet stood against the wall with a printer perched on top. Photographs of Bentley with local dignities at various local functions adorned the walls.

"Do you mind if I have a look around in here for a few minutes?"

"I'll leave you to it and go and write my list."

Miller heaved his large frame behind the desk and pulled open a drawer. Paper, pens, ink cartridges pencils and odds and ends of stationery supplies. He opened five of the six drawers and found absolutely nothing of interest. The sixth drawer was locked, but not for long. DCI Miller opened it with no difficulty whatsoever with the aid of a little lock pick he had confiscated from a burglar when he was a uniformed PC. It had come in handy once or twice over the years and Miller gave thanks for his foresight in 'forgetting' to hand it in.

The final drawer was empty save for a notebook. Miller quickly thumbed through it. There was a list of numbers on the front page which Miller surmised were passwords. Then there were a few blank pages, then some very cryptic notes with a set of initials followed by a series of single or double letters and a date.

The most recent entry read: JW – 11, BJ, A, VG 21.4.2016

Miller skipped this part and continued to turn the pages until he found the last entries. A list of initials again but this time followed by a telephone number. Gold dust!

Miller pressed the button and the computer hummed into life and a request for a password flickered into view. Methodically he began to type in the passwords from the notebook one at a time until on the third attempt the computer allowed him to access its contents. You'd think he would have had more sense being a bank manager but it just shows that brains and common sense are not the same thing, he mused as he examined the list of folders.

He opened a few documents but found nothing that seemed significant. He clicked on the pictures icon and the screen filled with an image of a lad about ten years old performing oral sex on a middle aged man in a hood. Miller felt a mixture of anger, disgust and pity for the child. If Bentley were still alive he would have been happy to kill the bastard himself.

He looked up as Mears cleared his throat in the doorway. "You ready Guv?"

"Yeah, I'll tell you what I've found in the car. Help me unplug this thing and we can carry it to the car between us – and don't call me Guv!"

He paused to tell Mrs Bentley that he had found some disquieting stuff on the computer and he would be sending a team in tomorrow to do a full scale search of the house if she had no objection. If she had said no, he would simply have got a search warrant but it was easier if there was no paperwork. He handed her a receipt for the computer and notebook and wished her goodnight. He was half way down the front step when he turned and asked. "I should have asked you this earlier but it slipped my mind. Are there any fireworks in the house?"

"Oddly enough there are. Darren used to organise the Rotary Club bonfire night firework display and there were a few left over. He stored them in a locked steel cabinet in the garage."

"Bugger!" Miller thought. Motives and suspects by the score and now bloody fireworks in his garage. How the hell was he going to make sense of this surfeit of information?

Chapter 8

Mr Spurgeon packed his shopping bag with a flask, a packet of sandwiches and his library book. He tucked his notebook and pencil into the inside pocket of his jacket and stooped to stroke Lady Mae.

"I'll probably be out all day my beauty, so behave yourself while I'm out." He tickled her behind the ears and after carefully locking up made his way to the bus stop.

He had a twenty minute wait while he changed buses and spent the time reading about the derring-do of Albert Campion. He found his thoughts wandering from the page and it came to him that he ought to try to get hold of some of the earlier works of Leslie Charteris. The Saint had been a vigilante, unafraid to put paid to the ungodly in the early books. A very different person to the character that he developed into in the later novels and utterly unlike the anodyne creature portrayed by Roger Moore in the television series. Quite like himself in fact.

The arrival of his bus interrupted his thoughts and he moved as quickly as his old bones would allow. He flashed his bus pass at the driver and took a seat near to the door to make his exit easier. Some bus drivers had no consideration for the elderly and seemed to take a perverted pleasure in slamming on their brakes and accelerating away without a thought for how an old person would retain their balance. It wouldn't have happened when there were conductors who would have ensured that everyone was safely on and off the bus before ringing the bell to signal to the driver that he could move off. No blessed standards any more, the whole country was going to the dogs.

He alighted at the nearest stop to Ms Tomlinson's house and began to walk nonchalantly up a slight incline that he knew, from the street map he had consulted, led to his new target's abode. He turned a sharp corner and rapidly discovered that the slight incline he was expecting was in fact a very steep hill. He soldiered on, endeavouring to look as if he were simply returning from a shopping trip should any casual observer notice him. Another fifty yards and he was forced to take a short rest, sitting on a convenient bench that the council had erected, presumably for just these circumstances. He wondered idly if it was Ms Tomlinson's department that was responsible or if it was down to the Highways Department. It amused him that Ms Tomlinson might be unknowingly assisting the man who was going to kill her and he smiled grimly at the thought.

As he caught his breath he took the opportunity to give the houses that fronted the road the once over lightly. They all had decent sized front gardens and were set well back from the road. Good, that greatly reduced the chances of being observed when he commenced his nefarious activities. With a great effort of will he coaxed his tired muscles into action and once more began to trudge up the hill.

The woman's house was in fact a bungalow. It was the last building in the road and perched on the very crest of the hill. She wouldn't mind living up here would she, she would never have to walk up that damned hill, she had her own set of wheels, he thought ungraciously. The bungalow was nothing special but it had a large garage to one side that had the type of old fashioned wooded doors that folded outwards rather than the more modern up and over metal kind. What would have been the front garden was now laid mainly to tarmac with just a little raised bed of annuals on either side to add a touch of brightness to the dour exterior of the property.

Mr Spurgeon had seen all there was to see and wasn't at all sure his attempt to emulate Edmund Hillary's ascent of Mount Everest had been at all worthwhile. He continued past Ms Tomlinson's home for a few yards and leaned against a farm gate.

He could do with a rest and didn't want to attract attention by turning around immediately and retracing his footsteps. A loud creaking disturbed his peaceful contemplation of the field, followed rapidly by the high pitched whine of an electric motor. Mr Spurgeon turned to see where the sound was coming from and was presented with the sight of Ms Tomlinson exiting her garage aboard a rather fancy looking mobility scooter. He watched in fascination as the huge woman powered the scooter down the short drive and straight across the road before turning left and accelerating down the hill. Well, he thought, she looks like Mr Toad so I suppose she might as well drive like him. All she needs to do is shout poop, poop and she could get a job in a production of Wind in the Willows at the drop of a hat.

Mr Spurgeon was now content. He knew how the execution could be committed. All it would take would be to interfere with that stupid woman's brakes and they would be scraping her off the wall at the bottom of the hill.

*****

DC Atkins usually enjoyed being out of the station but today he was up against it. He had interviewed Francis Danvers, the guy whose house had been repossessed first. Thankfully he had provided the bank with change of address details for his current (and currently badly overdrawn) account. Listening to the bloke grumbling about the unfairness of life had tried his patience and keeping him on the subject of the bank rather than the iniquities of the government had proved a hopeless task. In the end he had ended the stream of self-pitying whinging and left. The guy was a loser, completely defeated by life, he hadn't got the get up and go to pull off anything as technical and well planned as Darren Bentley's murder.

His second interview with George Smith who had lost his business seemed more promising. This guy wasn't defeated, he was angry and full of fire and vinegar. He was working on some spread sheets when Atkins had called and explained he was starting up in business again. It turned out that he had operated a small engineering workshop employing half a dozen people until the bank had pulled the rug from under his feet, Atkins' ears had pricked up when he learned that here was someone who did have the expertise to construct the bomb that had killed Darren Bentley. Sadly for Atkins, but just as well for the engineer he had a cast iron alibi. He had been pulled over for drink driving at 6.30 in the evening and had not been released from the station until 9.00pm. At least his alibi could be easily checked before he reported back to Mears.

His third trip to see the old fellow was wasted. The old chap was out and the only response he had received from his repeated ringing the doorbell was the faint meowing of a cat. He determined to call again on his way home that evening. There was no rush, this visit was for forms sake, not because he expected to be greeted by some sort of geriatric avenger.

*****

Rex Anderson the Editor of the Clingford Norton Star looked down at the letter and read it once again. It had to be a crank, but what was this business about a boat. It made no sense, Bentley had been blown up in a hotel car park that was miles away from the nearest water. Still, it wouldn't hurt to take it round to the nick. It would demonstrate that he was a responsible citizen to that fat bugger Miller and he might be able to pick up a little information while he was there. Miller had apparently threatened the wrath of God on any copper who leaked a dicky bird to the press and his usual sources had been sufficiently cowed by his threats to dry up completely. Sensibly he took a photocopy of the note before departing his office and walking the short distance to the police station.

*****

"Rex Anderson's downstairs Guv, reckons he's got some information for us, he's probably just trying it on to see what he can suss out about the Brentley case but you never know." Mears looked at his boss with a degree of caution. Miller was well known to dislike reporters with almost the same amount of venom that he reserved for senior officers but he's had a love hate relationship with Anderson for many years.

Miller sighed. "I'm only working on the daily report for the ACC so I'm not doing anything important. I'll pop down and see him in an interview room. If that bugger thinks he is coming up here, he's got another think coming."

He waddled down the stairs and spoke to the newsman through the plexiglass that kept irate members of the public from assaulting the officer on duty behind it. "How do Rex, come on through."

Anderson waved a packet of ginger nut biscuits at Miller and called "Two sugars in mine."

They sat facing each other, sitting on chairs that were bolted to the floor facing each other over a table that was similarly secured. Miller was squeezed in a little too tightly for comfort and scowled as he shifted about trying to get his capacious gut to fit comfortably into a space that was patently too small.

"Spit it out then Rex, I haven't got all day for social visits." He growled, as he dunked his biscuit into a liquid that was allegedly coffee although Miller would not have sworn to it in a court of law.

"How about a bit of tit for tat. I'll tell you what I know and you can give me an update on how the investigation is going."

"Bollocks. You want information you go to the press office like everyone else. If you've dragged me down the stairs on a fool's errand when I'm in the middle of a murder case, I'll bloody murder you myself."

Anderson passed a hand over his bald head and sighed. He had known that getting information out of Miller would be like drawing teeth but it had been worth a try.

"OK, but if my information is useful I want you to make sure that I get an exclusive interview with the arresting officer."

"Can't promise that Rex, but *if* the information is useful I will do my best to look after you. That's the best you're going to get, so spill the beans."

"I received this in the mail this morning." He handed the letter to Miller. He had placed it and the envelope that it came in into a poly pocket so that it could be handled without fear of compromising any forensic evidence.

Miller looked down at the letter. His eyes widened slightly as he took in the line about Bentley being blown up by a boat.

"Thanks Rex. I owe you one. This might be the work of a crank but it will have to be chased up just the same. I'll pass this on to forensics and see what they can come up with. If I make an arrest as a result of this letter you can have that exclusive interview and spread the part the Star played in the arrest all over the front page, but for now I'd be grateful if you would sit on this information."

"Come on Dusty, we're old mates. You know that I can't do that. If there is anything to that letter, I've got to publish. The Star is like all local papers, we're losing out to the internet and our circulation is going through the floor, a scoop like this would do wonders for our sales."

They argued back and forth until at last a compromise was reached. The Star would publish the letter but the line about the boat would be redacted. Anderson was free to report that the police were taking the letter seriously but were continuing with other promising lines of inquiry. Any other letters the Star received would be up for negotiation. In return Anderson and the Star would be given most favoured status above all other media and would be given snippets of information regarding the on-going investigation on an ad hoc basis.

The two men shook hands and Rex Anderson hurried back to his office to write a front page editorial about the vigilante who was stalking Clingford Norton.

Miller made his way back upstairs as though he had all the weight of the world on his shoulders. Now, to add to the plethora of motives and possible suspects, he had a bloody loony toon to deal with – and the big problem was the loony toon knew about the boat. Was this a false trail being laid by someone with a different motive for killing Darren Bentley or did he have a genuine vigilante on his hands? He was dreading having to break the news to the ACC who would throw a blue fit and only gained a little pleasure from the thought that the ACC had then got to suffer the same fate as him when he reported to the Chief Constable.

Miller briefed the ACC by phone and gained his grudging agreement that he had made the best of a bad job then he called a team briefing for 2pm. Mears had sat in while he talked to the ACC and so was up to speed with events.

"We can't let this become our sole focus Guv. It could be a red herring. We've got to continue with the investigations that we've already got underway."

"I know, but it's going to be a bugger motivating the team to continue if they think the killer is some silly devil who thinks he's Charles Bronson. And don't call me Guv."

"I think we should play it like this, we have to investigate the possibility that the letter writer is a maniac but we think it more likely that it is the killer trying to divert attention away from himself. And that could easily be true." He added

"I agree, I was thinking something similar myself. Our biggest problem will be the media getting in our faces and the avalanche of letters and crank calls we'll get once people see the Star tonight."

Miller sighed and automatically fed a ginger nut into his mouth. Who'd be a poor bloody copper?

*****

Miller was once more back in his office trying to catch up on the paperwork that a large scale investigation inevitably generated. He was content that his team had, by and large, agreed that it was more likely to be the killer covering his tracks than a real vigilante and they had returned to their investigatory duties buoyed up by his words of praise for their continuing efforts. That praise had been earned.

Karen Bentley's lovers were being interviewed although nothing significant had reared its ugly head yet. The search of the Bentley house had revealed nothing except for a stash of indecent photographs of children behind a water tank in the loft. The fireworks were where Mrs Bentley had said they would be and they matched the list that the Rotary Club Secretary had supplied. Apparently none were missing. The canvassing teams searching for suspicious sales of fireworks had followed a couple of leads but they had only led them to a twenty-first birthday party and a retirement do for a local restaurateur. As yet nothing on the sale of any rubber inflatables either. At least they were whittling down the workload and might soon be able to see the wood for the trees.

He picked up the phone to ring forensics to chase any information on the letter or Bentley's computer but thought better of it, if they had some information they would call him and chasing them wouldn't speed things up. Instead he buzzed Mears and asked him to join him for a chat.

Mears sat down and looked at his boss. He looked harassed and a tad distracted. Nothing a good concrete lead wouldn't put right he thought.

"Sit down Jimmy, take the weight off."

"Cheers Guv. I've sent a constable over to the Star to collect a copy of tonight's paper as it comes off the presses by the way.'

"Good thinking Jimmy. I can't wait to see what Rex puts on the front page." He added, his words dripping with sarcasm. "I'll tell you what bothers me more and that's this paedophile angle. It opens up a whole new can of worms. I ought to have contacted the Paedophile Unit at the Yard but I've held back to see what forensics find on his computer first. With luck the names of anyone who shared his disgusting tastes and if they murdered the bastard we can send them a letter of thanks and a fiver out of the till before we bang them up. If they didn't, we can bang them up for kiddie porn offences anyway."

"Star sir." The red faced constable who had apparently been hurrying to get the evening paper to his D I reached into Miller's cramped office and dropped the Star onto the desk."

"Thank you, constable." With that Miller looked down at the front page. It was more or less what he had expected but it still sent a chill down his spine. The rest of the media would be on to him as soon as they saw the story and every nutter for miles around would be adding to the workload of his overworked officers.

The banner headline read.

Vigilante Killed Bank Manager

It was followed by a brief rehash of the case and then said, see pages, 2, 3, 4, 5 and 6.

Below the letter was reproduced with the information about the boat blacked out. At the side of the letter was Rex Anderson's editorial comment.

The Star Helps the Police

When the extraordinary letter that is reproduced opposite was received at the Star's offices this morning we took it immediately to the police. Neither they nor we know if the letter is genuine but it is being treated seriously by the investigating officers.

We at the Star hope that this letter is a hoax. That would be a grave matter and if the perpetrator is caught we hope that the full force of the law is invoked and the punishment he or she receives is appropriate to such a serious crime. But however heinous an offence a hoax would be, it would be infinitely better than the alternative – having a bloodthirsty maniac stalking the streets of Clingford Norton killing its citizens for his own perverse reasons. Make no mistake this is no vigilante keen to hand out justice, this is a murderer trying to justify the appalling act of blowing up one of our most respected citizens for no other reason than the job he was doing. The Star will stand four square with the police and support them in every way we can until this brutal killer is brought to justice and the citizens of our fair town can once more sleep safely in their beds.

"Could be worse, it's a bit flowery though, our fair town indeed, who's he think he is John Betjeman?" said Miller handing the newspaper to Mears, "But you watch him change his tune if we don't catch this so called vigilante double quick. Then it will be all about how useless we are and we ought to call in the Regional Crime Squad."

*****

Mr Spurgeon looked up from his book. Who could be ringing his doorbell so insistently at this time of night? In another hour he would be tucked up in bed and he liked to relax with a good book before retiring for the night. His legs were stiff from his hill climb and descent earlier in the day and he made a bad job of walking to the door. His hip had never quite been the same after that fall outside the bank and now it was throbbing quite painfully.

When he reached the front door he called out. "Who is it?"

He was horrified to hear the reply. "D C Atkins, Clingford Norton CID, could I have a word Mr Spurgeon please?"

Surely they hadn't found out. He had been so careful. Even if they suspected they couldn't prove anything. Better to brazen it out. He slipped the chain from the door and saw a tall figure standing on his step displaying his warrant card.

"Come in please."

The much younger man followed Mr Spurgeon through into the sitting room and the older man's inherent courtesy took over. "Please sit down Detective Constable. I was just about to pour myself a nightcap, would you care to join me in a tot?"

Atkins, relaxed as he sank into the chair, it had been a long, tiring day and this old fellow was struggling so much to get about he couldn't possibly be a serious suspect. "That's very kind of you sir, I'll join you with pleasure."

As Mr Spurgeon busied himself pouring the drinks Atkins explained that they were interviewing anyone who might have cause to wish Darren Bentley harm. They were aware of the incident at the bank and just wanted to hear his side of the story. It was just routine but they needed to talk to him before they could cross him off the list.

Mr Spurgeon felt the tension leave his body. Just routine, he might have expected this if he had thought about it. He handed a glass of scotch to the detective and told him all about it – apart from killing Darren Bentley of course.

The detective sat and sipped his scotch, listening and nodding from time to time. He could sympathise with the old man, these banks thought they could get away with anything and had tried something similar on his mother not that long ago. She was a canny old biddy though and had soon realised how much the interest rate had fallen and had shifted her savings into an account that paid a reasonable return. The idea that this old fellow was capable of planning and carrying out a murder was almost laughable.

"Have you seen tonight's Star Mr Spurgeon? You can have my copy if you like, I've read it and there's any number back at the station."

Mr Spurgeon accepted his kind offer and tucked the paper away for a quiet read in the morning. He had had enough excitement for one day and just wanted his bed.

When, after another glass of Mr Spurgeon's excellent scotch, he finally said goodnight, he knew that all three suspects he had interviewed that day could be crossed off the list and he could move on with something that might give a better result.

Mr Spurgeon saw him off the premises and dropped the chain back into place. "Well Lady Mae, that went well." He said as he walked into the kitchen to wash up the empty whisky glasses. "Such a nice young man, it was a very pleasant change to have a visitor in to share a drink and a convivial chat. You are good company but you don't have a lot to say for yourself you know."

Chapter 9

Mr Spurgeon was furious. He had enjoyed his breakfast of soft boiled eggs and soldiers washed down with a nice cup of tea before repairing to his customary seat on the sofa to read the previous day's edition of the Star. He had fondly imagined that they would have been broadly sympathetic towards the efforts of one individual to rid the town of scum like Bentley but they had called him a bloodthirsty maniac! How dare they? Were they so stupid that they couldn't understand that he wasn't a murderer, what he had done had been for the good of the town?

Mr Spurgeon threw the paper to one side and rose to his feet. He was too angry to sit still and began to pace around the room as he turned the Star's totally unjustified description of him over in his mind. After a while, during which time Lady Mae had run through to the kitchen after being nearly trodden on several times such was Mr Spurgeon's depth of thought, he began to calm down. He needed to get moving with the Ms Tomlinson execution. That would show them. He wasn't a bloodthirsty maniac, murdering innocent people, he was just an ordinary chap who was trying to make a difference. When he had removed a few more worthless characters they would treat him with the respect that he and his crusade deserved.

He knew how he was going to kill Ms Tomlinson, the actual execution would be the easy part. It was getting to her bungalow that would be the problem. He would have to wait until she had retired for the night to gain access to her garage and that meant having to use the Morris. He didn't like the idea of using his faithful old motor. Since he had ceased driving he hadn't taxed or insured it and had applied for a Statutory Off Road Notification that kept the vehicle on the right side of the law. Taking the car on to the road without tax or insurance was a clear breach of the law and Mr Spurgeon regarded himself as a law abiding citizen. But needs must when the devil drives as his father used to say. The only alternative to using the Morris would be a taxi as the buses would long since have finished running when he intended to visit Ms Tomlinson and he couldn't imagine asking a cab driver to wait while he sabotaged the mobility scooters brakes.

He would do it tonight. There was enough petrol in the tank to take him across town and back easily and these people needed to be shown the vigilante should be treated with respect as quickly as possible.

Mr Spurgeon went down to his workshop and began to assemble the equipment he would need for his little expedition. He placed some narrow nosed pliers, some ordinary pliers, a rasp (to be used as a lever not a file) a selection of spanners, a spray can of lubricant, a reel of sticky tape, disposable gloves, a torch, a roll of cling film, a selection of screwdrivers and a small plastic bowl. He wrapped everything individually in rags to prevent his tools making a noise and placed everything in a canvas shopping bag. He felt much better for being active and returned to the house with a spring in his step.

He was humming when he entered the house and put the kettle on for a brew. His hip and leg muscles were still aching from yesterday's climb up the steep hill and he decided to take it easy. He took tomatoes, lettuce (proper lettuce not those awful leaves you get in plastic bags) and cucumber from the fridge and prepared a salad for his lunch. He sealed the bowl with cling film and set it on the work surface to come up to room temperature. Mr Spurgeon abhorred salad straight from the fridge. He opened a tin of red salmon and tipped it into a dish. Using a fork, he carefully removed the bones and few remnants of skin which he placed into Lady Mae's dish along with a small share of the actual fish. Next he broke up the remaining salmon that was for his lunch and added salt, pepper and a dash of malt vinegar before placing that dish in the fridge. Mr Spurgeon abhorred warm fish. Having faithfully reproduced the way his mother would have prepared the meal Mr Spurgeon took his tea into the living room for a nice sit down. He scowled when he saw the Star resting on the carpet where he had tossed it in his fit of pique. That wouldn't do at all. He picked up the offending newspaper and carefully folded it before placing in the magazine rack. A place for everything and everything in its place still applied, despite the newspaper's dubious content.

After lunch Mr Spurgeon watched television. For a change there was a decent afternoon film on BBC2. It was an Ealing Comedy and one he hadn't seen for many years. It was called "The Lady Killer's" and Mr Spurgeon was quite taken with the irony of the title but not with the efficiency of the so called lady killer's. Later tonight he would show them how it should be done.

That evening while he was waiting for the clock to tick round to midnight, the time he had decided to begin his journey to visit Mss Tomlinson's bungalow, Mr Spurgeon composed another letter.

To Whom It May Concern

Ms Tomlinson has presided over the destruction of the libraries of this county while willingly agreeing to the council's limited resources being spent on lesbian workshops and glossy pseudo newspaper propaganda sheets glorifying the council and other such fripperies.

She was being paid in excess of thirty thousand pounds a year to do a non-job that would once have been performed by a willing volunteer for nothing. She was a leech who used her position for personal gain and she could not be permitted to continue to destroy our libraries with impunity.

Someone had to take a stand in defence of the public and I have answered the call. Other people in public life who are lining their pockets at the expense of hard working ordinary people had better beware. Ms Tomlinson was only the second on my list and my crusade will continue until justice and fair play are once more established throughout Clingford Norton.

Sincerely

The Vigilante

Mr Spurgeon re-read his letter before signing it in red ink. A touch theatrical he thought, but it underlines my message nicely. He placed the letter directly into a poly pocket without bothering with an envelope. This letter wasn't going through the post. The poly pocket he placed into his canvas shopping bag and he was ready for the off. As his literary hero Sherlock Holmes would have said "The game's afoot."

Mr Spurgeon left his house promptly at midnight. He closed his front door as silently as he could and walked the short distance to his lock up garage. For once he was glad of the council's budget cuts which had resulted in only every other street lamp being illuminated up until midnight and being switched off completely thereafter, which greatly increased his chances of being unseen. The streets did appear to be deserted but prying eyes could be watching from the shadows so Mr Spurgeon kept his head down and hurried as quickly as he could to where his Morris Minor awaited to transport him on his journey to transport Ms Tomlinson on her final journey.

He had taken the precaution of lubricating the hinges of the up and over door and it glided up silently into position. He started the car, moved it into the yard and returned to close the garage door. The open door might be spotted and he wanted to take no chances that might betray his movements. The drive through the dark streets was swift. There was virtually no traffic to impede his progress and he was pleasantly surprised when he arrived at his destination at a little after twelve thirty. He drove past the bungalow, switching off his lights as he did so and reversed the

Morris through a gateway and into a field. He was pleased that the lack of rain recently meant that he had no fear of becoming bogged down in mud and that the car was out of sight of any passers-by unless they actually entered the field.

He lifted the shopping bag off the front passenger seat and exited his vehicle, being careful to close the door as quietly as he could. He paused at the gateway and peered in both directions. Satisfied that he was alone he walked purposefully towards the bungalow, it was in darkness and there was no sound emitting from Mrs Tomlinson's dwelling. He quickly glanced around before moving smartly up to the garage door. He was in shadow but checked again that he was unobserved before taking out his can of lubricant and spraying the hinges that had creaked yesterday morning. As he waited patiently for the oil to do its work he pulled on his disposable gloves. When he thought it had been given sufficient time he turned the door handle and gently pulled it towards him.

It was as he had hoped the door wasn't locked, after all who would want to steal a mobility scooter? He pulled the door open until he could squeeze through and then closed it silently behind him. Inside the darkness was total as there was no side window to allow even a little moonlight to penetrate the garage. He felt around in his bag and located his torch. He quickly switched it on and took a look around. Apart from a few storage boxes at the rear of the garage it held only the shiny, new and powerful mobility scooter.

He shone his torch over it, searching for the braking system. He lifted a side panel and it was displayed directly in front of him. It was very straight forward. Disc brakes that worked from a master cylinder with a reservoir of fluid above it. This would be easy. Mr Spurgeon placed the bowl beneath the reservoir then punched a hole into the bottom of its plastic case where it projected above the master cylinder. The fluid oozed slowly out until Mr Spurgeon unscrewed the filler cap and the oozing became a steady flow.

He waited until the system had drained itself then covered the bowl with cling film. There would be some fluid left but not enough for the brakes to work. He considered doing something to the steering but decided that he couldn't guarantee that the steering wouldn't fail before she left the garage so deciding against the belt and braces approach he turned his attention to the small dashboard.

The panel that contained the odometer and an array of warning lights was only held in place by a screw at either side and it was the work of moments to remove the plastic screen, extract the bulb that indicated a brake problem and refit the screen. Almost done.

The last thing that Mr Spurgeon did before leaving the garage was to use his reel of sticky tape to fix the poly pocket containing his letter to the underneath of the seat. He gathered his tools together, picked up the bowl of brake fluid and stole quietly from the garage. He had to put his things down in order to fasten the door and he took the opportunity to check that he was still unobserved before picking up the bag and bowl and walking quickly back to his vehicle. He lifted a corner of the cling film that secured the brake fluid and emptied the contents of the bowl at the side of the field as he didn't want it to spill in the car. He reapplied the cling film to the bowl, ensured that he had a good seal and placed the dirty bowl in the shopping bag with his other tools. He stowed the bag in the front passenger seat foot-well, entered the car and drove back to his garage at twenty-nine miles an hour. He saw no-one on his journey and he was confident that no-one had seen him.

Mr Spurgeon slipped into his house like an old grey ghost. He put his bag in the kitchen where it would be handy for the work shop in the morning, took off his coat, fussed the cat and poured himself a scotch. Now all he had to do was wait.

*****

DCI Miller was not a happy man and he made sure that every single member of his team was aware of that fact. He addressed the team meeting in a voice that resembled a growl, his disappointment and anger permeating each word.

"Here's what we've got so far." He paused and then roared. "Bugger all!"

His officers sat stony faced as he launched into a king sized bollocking. They knew that he wasn't being fair, that they had been working their socks off to get a result. They knew that he knew that too and was just using them to vent his frustration at the lack of apparent progress.

"The sum total we have so far is that everyone who met Bentley took an instant dislike to him because it saved time. He was an arrogant bully with paedophile tendencies whose wife was shagging anything in trousers, or preferably out of them. We have interviewed everyone with a connection to Bentley, including his wife's lovers and apart from a common thread of loathing for the man we have nothing to show for all the hours that have been spent interviewing. Nothing. Zilch. Zero. Those with a reasonable motive for wishing him dead either have an alibi, are physically incapable of setting the bomb or wouldn't have the expertise to construct the detonator. We are still waiting for forensics to complete their work on his computer and we ought to have that information at some stage this morning. Until we get that information this investigation is going nowhere. You're doing no good in here, I want you all back out on the streets. Interview everyone again. Check alibis. Go through the CCTV footage from the garages again, the perpetrator must have bought the petrol from somewhere. I want the radius for checking sales of fireworks and rubber inflatables increased to include all towns within twenty miles of the Bentley home."

He looked at the expressionless faces in front of him and sighed. "OK, that's it, bugger off and do something useful."

His disconsolate team hurried from the room, grateful to escape from his withering criticism. He turned his attention to Jimmy Mears. "Let's have a coffee and see if we can think of a new angle."

The fat man walked towards his office, his whole demeanour reeking of piss and vinegar. His tall, thin colleague trailed behind thinking that a coffee would be nice but doubting that they would come up with any fresh ideas.

For all the good their pooling of ideas did they may as well have acted like the comedy couple they resembled with Miller saying, "Another fine mess you've gotten me into" and Mears responding with a blank look while he played with the hair on the top of his head.

Miller had consumed almost a whole packet of rich tea biscuits while they had been talking through the case and now stuffed the last biscuit into his greedy maw. "I just don't know what else we can do." He spluttered sending a cascade of biscuit crumbs over his desk and his junior colleague. "If the computer doesn't give us something to work on we're pretty much at a dead end."

Mears nodded, he knew that Miller was right. If a murder wasn't solved in the first few days of the investigation the chances of it being solved at all receded dramatically. "The trouble is Guv, there are so many people who hated the bloke that we have too many suspects and apart from knowing that a rubber inflatable was used to hold petrol and gunpowder we have no firm evidence of anything. The letter has given nothing. Cheap stationery from Tesco that is sold in the thousands. There are no witnesses to the actual explosion let alone anyone seeing the killer setting the device. We thought that Karen Bentley's lovers would be a fruitful line of inquiry but that has drawn a blank too. As far as I can see getting the team to go over everything again is our only option unless or until the computer gives us something."

*****

Ms Tomlinson would never admit it but the reason she needed assistance in getting around was due to the strain on her joints caused by chronic obesity. As a child she had been acutely aware that she was neither pretty nor lovable. Her sharp mind and sharper tongue had ensured that she had no friends and, as the years rolled by, even her parents had disliked her company and had been relieved when she had left home to live in a small bedsit.

Her career, she was convinced, had been hindered by her lack of looks, bosses tended to be shallow, promoting the pretty girls who smiled a lot rather than her, even though she was much better at her job and much more suitable for promotion. She gradually became more and more bitter and frustrated, finding her only comfort in eating excessive quantities of food.

On the spur of the moment she joined the Conservative Party and, to her surprise, found her spiritual home. She took to the political infighting and backroom machinations like the proverbial duck to water. Having no social life to speak of, she worked hard in the background and enjoyed pulling the strings that made others dance to her tune. At last she felt contented.

She was aware that her looks would be likely to affect her rise within the party in the same way that they had her career, and she accepted that as her lot in life. Then one day a candidate for the borough council had died only a couple of days before the closing date for nominations. With no-one else willing or able to step into the breach she had found herself a candidate for the Kingsley Ward of Clingford Norton. Her looks were no deterrent to winning the seat, the electorate there would have voted for Quasimodo if he had been wearing a blue rosette, and she was elected with a substantial majority over her Labour and Liberal opponents. That was the beginning of her rise to becoming a figure of power and influence on the borough council. After a few years she stood for the county council and now held the duel position of Borough Councillor and County Councillor.

Ms Tomlinson mulled over her rise to her present position as she plotted her next move. As Leader of the council she would hold the appointment of the various Chairs of Committees in her hands and would be able to reward or punish as she liked. Mrs Tomlinson liked power. She liked power a lot. She had pressurised, blackmailed and coerced her fellow councillors until she was sure that she had sufficient support to oust the current Leader at the next full meeting of the council. She exposed her teeth in a rictus that could have been mistaken for a grimace of pain (Ms Tomlinson wasn't very good at smiling as she got little practice), as she clambered aboard her mobility scooter.

She shuffled her enormous buttocks around on the seat before turning the ignition key and easing the vehicle forward until it gently nudged the garage doors apart. Once they were open sufficiently to let her vehicle through she stabbed a swollen foot hard onto the accelerator and shot down her short drive and straight across the road. She loved riding her mobility scooter, it gave her a sense of freedom as she drove it far too fast through the streets of the town. The severe incline that she was descending combined with her fierce acceleration and her very substantial weight sent the scooter hurtling down the hill. The wind whipped against her face and she once more attempted a smile as the houses on either side of the road rushed past in a blur.

She didn't begin to panic until she was almost at the foot of the hill. She took her foot off the accelerator and pressed on the brake. Nothing happened. She tried again. Still no result. She looked up and saw to her horror that she was rapidly approaching the sharp turning at the bottom of the hill. She continued to pump the brakes as she attempted to steer the vehicle safely around the bend. Gripping the steering tiller she turned it a little too far, for a split second thought that she was going to make it and might be able to coast to a stop on the flat area at the foot of the hill. That was when the mobility scooter tipped over. The scooter and Ms Tomlinson continued their journey separately. The scooter crashed into a car parked on the opposite side of the road as Ms Tomlinson's face contorted in panic and she screamed like a banshee before she smashed head first into the side wall of the Co-operative convenience store.

Her death was instantaneous, which was a blessing as she never shopped at the co-op as it was a socialist organisation and she would have hated to know that they had contributed to her demise.

Chapter 10

"Forensics report Guv." Mears said as he lay a manila folder on the desk in front of Miller.

"What does it say, Jimmy, I know you've already had a shufti so save my tired old eyes and give me the gen."

"Yes Guv. They think the code is just initials followed by a date. JW would be the boy's initials, 11 his age. BJ is blow job and A is anal. Finally, the six digits at the end are simply the date when he abused the lad."

"The dirty bastard. I'm beginning to lose interest in solving this one Jimmy. I reckon whoever did him in did the world a favour."

"I feel much the same way Guv but you'd better here the rest. There was nothing on his smart phone to interest us. As far as the computer goes it's a different matter. No face book or social media at all. The usual accounts and records of savings etc but there was, according to the techies, over a hundred thousand images of child abuse. Mostly young boys but some of little girls. He probably kept those for trading with other paedos. He was in regular contact with a dozen or more other blokes who were into his perversion and the techies have managed to trace all but one of them. The majority live abroad, mainly in America but there are a couple resident in the UK and one of them only lives about twenty miles away. His name is Arthur Cadbury and he's the local vicar."

"Right." Miller exploded into action, at last he had something to get his teeth into. "I want a team assembled and ready to go inside ten minutes. We're going to pick the bastard up and turn his gaff over. Tell the local nick that we are going to be on their patch. I'll see to the warrant."

Exactly an hour later a small convoy pulled up outside a large Victorian house that served as the rectory for the village of Little Crittington. Miller, closely followed by Mears, marched up to the front door and rang the doorbell, keeping his finger pressed on the button until the door was opened by a flustered looking man wearing a clerical collar.

"Are you Arthur Cadbury?"

The flustered man gulped, his face showing his panic as he stammered, "Yeeeees."

"I am Detective Chief Inspector Miller of Clingford Norton CID and I have a warrant to search these premises. Kindly step out of the way."

Miller barged the dazed man out of the way. "Right lads you know what to do, start at the top of the house and work your way down. I'll be down here having a chat with Mr Cadbury." He gave the shaken priest a malevolent look that left the vicar under no illusions as to what sort of chat it would be.

Cadbury visibly pulled himself together and said. "What is the meaning of this intrusion? You have no right to come barging into my home in this way."

"Yes, I do Mr Cadbury, this warrant gives me the right to search these premises, anyone who is present on these premises and to remove anything that I believe to be illegal or which might pertain to criminal activities."

The DCI pierced Cadbury with a stare that would have frightened a mafia hitman and barked, "Is there somewhere we can sit and have a chat then Mr Cadbury?"

"My study."

"We'll go there then. Is there anyone else present in the house?" He added.

"No, my housekeeper only comes in for a few hours in the mornings."

"OK." He turned to a constable who was standing guard by the front door. "You lad, DI Mears and I are going to question the good vicar in his study. You can leave the door long enough to find the kitchen, make three coffees and bring them and some biscuits to……….?" He paused and the vicar explained where they would be to a constable who thought making coffee was a poor use of his ability.

The two policemen and a terrified clergyman entered a room that was a credit to the priest's organising ability. Filing cabinets stood against the wall and shelves were packed with lever arch files that were neatly labelled with their contents. Two visitor's chairs were placed before a large desk that had a desktop computer on one side and a space for working on documents on the other. The vicar went to sit behind the desk but Miller stopped him with a sharp "This side of the desk sir please, we don't want you pressing any buttons on the computer by mistake do we?"

The cleric slumped into a visitor's chair and watched Miller drop heavily into his executive type leatherette swivel chair. He was finished, there was enough evidence in his computer to ensure that he was going to prison for a very long time. This time there was no friendly bishop to help him cover up his dirty secrets. His already slight frame seemed to shrink even further as he looked at the plump policeman.

"This is an informal chat Mr Cadbury and a formal statement will be taken later at Clingford Norton police station. You do not have to say anything but anything you do say will be taken down and may be used in evidence against you. Do you understand?"

The frightened clergyman said that he understood and Miller immediately began to fire questions.

"How long have you been a paedophile?"

"I don't know what you mean, how dare you." Cadbury spluttered in a vain attempt to appear both innocent and indignant. "This is outrageous."

"We found enough evidence on Darren Bentley's computer to put you away for a very long time. There is probably further evidence on your hard drive, so stop being a silly bugger and tell the truth. Judges tend to go a little easier on people who plead guilty and co-operate with the forces of law and tend to be tough on those that waste the time of the police and the courts. Now answer the question. How long have you been a paedophile?"

"I've been involved with Bentley for years but all I've ever done is look at the pictures. I would never hurt a child, I love children."

The classic excuse Miller thought. It's going to be a pleasure getting you sent down, with luck you'll have to share a cell with a muscle Mary who will bend you over and give you a dose of your own medicine. His mobile rang but he ignored it and spoke to Cadbury. "Who else is involved?"

The cleric turned a defeated face towards him and said hoarsely. "There are fifteen in the circle, I don't know who they are apart from Bentley and a chap called Smedley who lives in Winchester, we all use code names. It was supposed to be safer." He added resentfully, as if being caught was an affront to their security measures.

"And what exactly does this circle do?" Enquired Miller with deceptive kindly interest.

"Some of us just swap photographs but others do more." He stopped as though uncertain how to explain exactly what "more" was.

Miller's phone had stopped ringing and now Mears' mobile began to ring. He pulled it from his pocket, said "Mears," and then listened intently.

"Guv, we've got another one. A dead councillor this time."

"Jesus Christ, I suppose that means I won't get that coffee," Exploded Miller, "Get Sergeant Meredith down here. Now!"

Miller turned to the clergyman, "Don't think you are off the hook for one moment but I am going to temporarily suspend this interview while I deal with another matter."

A uniformed Sergeant entered the room and stood smartly in the doorway. "Sir?" said Meredith.

"You must be psychic, we were just about to send for you. DI Mears and I have to return to town pronto. I want you to take charge of the search. In particular, I want that computer, DVD's, videos etc in the incident room. Look for a laptop and if you find one, bring that too. You know the drill, I want this place turned inside out. When you have examined everything from a speck of dust to an elephant's foot umbrella stand I want you to escort the Reverend Cadbury to the station. He has been cautioned. Lock him up and put him on suicide watch. I don't want him taking the easy way out."

Cadbury had been listening to this exchange with increasing horror. Now he put his head in his hands and began to weep.

*****

Mr Spurgeon had enjoyed a little lie in that morning. It wasn't something he did often as he firmly believed that being in bed after six o'clock in the morning was something in which only invalids should indulge. He had standards after all. He wasn't like those young people who lived on the council estate only getting up before noon on the days their dole money was paid into the bank. And that was another thing, why were these spongers mollycoddled. They could sign on when they left school and not do a stroke before they retired on a full pension. All paid for by the muggins tax payers like him. And what did they do with the money that was so kindly doled out – they spent it on cigarettes and beer. If they ran out of cash they just went thieving. Stealing from people who had worked hard for their money. And what happened when they got caught? Nothing. Let off with a warning like as not or a fine that would be paid in weekly instalments from their state stipend. And if they did get sent to prison it was a cake walk, colour tellies, video games and three square meals a day. They lived better than most pensioners. He was OK, he had worked for the same company all his life and had retired on a good pension before the big crash but he was in a minority. Most pensioners would look on a prison sentence as being similar to a stay in a holiday camp, something that they couldn't afford to pay for but would be very welcome if they had the opportunity to enjoy a break from their day to day struggle to get by.

Mr Spurgeon was beginning to think of himself as being the pensioner's champion. Of course, what was good for them was good for everybody but he felt an affinity for the downtrodden elderly and wanted to help them more than any other group.

He was reading the Daily Telegraph, letting his breakfast go down a bit before tackling the washing up. The paper was full of Brexit and what it would mean for Britain if we voted to leave the European Union. Mr Spurgeon wasn't interested, as far as he could see one bunch of crooks was much like another and in or out would make not an iota of difference to him. He scanned the foreign news pages. As usual they were full of reports of worldwide economic meltdown and concerns about Russia flexing its muscles again. Like most people he had thought that Russia had turned over a new leaf and was disappointed to learn that Mother Russia wanted to re-adopt the child nations she had freed twenty years ago. At the end of the article readers were reminded that a huge amount of Europe's gas was imported from Russia and that the uncertainty could well result in disruption to supplies and would also give the power companies an excuse to inflate their charges again.

Mr Spurgeon had intended to spend a little time thinking about who his next target should be when he left the kitchen for the sitting room but he was spoilt for choice. As a lifelong Tory he would have ideally liked to emulate Geoffrey Household's "Rogue Male" and go toddling off to assassinate a dictator but he realised with regret that such a thing was beyond his powers. Maybe the boss of an energy company? They increased their prices as soon as the wholesale price of gas went up but never put their prices down when the wholesale cost fell. If anybody exploited ordinary citizens it was them. Definitely one to add to his list.

Then there were the supermarkets. All of them catered for families and not for single people of pensioners. They always had special offers on family sized packs and never on small sizes. And never on Werther's Originals. And they had been adding horsemeat to their beef products to increase their profits. Of course they said they hadn't known but as Mandy Rice Davies would have said, "They would, wouldn't they." A supermarket manager was added to his mental list.

Mr Spurgeon hummed to himself as he began to clear the table. Possibilities, possibilities. This morning it seemed as if the world was full of possibilities.

*****

Miller briefed Mears as he drove far too fast back to Clingford Norton.

"The details are a bit sparse Jimmy. All we know for sure is that a prominent local councillor, a Ms Janet Tomlinson crashed her mobility scooter into a brick wall and was killed instantly. Foul play was not suspected and it was only when the body had been removed to the mortuary and the scooter was being put on a low loader that they discovered a note from chummy claiming he had killed Mrs Tomlinson."

"Looks like we've got a serial killer on our hands Guv. How do you want to play it?"

"Mark an X on the coupon for no publicity for a start Jimmy, and don't call me Guv. There isn't much doubt about the cause of death so we are going directly to the scene of the crash, then on to her home for a quick look around. After that God knows."

"At least we can release some of the team from questioning Karen Bentley's lovers. It would be too much of a stretch to imagine any of them could be the vigilante."

"True Jimmy, but where do we start on this one? If it is a nutcase knocking off people he thinks are a waste of space, he may never have even met his victims. You'd better ring the nick and get someone to collect her house keys from her effects and meet us at her house. They can take a photocopy of the note and bring it with them too, then make sure the original goes to forensics with a most urgent sticker on it. If this mad bugger doesn't have a personal connection to his victims the techies are about our only hope of cracking this case."

"I read a detective novel donkey's years ago, Agatha Christie I think it was, where a bloke killed several people apparently at random. He only needed to kill one to inherit some money and he killed the others because he had no reason to and it disguised his real victim and therefore his motive. I'm not saying this is the same but I don't think we can back pedal too much on the standard, means, motive and opportunity Guv."

"You're right, we have to cover all the bases on this one. We are going to be under the microscope and now we have a political aspect to cope with too. You can bet that Councillor Tomlinson's party colleagues will be on the blower to the ACC as soon as they know her death wasn't accidental"

They sat in without speaking further as the miles melted away, deep in thought. As they entered the town's outskirts Miller broke the silence. "We might have to bring in a profiler."

"They mostly tell you the bloody obvious and when they tell you something that we hadn't thought of it's usually bollocks."

Mears had once had a secondment to the Regional Crime Squad and had actually worked with a profiler on one occasion. It had not been a happy or successful experience and the killer had struck another three times before being caught by an off duty bobby who saw him dumping the body of his latest victim on some waste ground. The profiler had indicated that they should be looking for a middle aged white male from the professional classes who was married and probably sexually impotent. The killer turned out to be of West Indian origin, in his twenties, a fork lift truck operator with a dozen kids by various women.

"I've never worked with a profiler and I hear what you say but what you have to consider is this. We have to be seen to be doing everything we possibly can. This is going to be all over the media and if we don't catch chummy we'll be crucified. That doesn't make a lot of difference to me, I'm going soon anyway but your career is on the line. You're only an "acting" DI and if you want the promotion confirmed we'd better show that we are pulling out all the stops. Mind you the bean counter may say no anyway, you know how tight he is and two high profile murder cases are going to tear a hole in our budget you could drive a double decker bus through."

"If we have to, we have to, but all I'm saying is we need to treat anything a profiler tells us with extreme caution. Personally I'd just as soon consult a fortune teller on Margate pier or sacrifice a goat on my front lawn and read its entrails as take any notice of one of those charlatans."

"Harsh words Jimmy. Over the years profilers have come up with the goods on more than one occasion."

Mears subsided into silence and once more became wrapped up in his thoughts.

*****

When the detective duo arrived at the scene of the crash, Miller exited the car with the speed of a leopard springing on a defenceless lamb. The mobility scooter was still in situ but the corpse had been removed in an ambulance as the note hadn't been discovered until after the body had been moved – much to Miller's displeasure.

"What do we know?" he threw at the nearest uniform, who was trying unsuccessfully to blend into the background.

"I was in the Co-op when it happened sorting out a shoplifter. There was one almighty crash and I was here within a few seconds. I checked the woman over and it was obvious there was nothing that could be done. The front half of her head had been caved in, she wouldn't have felt a thing."

"Yes, yes, get on with it," Miller interrupted impatiently.

"It looked like a straightforward accident. Either her brakes failed or she had had some sort of seizure, passed out and lost control. A traffic car arrived shortly afterwards and the officers thought the same as me – an accident. It was only when her body had been taken away and photographs had been taken of the scene that the tow truck arrived to take the scooter away for examination. That's when the note was found. I rang the station to report in and cordoned off the scene. Then I just waited."

"You've done well lad. You kept your head when it would have been understandable to be overwhelmed. I'll make sure that your Sargent is aware of it."

Miller turned his attention to the scene. There were half a dozen uniforms standing in a group awaiting instructions and a few onlookers with nothing better to do than to stare at the spot where a woman had died.

"Inspector Mears, send those ghouls packing, ensure that the scene is properly photographed and then get these boys cracking on a fingertip search. I want the whole road checked from her house to the point of impact. When that is done you can reopen the road and report to me at the station. I'm going to search her bungalow. I might have a look at the scooter later if I've nothing better to do but forensics should be able to tell us anything we need to know. You'd best call me before you go back to the station, I might still be at the top of the road and you can join me there."

"Anything you'll be looking for particularly Guv?"

"Haven't got a clue but it's what it says you should do in my bumper book of how to be a detective, so that's what I'll do. And don't call me Guv."

Mears passed Miller's instructions on to the team and watched as his boss manoeuvred his large posterior into the driving seat of the pool car in which they had arrived. He'd have to cadge a lift back to the station, still it was too much to expect Miller to walk up such a steep hill, he's probably have a coronary half way up and then he'd have two bodies to sort out. He sighed, it looked like being another long day.

Miller parked the car in the field entrance that Mr Spurgeon had used the previous night. His motive was different though. He didn't want to contaminate the crime scene. He was pulling on a white paper overall when a panda car from the station drew up and a rather nice looking female officer passed him the house keys and a polypocket containing a photocopy of the note.

"Anything else I can do sir?"

Miller had an impure thought about how exactly she could brighten his day but in the interests of preserving his pension he kept them to himself.

"That's all constable, thank you." He smiled as he spoke, managing by sheer willpower not to turn it into a leer.

He read the note before proceeding to the house.

To Whom It May Concern

Mrs Tomlinson has presided over the destruction of the libraries of this county while willingly agreeing to the council's limited resources being spent on lesbian workshops and glossy pseudo newspaper propaganda sheets glorifying the council and other such fripperies.

She was being paid in excess of thirty thousand pounds a year to do a non-job that would once have been filled by a willing volunteer for nothing. She was a leech who used her position for personal gain and she could not be permitted to continue to destroy our libraries with impunity.

Someone had to take a stand in defence of the public and I have answered the call. Other people in public life who are lining their pockets at the expense of hard working ordinary people had better beware. Mrs Tomlinson was only the second on my list and my crusade will continue until justice and fair play are once more established throughout Clingford Norton.

Sincerely

The Vigilante

Sweet Jesus he thought as he raised his eyes from the sheet of A4, a twenty-four carat nutcase. And he'll do it again if we don't stop him quickly. He pulled on a pair of blue rubber gloves and marched determinedly towards the front door of the bungalow. He spent a fruitless hour examining the Councillor's home. He started his search in her bedroom and found nothing more interesting that a copy of *Fifty Shades of Grey* in her bedside cabinet. He checked the spare room and stuck his head into the loft trapdoor. The loft was completely empty other than a water tank. She was disabled, what could he have expected to have found? The sheer bulk of the woman would have prevented her from getting through the hatch even if she could climb a set of steps he mused. The drawing room and dining room offered nothing helpful but the computer on her study desk provided the first interesting piece of information.

He had been surprised to find that no password was required to access the computer but on reflection, she lived alone so who would she hide confidential information from? He quickly skipped files that were labelled with Council business names and moved rapidly into her diary and bank statements. It was almost too easy. Meetings with JM were almost always followed by a cash payment into her bank account. The sums varied but were never less than a thousand pounds and averaged around five thousand. Either she was taking a bung or was blackmailing someone with the initials JM. Whatever, the payments provide a motive. Perhaps the vigilante had reasons for knocking off the Councillor that had nothing to do with public libraries? It was a lead anyway and would have to be properly investigated. He sighed, it would have been easier if he hadn't looked in the computer, then he could have concentrated on the vigilante instead of having to spread his resources in two directions. He shut down the computer, locked the door behind him and made his way back to the station.

Chapter 11

Mr Spurgeon was had spent the morning listening to the local radio station. It wasn't as entertaining as Radio 4 Extra but he wanted to listen to the news for any reports regarding Ms Tomlinson. The forced cheerfulness and sheer inanity of the pseudo American idiot who interrupted the music with his banal comments soon got under his skin. By the time the first news came on giving sparse details of the accidental death of a leading local Councillor he was almost incoherent with frustration and had added local radio presenters to his ever expanding list of targets. The mid-afternoon news had more up-to-date information.

"The death of Councillor Ms Janet Tomlinson this morning is now being treated as suspicious by detectives investigating the apparent road accident. No further information is available at the moment but we will keep you updated with more details as soon as we have them."

They had found the note then. Good, let them investigate as much as they liked, he was satisfied that they would find nothing to link him to the execution. He began to peel potatoes for his evening meal, tonight he would be dining on steak pie, mash and sprouts followed by apple crumble and custard left over from yesterday. Waste not want not as his mother used to say. He hummed contentedly as he prepared his meal, his hands moving rhythmically as he peeled the skin from the King Edwards. After supper he would sit down and have a proper think about his next target. The problem was there were so many to choose from.

*****

When Jimmy Mears returned to the station Miller was busy in an interview room questioning Arthur Cadbury about his activities. Mears was glad of a few minutes to catch his breath and busied himself in Miller's office making coffee. He placed a fresh packet of bourbon creams strategically on the DCI's desk to mitigate his trespassing in the boss's office and settled down in a far from comfy chair to enjoy a coffee while he reflected on the day's events.

He was about to make a fresh cup when Miller waddled through the door. "Making yourself at home then," He muttered grumpily, then spotting the biscuits, he brightened.

"I'll have one as you seem to be in charge of the catering."

"Yes Guv, how did it go with the paedo priest?"

"He's coughing his heart up. We should be able to do him and one or two of his funny friends. The foreign contacts we'll pass on to the Met and they can sort 'em out. How did you get on? Come back with lots of nice big clues so we can close this lot down before I retire?"

"Sorry Guv, nothing like that. There were a few traces of brake fluid on the garage floor and on the road near the house but that's it. We've done house to house near her bungalow and no-one has seen anything remotely suspicious. A couple of witnesses saw her driving down the hill like a fury but that is her usual style apparently. An elderly couple saw her trying to brake as she neared the corner, obviously without success. And that is the sum total of today's endeavours."

Miller had cursed himself when Mears had mentioned the garage. How could he have been so careless as to forget something so startlingly obvious that a bobby on his first day would have investigated as a priority?

"I found something that may or may not be helpful." Miller went on to explain about the computer and what it contained.

"Blimey Guv, this is getting out of hand. We start off with a simple murder and before you know it, we've got two murders and more promised, a paedophile ring and now bribery and corruption at the town hall. We just haven't got the bodies to investigate it all."

"I know. I'm seeing the area commander in the morning and I'll try to offload the bribery and the kiddy fiddling. Failing that I'll throw myself on his floor and cry until I get more officers. And don't call me Guv."

Miller dipped a biscuit into his coffee and munched contentedly until Mears broke the silence. "One other thing you ought to know. We have a leak. Local radio is reporting that we are investigating a suspicious death and not an accident. You can expect the local rag to have the same information. This is likely to be picked up by the nationals too, it's just the sort of thing the tabloids love. Forget about the peripheral stuff, a serial killer will have them champing at the bit. I reckon we are going to have TV cameras and the press all over us."

"Shit, bugger and bollocks! I'd best forget about seeing the area commander tomorrow and see if I can get an interview with him before he buggers off home or disappears to the golf club. Call a briefing session for seven o'clock in the morning. I want everyone present and no excuses. I intend to read the riot act about keeping this investigation confidential and if I find out who is leaking they'll be out of the door so fast their feet won't touch the ground. I want you to prepare a list of duties that reflects that this is now a double murder case. I want everybody we have already interviewed spoken to again. Is there a link between the two victims? I want a rocket up forensics arse. What have they found on the scooter? Did he leave any traces in the garage? I want her colleagues on the council spoken to, who has she upset lately? Same with her neighbours. Does she have a family? Any friends who might know something. All the usual stuff, but prioritise the council. Whether or not the vigilante is right about her, she has upset him big time so who has kicked up most about library closures? Was there a campaign against the cuts? Who was involved? And anything else I've forgotten."

Miller grimaced as he drank the last of his cold coffee and picked up the phone. He paused before dialling. "You still here?"

"On my way Guv."

As Mears closed the door behind him Miller took a deep breath and prepared to do battle with his commander.

*****

Detective Chief Superintendent Wildchild was a fast track copper who had joined the force direct from university. He had enjoyed accelerated promotion and although a good ten years younger than Miller was positioning himself for the Assistant Chief Constable's job when the present incumbent retired in a year's time. His dress was always impeccable, his suit well cut and expensive, the shine on his shoes almost as lethal as a laser beam in a James Bond film. He smiled easily, though the smile seldom reached his eyes and when one got past his rather obvious good looks his mouth seemed thin and mean. Physically he looked to be as fit as a butcher's dog. His office reflected his personal appearance. Photographs of him in rugby kit or meeting some local bigwig adorned the walls. His highly polished desk was bare of anything except a pristine foolscap notepad and a pencil placed on his blotter.

Miller entered the office knowing that he had a battle on his hands. Wildchild was not his favourite person and he wasn't exactly flavour of the month with the DCS and never had been. The two men were like chalk and cheese, sometimes that sort of relationship worked well with each adding their own personal strengths to their mutual benefit. But not for Wildchild and Miller, their shared antipathy was so strong that there was no chance of a harmonious relationship and Miller avoided any contact with his boss that wasn't strictly necessary. Now it was.

"Sir." Miller greeted the DCS.

"Sit down Cedric and fill me in."

I'd love to thought Miller. Only his mother and his wife when she was mardy ever called him Cedric. His friends called him Dusty and the DCS knew that very well, only calling him Cedric to wind him up. He gave a brief resume of the Bentley killing, the paedophile connection and the arrest of Arthur Cadbury then a more detailed account of the day's events, including the possible blackmail or corruption. Finishing with the leak and the imminent invasion by the national media.

Wildchild had been listening with an unhappy expression on his face until the media had been mentioned. Now he perked up, getting his picture in the paper or even being interviewed on TV would raise his profile and do his promotion prospects no harm at all.

"So what do you want from me?" The DCS asked, suspicion colouring an otherwise reasonable question.

"Ideally I need to hand over the paedophile and corruption enquiries so that me and the team can concentrate on the murders. More bodies to perform the routine questioning would be helpful too."

"What about the blackmail aspect."

"Not very likely sir, she was heavily involved in council work and I think that is going to be the most productive area to pursue."

Wildchild considered what he had been told, his HB pencil tapping on his unmarked notepad as he went over the ramifications of Miller's account. Miller waited patiently for the DCS to come to a decision. After what seemed a long period of thought Wildchild dropped his pencil onto the notepad and addressed his junior officer.

"OK Cedric, this is what I am prepared to do. I will take control of all press briefings and statements, that should relieve you of a little burden. I will give the paedophile aspect and the corruption case to DCI Cope and I'll arrange for an additional Sargent and six constables to be seconded to you until further notice. In return I want to be briefed every day and more often if there is an important development. I will have a word with the ACC to let him know that I will be reporting to him from now on."

Miller couldn't believe his luck, he had got everything he had wanted and more. He had already known that the publicity seeking DCS would take over press relations and if he hadn't he would have referred them to the press office anyway, but to get extra resources and pass on some of the workload was better than he could ever have expected. He surmised that Wildchild wanted the case cracked as fast as possible, to take as much credit as he could in order to consolidate his bid for promotion. He wouldn't be smiling when Rex Anderson was on the phone demanding that his paper be given preferential treatment. Then Miller could expect a call from his boss that would be far from cordial. He'd worry about that when it happened.

"Thank you sir, that will be very helpful."

As Miller rose to leave Wildchild added, "I've given you everything you asked for. You have got to deliver, I want a result and I want it quickly. Understood?"

"Yes sir, you're perfectly clear."

As Miller left the DCS's office he knew that he had to succeed. Now Wildchild had given him the resources he had asked for there was no excuse for failure.

Chapter 12

Mr Spurgeon had washed up and put away the dishes. He had enjoyed his meal, the steak pie had had a decent amount of meat and plenty of thick gravy, so important for flavour. The pie had been cheap too, reduced to half price for a quick sale as it was due to go off at midnight. Mr Spurgeon didn't believe in sell by dates. If you thought something was off you sniffed it, and if it smelled alright you ate it. He had even noticed a use by date on a canister of salt he had bought in Tesco's. What nonsense! Salt was dug from the earth where it had rested for thousands of years, it was a preservative for goodness sake. Talk about the nanny state! Anyway his pie had been fine and he had another three tucked away in his small freezer that he would eat over the next few days. As a pensioner he had to watch the pennies. Look after the pennies and the pounds will look after themselves as mother had said.

Now he was sitting in his armchair, Lady Mae was on his lap purring and he was stroking her absentmindedly as he considered his next move. Killing was easier than he had expected. Even killing that grotesque woman hadn't bothered him at all. He vaguely wondered if that was a normal reaction but dismissed the thought. He was an agent for justice not a murderer, so the normal rules didn't apply to him. He had to decide who was going to be next on his death list and get on with it. He wasn't a spring chicken anymore and although his health was good for a man in his seventies he might not be as fit as he was for much longer, and there was so much to do before he retired from his self-appointed role as the Vigilante.

He mulled over various targets, another councillor? Someone from a utility company? What about one of those awful people who kept phoning him, offering to help him get money that he didn't deserve for PPF or some such set of initials? Those people who advertised loans on the television at percentage rates that were close to stratospheric, taking advantage of vulnerable poor people needed sorting out too. There were plenty of politicians who would not be missed either. He chuckled to himself at that, realising that, subconsciously he was quoting the Lord High Executioner from Gilbert and Sullivan's The Mikado. "I've got a little list, he never will be missed." He hummed gaily.

Without coming to a decision on the next step he eventually gave up and went to bed. Telling himself that he needed to sleep on it and he would decide in the morning.

*****

It was the headline in the morning paper that decided the matter.

"Gas to Rise by 10% as Wholesale Prices Fall."

Mr Spurgeon read the article that accompanied the headline with feverish interest. As a pensioner he was acutely aware that heating costs were a major part of his budget. As the Vigilante he was the representative of all downtrodden people, especially pensioners. Basically, it was all in the headline. The shysters who owned UKgas were putting up gas prices by ten percent at the same time as the wholesale price of gas had dropped by twelve percent. The article ended with a warning that a similar rise in electricity prices was forecast.

That settled it. A representative of UKgas would be the next target. Someone as senior as possible ideally, to drive his message home to the fat cats in the boardroom. They wouldn't have to make a choice between eating and heating when the winter came. They would be nice and snug in their well heated homes eating piping hot food while the old and poor died from hypothermia. The sheer gall of these people made him sick to his stomach with righteous indignation. Another trip to the library was called for.

*****

Mrs Dacre was on duty again and they exchanged their customary cordial greetings as Mr Spurgeon passed her desk on his way to the computer section. He settled himself into a chair at the far end of the row of terminals and commenced his trawl through the internet. He tried UKgas's website to start with but without success. He could find the names of various directors but had no way of finding their addresses. A dead end. Just when he was ready to give in his luck changed. As a last resort he had visited the website of the local paper and typed UKgas into the search facility.

He found several articles relating to road works, gas prices and the opening of a new office in the town, but the one that caught his attention was:

"Local Boy Makes Good"

The article was a puff for UKgas using the promotion of a local man to Regional Manager as a reason to publish. Nigel Johnson had attended the local grammar school before taking his degree in environmental studies at a redbrick university. He had worked his way up the greasy pole and had achieved his present position within the organisation at the age of forty-two. He was unmarried and his only hobby was fishing at a local lake where he maintained a caravan. The photograph accompanying the article showed Johnson with a rod in his hands as he stood outside his mobile home. The caravan's name was painted on the side – Carpe Diem, Latin for seize the day and one of his father's most quoted sayings. Mr Spurgeon smiled to himself. It was a poor joke, based on the fact that it was a carp lake he supposed. Mr Johnson sounded perfectly dull and perfectly decent. If it wasn't for his job Mr Spurgeon would have intended him no harm. But he worked for UKgas in a senior capacity and lived locally, so he had to die. The beginnings of a plan were already buzzing through Mr Spurgeon's fertile mind as he bade farewell to Mrs Dacre and exited the library.

*****

"Look Mr Wildchild, did you or did you not find a note from the vigilante at the scene of Councillor Tomlinson's crash?" Rex Anderson was becoming more and more frustrated at the DCS's stonewalling of all but the least important questions he had asked.

"I have no comment at this time."

"I had a deal with DCI Miller."

"I am in charge of all press communications now so any arrangements you had with Millerares null and void."

"Are you going to tell me anything?"

"You will be informed of any developments at the same time as all other members of the media."

"You might find that keeping the right side of the local press is going to be more useful in the long term than chumming up to the nationals. As soon as this case is finished they'll be off to London but I will still be here."

"I will treat every media person in exactly the same way. I do not play favourites."

"Very well Mr Wildchild, just don't ask me for any favours when you need some good publicity. You'll find I don't play favourites either."

Anderson slammed the phone down, pushed his chair back from his desk and reached for his mobile. It went to voicemail. Biting down his anger he left a message.

"Dusty, its Rex. Just been talking to that shit Wildchild – or rather he's not been talking to me. Give me a bell when you can. Cheers."

*****

Mr Spurgeon had visited the bus station after his trip to the library and found, to his delight that a bus stopped at the lakeside every hour on its way to the next town. Deciding that there was no point in returning home. He called in at a local bakery and bought a sandwich and a bottle of water for his lunch then returned to the bus station to await the arrival of the bus to the lake.

Mr Spurgeon passed the short and uneventful journey working out that his small bottle of water was around three times more expensive than the equivalent quantity of petrol. He didn't add the manufacturers to his list but he was sorely tempted to, they were obviously rip off merchants of the worst kind.

He arrived at the lake and followed a footpath that led down to the water's edge and then diverged to the left and right, following the lake shore. Unsure of which path to take, he opted to go left as there seemed to be more caravans parked in that direction. He ambled slowly along, both because he was enjoying the fresh air and the view over the lake and also because he wanted to give the impression that he was a harmless old man out for a ramble on a sunny afternoon. He reached the end of the row of static caravans without finding Carpe Diem and turned to retrace his footsteps. He didn't mind the wasted time, it all added to the impression that he was just enjoying a stroll. He sat for a while and ate his sandwich, washing it down with the liquid gold masquerading as water. When he had finished, he placed his litter in one of the rubbish bins provided, dispose of your litter properly or take it home, his father had said, then ambled up the right hand path confident that Carpe Diem was within reach.

It turned out to be the last caravan in the row and Mr Spurgeon was feeling a little tired after his walk in the sun, his head was beginning to ache and he was glad to spot a convenient bench. He took a seat and looked over the lake as he rested his hip. As he gazed over the beauty spot he scanned the caravan and the surrounding area cautiously, not wanting to attract attention to himself by staring at the mobile home. Except it wasn't mobile, it was resting on piles of concrete blocks and didn't look as if it had moved in years.

The nearest caravan to him was about twenty feet away, adequate for what he had provisionally planned. It looked empty and probably had been for some time. There were no other buildings that overlooked his target's mobile home, all the caravans being arranged along the lakeside in a row. Mr Spurgeon noted that all the mobile homes had two gas bottles standing at the rear. Presumably one was a spare so that when the gas ran out a fresh bottle could be connected without disruption to any cooking that was in progress. It occurred to Mr Spurgeon that it was a form of natural justice for him to be planning to use gas to blow up an employee of UKgas. It just seemed right. Now all he had to do was work out how to detonate the gas at a time he knew Mr Johnson to be staying at the lake and he was home and dry.

*****

That evening Mr Spurgeon spent most of his time in his workshop, hoping that inspiration would eventually arrive. If the gas bottles had been in an enclosed space the answer would have been easy. Light a candle, turn on the gas and exit as quickly as possible. The fact that the gas was outside was what made it difficult and try as he might he couldn't come up with a solution. He was nearing the point when he would have to consider other options when the answer, or at least part of the answer came to him. He needed to put the gas in an enclosed space of his own devising. Now all he had to do was figure out how to do it.

*****

Miller was holding the phone away from his ear with a pained expression on his face when Mears tapped on the door. Miller gestured to him to enter and take a seat at the same time mumbling bland assurances into the telephone. After a while he ended his end of the call with a brisk, "Yes sir, absolutely sir, it won't happen again sir."

He grinned at Mears who had cocked an eyebrow in silent inquiry. "The Wildchild is in a bit of a mood. Rex has been on to him and I gather the call was far from cordial. Not that I give a monkey's, I will be walking out of here and into the sunset in a few week's time, so sod 'em all."

The morning's briefing had gone well, and so it should have, Mears had been up half the night working out rotas and selecting which officers would be doing what. Miller had thrown his toys out of the pram over the leak and promised hellfire and brimstone, not to mention loss of employment and pension to anyone who leaked information to the media about any of the ongoing cases. The officers on the receiving end of his diatribe had reacted well to his abuse, knowing that he was right to be upset. When he had wiped the floor with his officers Miller changed tack. Praising their efforts to date and entreating them to continue to give him their best. When he ended his address by saying that in all likelihood this was his last case and he wanted to go out on a high the assembled team gave him a spontaneous round of applause, which rather took the wind out of his sails. Embarrassed by this show of affection and support he hastily ended the meeting by telling his team to bugger off and get on with the job.

"I'm beginning to wish that I could trade places with you Guv, I'm knackered and the idea of a good night's sleep seems like the ultimate fantasy at the moment."

"You've been working your socks off Jimmy, let's just go over the case again from the beginning and then you can slide off home and catch up on some shut eye. I think that I can just about manage to run things in your absence for the afternoon."

"OK Guv, shall we start off with Darren Bentley? I'll put the kettle on before we start and perhaps you could look in your drawer to see if there's an odd biscuit or two?"

The two men took it in turns to discuss every aspect of the case and to question any conclusions that had been reached. Miller spitting crumbs as he became excited over a point he was making and Mears fighting back yawns and attempting to make incisive comments. It was late afternoon by the time Jimmy Mears finally left the station and they were no further forward than they had been when they started. Nothing of any importance had emerged from their painstaking reconstruction of the investigation into Darren Bentley's death and they were no further forward with the Councillor Tomlinson case either. It seemed that both cases had reached a dead end and as Miller despondently remarked as Mears left his office, "What we need is another murder then maybe the bugger will leave us something to go on."

It wouldn't be too long before his wish came true.

Chapter 13

Mr Spurgeon was feeling happy as he popped his sandwiches and a vacuum flask of tea into his shopping bag. It would be tea today, no more paying inflated prices for a something that fish swim in, not to mention doing other unsavoury things that he didn't want to think about. At least the water from the tap was boiled and had been properly treated by the water authority, something he couldn't be sure of with the French spring water he had been forced to drink the other day. His father had always called tap water Corporation pop although Mr Spurgeon, or Master Spurgeon as he was then would sooner have had proper pop, lemonade or Tizer for choice.

Today he was off to London on the train to purchase a play house, ostensibly for his non-existent niece, in reality it would bring the outdoors inside and enable him to blow Mr Johnson to kingdom come.

He was leaving later than he would have liked but British Rail or whatever they were called these days made travel before nine o'clock much more expensive. They said it was to encourage leisure travellers to make their journeys after the rush hour had ended but Mr Spurgeon believed that it was so they could rip off commuters who had no option but to travel at peak times. When he got to the station and queued to purchase his ticket he got as close to losing his temper as he ever had in his life. The grinning, greasy haired, dandruff coated buffoon who was working behind the counter seemed to think it was amusing to confuse an elderly gent by reeling off a list of options that rivalled the choices on a Chinese menu. Super saver away days, senior citizen rail cards, when was he making the return journey, was he travelling alone as there was a discount for a second person, first or second class, quiet carriage, back to the engine or facing it. He was still reciting his list when Mr

Spurgeon interrupted him and that was most unlike his usual courteous way of dealing with people.

"I want the cheapest possible day return to London please."

The ticket office clerk smiled smugly as he pressed buttons to dispense the tickets, another little triumph over the travelling public. Then he quoted a price that would have been sufficient to purchase a small car a few years ago. Mr Spurgeon breathed deeply as he slowly counted out the banknotes, making an effort not to demean himself by blowing his top. The clerk counted the money twice to ensure it was correct than threw a few coins, his tickets and receipt into a little metal dish and pulled a lever that moved the money and tickets to Mr Spurgeon's side of the counter. He fished out his change and travel passes and stalked out of the booking office and onto the down platform. British Rail had just moved to the top of his target list and he vowed that as soon as he was done with UKgas he would take steps against the minions of the railway system starting with the ticket office clerk. A Mr Mick Jones according to the grubby name badge pinned to his equally grubby shirt.

*****

Cedric Miller sat in his office brushing biscuit crumbs from the front of his waistcoat. The garment was a little on the snug side but he wanted to make a good impression when he returned to interview the widow Bentley. He needed something to do that at least gave the impression that it might be productive and if he had to interview someone it might as well be an attractive woman who caused his trouser furniture to rearrange itself whenever he was in her presence. Every member of his team was out talking to people who had been questioned before in the vain hope that something fresh would emerge. He knew it was a long shot but it had to be done. He had been hanging on at the office, awaiting the arrival of a forensics report on the Tomlinson case before leaving to question the non-grieving widow.

When the report arrived it was several pages thick and said not much more than bugger all. The cause of the accident was brake failure due to the mobility scooter having no brake fluid in its system. There were marks on the pipes and master cylinder that could have been caused by someone draining the system or just as easily by the accident itself. The garage provided no clues at all, no signs of forced entry and no drops of brake fluid on the floor other than the thin trail that had been left when Mrs Tomlinson had exited the garage on her last journey in the mortal world. If only real life was like television. If this was CSI the techies would dab a chemical around the garage, shine a light on it and a hologram of the murderer would appear signing a confession. His only chance of moving forward was locating a witness who saw something on the night of the murder. Wildchild was supposed to be organising an appeal through the media for anyone who had been in the area of Ms Tomlinson's bungalow on the night of the accident to come forward. Miller wished the DCS luck when he asked Rex Anderson for his co-operation, he'd have liked to be a fly on the wall when that conversation occurred.

*****

"I'm afraid none of our play houses are waterproof sir, they're designed for indoor use or outside when the sun is shining." The salesman spoke to Mr Spurgeon as if he were the child that would be using the toy instead of the doting grandparent that he purported to be, the patronising so-and-so.

"Not to worry, I would have preferred something waterproof to save having to move it in and out of the house but one of these will do. But I want something that is lightweight and easy for an old chap like me shift about."

"All the play houses are quite light sir, the rods that hold it in position are either plastic or metal but the fabric doesn't vary a great deal in thickness so there is little to choose in terms of weight."

"Show me one of your better quality ones then please."

Mr Spurgeon had ended up inspecting the young man's entire range. He was disgusted at the flimsiness of the cheaper versions, they wouldn't last ten minutes in the hands of a couple of boisterous toddlers and horrified at the cost of the sturdier types. His father had bought the small terraced house he lived in in the nineteen-thirties for the princely sum of three hundred pounds. Some of these kid's toys were dearer than the price of the house he lived in when his parents had bought it. He gritted his teeth and took his debit card from his wallet, he hated using plastic to pay for goods but after paying for the exorbitantly priced train ticket he didn't have sufficient cash to pay for the play house. He knew it would have been safer to walk to a cash machine and withdraw the money he needed but the journey down and walking the streets of the capital had made his hip ache. His head ached too, a dull throbbing pain that was becoming more and more insistent. He wanted to go home and put his feet up. The chances of anyone discovering that he had purchased the play tent in London he considered so remote that he took the easy option and used plastic to pay.

The young man asked if he would like the item gift wrapped and Mr Sturgeon replied in the affirmative. Just as when he had purchased the boat, the wrapping paper would disguise the nature of his package from his neighbours prying eyes. Apart from the price he was pleased with the play house, he had opted for one that was more or less a four foot cube under a pitched roof and with a zippered entrance. He had selected one with plastic rods as they would burn more easily and the less forensic evidence for the police to examine the better. Best of all it only weighed in at nine kilos and he could manage to transport it without giving himself a hernia. Not that he approved of the metric system, he had had to use it at work from time to time but in his private life he remained steadfastly wed to imperial measurements. More interference from the dratted Europeans, with their bans on odd shaped vegetables and insistence on health and safety, even schoolchildren couldn't go on trips in case they had an allergic reaction to the seaside. Just as well the bureaucrats who ran the show lived in Belgium or he would have pushed them straight to the top of his list.

His only problem now was how to ensure that the gas remained within the play house. He had been mulling that problem over on the journey down and now that he had seen the fabric that had been used to manufacture the play house he was content that he had the answer. He needed to coat the fabric in something that would prevent the passage of air and he was going to use cooking oil. That would be easy to apply after he had erected the tent at the rear of the caravan. A four inch paint brush would do the job in a very few minutes and the oil would burn too and help to destroy the play house completely.

Mr Spurgeon left the department store confident that his plan was viable. He needed to move fast though, as rain was forecast over the weekend and the moon was beginning to wax. He needed a night that was dark and dry to perform his self-appointed task. The only snag with the play house was its bright colour, a sort of fluorescent pink that would appeal to small girls. It would stand out like a sore thumb in the moonlight so it was tomorrow night or he would have to wait for the moon to wane before he could complete his plan.

*****

Miller was trying without much enthusiasm to go over Mrs Bentley's statement, hoping that something might emerge that would give him a clue as to the murderer's identity. It was difficult to concentrate on going over old ground with the merry widow wearing a negligee over very little in the way of undergarments. Not that he was unhappy at having to look at her in a state of semi-undress. She had a body that many younger women would have envied. Long legs and a fine, proud bosom that was in danger of spilling out every time she bent forward. She must have known the effect she was having on the fat policeman as she continually found excuses to lean over, offering him a biscuit from a plate of chocolate digestives or topping up his coffee cup. He knew that she was only teasing him, he was portly and not a handsome man, far, far down the pecking order of potential men with whom she would want to enjoy an afternoon of red hot sex. Nonetheless his body was reacting in the most natural way in the world and he was concerned that he wouldn't be able to disguise his tumescence when it was time to take his leave. He was a little surprised and quite proud to have reacted with such a display of youthful enthusiasm. Things had been a bit quiet in that department lately, perhaps he would give his wife a pleasant surprise when they retired to bed that night?

He brought his wandering mind back reluctantly to the interview. "So you can think of absolutely nothing that might assist us in our inquiries?" He asked ponderously.

"Nothing Mr Miller, everything is in my original statement. I've wracked my brains to think of something that would help you find the man who killed Darren. I've said before I thought he was an unpleasant man but he didn't deserve to die in a fireball and if I knew anything I would tell you."

"Fair enough Mrs Bentley, if you do happen to remember something, any little scrap of information, please call me at the station. Our job is like assembling a jigsaw puzzle, we take all the little fragments and put them together to make a picture of what happened. On their own one piece frequently means nothing but when it is placed with others the truth can sometimes emerge."

He stood to take his leave, bending forward as if suffering from a mild backache as he did so, in order to disguise his erection.

"Trouble with your back Mr Miller?" The widow enquired mischievously, her eyes revealing that she had a good idea of the cause of his discomfort.

"Just old age creeping on, it will pass In a short time." But he was half way back to the station before his hormones subsided and he could sit comfortably and concentrate on his driving.

Chapter 14

Mr Spurgeon was a little worried. He had everything ready to put his plan into operation but he didn't know if Mr Johnson would actually stay at the caravan that night. His best guess was that he would, making an early start to his fishing on Saturday morning before the forecast rain descended. He knew that, as much as it went against the grain to break the law, he would have to use the Morris again. He simply had no other option. He couldn't commence his activities until Mr Johnson was fast asleep and all activity amongst the other caravans had ceased. There was no point in performing a dry run to check if he was at the site, that would simply double the chance of being observed. He would wait until midnight and hope that luck was on his side.

He spent the afternoon preparing for his planned nocturnal activities. He went into town and bought a large bottle of the cheapest cooking oil he could find and added a few bits and pieces to his basket so that his purchase of the oil would not stand out in the till girl's memory. Not that she looked as if she had a memory or any sort of brain function at all. She waved his purchases through the barcode scanner as if she was an automaton, her bovine eyes registering no interest at all in what she was doing, her jaw moving lethargically as she chewed on a piece of gum. She didn't even look at him when she announced the total price of his goods. At any other time he would have been miffed to have been treated with such arrant discourtesy but today it suited him to be ignored and he left the supermarket content that he had attracted no undue attention.

After his trip to town Mr Spurgeon turned his attention to the gift wrapped parcel. The wrapping paper was pink and that would be too bright even in the darkness of the lakeside. He tore off the paper and, after inspecting the brightly coloured box decided that he would have to rewrap the play house in something darker to tone down its almost radioactive colour scheme. He decided that the sound of paper being removed in the silence of the lake area was likely to sound louder than he would like. His target would be sleeping a few feet away with only the thin wall of a caravan to deaden the sound. He opted instead to wrap the box in one of Lady Mae's old blankets and secured it with string. He added a couple of straps that he cut from an old knapsack that he had used when he went on hiking holidays and he had a parcel that he could carry on his back the way that young backpackers carried their worldly goods when on a gap year abroad.

All he needed now was a strong, sharp knife, the oil, an old paint tray to pour the oil into, a box of cooks matches and the enormous church type candle that his nephew had given him for Christmas a few years ago. Apparently it gave off a scent of vanilla when it was lit but Mr Spurgeon had never bothered to find out and the candle was with so many other unwanted knick-knacks in a cupboard in the dining room. Its sheer size was what made it perfect for the job. Thick enough to stand on its own without the need to stabilise it on a saucer. It would also burn for a long time, so if the gas took longer than expected to build up there would still be a naked flame to cause ignition.

The final and vital piece of equipment was his folding sack barrow. He wouldn't need it to transport the play house but when he shifted the gas bottles he would be glad to use it. Full bottles weighed over sixty pounds and that was a fair weight for a man in his eighth decade to lug about. He assembled his equipment and then went to bed for a nap, he wasn't used to late nights and he needed to be alert and on top of his game when he was creating his home-made bomb.

*****

Jimmy Mears returned his mobile to his jacket pocket and sighed. "That's the last of 'em Guv, all the teams have finished for the day and no progress made whatsoever."

Miller looked at his watch, "It's after eight o'clock Jimmy, time to call it a day and go home to our loved ones – or our wives."

Mears smiled automatically at Miller's tired old joke and nodded his agreement. "We're not doing any good here Guv and that's for sure. There are still a few people to see tomorrow but if that doesn't get us anywhere I'm blessed if I know how to take the investigation forward."

"Don't fret Jimmy, something will turn up. Probably another body." He added in a voice that smacked of graveyards. "Now that would move things on."

"I know I shouldn't say this Guv but I think that is our only hope of solving this puzzle. If the so-called Vigilante stops now I think he's going to get away with it because we haven't got a shred of evidence we could use against him in court. At the moment our only hope is that he suddenly finds God and walks into the station to confess his sins."

"Chin up, it's never as bad as that. Just keep plugging away, something will turn up in the end. I'm going to see Wildchild tomorrow and ask him if we can get a profiler in from the Met, although I'm not sure there's enough to create a profile. By the way, speaking of profiles, we keep calling the Vigilante he, any chance it might be a bint?"

"Shouldn't think so, the boat bomb and fiddling with the braking system of the scooter point towards someone who is at home with a bit of do-it-yourself. Don't suppose we should rule it out though, there's a lot of women around these days who can change a light bulb."

"Okay Jimmy, see you in the morning. Oh, and Jimmy?"

"Yes Guv."

"Don't call me Guv."

*****

Mr Spurgeon had slept well and was now wide awake and driving the Morris towards the lake. He hummed a little tune as he maintained a steady fifty miles an hour on the main road. He was happy to be making progress and knew that his task would either be completed that night or he would need to postpone for a while until the moon was beginning to lose its power. He wanted to get the job done so that he could move on, but was not especially perturbed by the idea that it might take longer than he would have wished. He was pleased that he had remembered one small but important thing before he had left the lock-up. He had removed the interior light bulb. The last thing he wanted was to be illuminated as he left or re entered the car, after all if he was about after midnight there might well be other night-owls.

He pulled the car off the road into a small layby opposite the entrance to the lake. There were trees overhanging the parking spot and the dark coloured vehicle was virtually invisible to anyone more than a few feet away. He glanced at his watch, it was twelve thirty, hopefully Mr Johnson would be tucked up and fast asleep so that he could wake refreshed for a day's angling. He shrugged the package onto his back, picked up the lightweight sack barrow in one hand and a plastic carrier bag in the other and moved as swiftly as an old man could across the road and into the field.

There were still a few lights showing through the curtains of several caravans but they were all in the opposite direction to the way he was going and far enough away from where he would be to cause him no concern. He moved stealthily down the slight slope, now he felt confident that the grass would muffle any noise he made, he gratefully assembled the sack barrow and dragged it behind him rather than carrying it. As he progressed towards Mr Johnson's caravan he thanked his lucky stars that he had remembered to grease the wheels of the sack barrow that afternoon. As it was he was spookily silent and moved across the field with no more noise than a clumsy field mouse would have made.

His eyes were now becoming accustomed to the darkness and he could see the shapes of the caravans clearly against the gently lapping waters of the lake. At any other time, Mr Spurgeon would have enjoyed the serenity of the spot and the fresh air that was entering his lungs but he was on a mission and had no time for the beauties of nature. As he approached his destination he was able to discern the outline of a vehicle adjacent to the caravan. Good! That meant he was here and his journey had not been wasted.

He slowed as he neared the caravan and moved silently to the side of the caravan. He pressed his ear to the side of the mobile home nearest to the gas bottles and held his breath while he listened intently. After a moment or two he was able to make out faint snores. Bingo! He was in business.

He swiftly placed the sack barrow on the ground alongside his carrier bag of equipment then shrugged the package from his back and unwrapped the playhouse. There was no need to read instructions, even if the meagre light cast by the stars and the waning moon had been strong enough for him to do so. He slit the package open with a lethal looking knife that he had used when he was a boy scout and slid the contents gently onto the ground. Assembling the play house took only a few minutes even though he constantly paused his activities to listen for any signs of life.

Now for the tricky bit. He bent over the gas bottles at the rear of the caravan and slowly, and very, very carefully disconnected the live bottle from the pipe that led into the kitchen of the mobile home. Apart from the slightest scrape of plastic on metal the whole procedure was conducted in silence. He used the sack barrow to move the bottles to one side, using the cat blanket to muffle the metal base of barrow. He was doubly lucky as the spare bottle was full and the one in use nearly the same. Now he picked up the playhouse and positioned it up against the rear of the caravan so that the entrance was at the side and manoeuvred the bottles into the fabric tent. Full of his own cleverness he decided to check out the nearest caravan's supply of gas to see if he could add another bottle to the two he had already installed. Once again he was in luck and managed to wheel his barrow across the grass with a further full gas bottle which he added to the existing pair. He knew it was stealing and his conscience pricked at the thought of committing a robbery but he consoled himself with the thought that it was for the greater good.

He couldn't afford to hang about and quickly moved to the next stage. He unscrewed the top of the oil bottle and poured some of the slippery contents over the play house roof. The rest of the oil went into the roller tray. Swiftly he spread the oil over the external surfaces before darting inside and performing the same task on the interior. In the darkness he couldn't discern how efficiently he was coating the fabric but hoped that by applying the oil to both sides of the play house he would have made the tent sufficiently non-porous to prevent the loss of gas. Next was the dangerous part. He placed the toy's packaging along with the empty oil bottle, the paint brush and everything else he had used, with the exception of his sack barrow inside the play house and set the candle near the entrance so that he didn't have to enter the pretend building to light the wick.

He took a last look around then entered the play house and turned on the three gas taps. It took him a moment to grip a match through the latex gloves he was wearing but as soon as he had the candle lit and the entrance zipped down Mr Spurgeon beat a hasty retreat. He moved as rapidly as he could up the slope towards his car, dragging the sack barrow behind him. He glanced back to check that he was unobserved and saw the light of the candle clearly showing across the dark field. All he could do now was hope that no late night nosey parker interfered with his plan.

When he reached the road he picked up the sack barrow and flitted over the tarmac like Dracula after a virgin. As he approached the car his heart stood still and he felt an almost irresistible urge to vomit. There was a car parked behind the Morris! He stopped in his tracks, trying to still the rapid breathing that the scare had engendered. Low noises were coming from the other vehicle. Moans as if someone were in pain. Then the light dawned and he realised that a couple were having sexual congress only a few feet away. Shocked by their lewdness he moved quickly and silently to place the sack barrow in the front passenger's foot well, then climbed into his vehicle, started it up and moved off without turning on his lights. He drove for a mile or so before he risked switching his headlights on and took a circuitous route back to his home that avoided the main roads.

He had been driving well within the speed limit and was just entering the town when a mighty explosion shattered the peaceful night. He pulled over at a post box and slipped in a thin envelope. He had done it again! His only concern now was getting home without being spotted. Apart from the remote possibility that the couple in the car had seen him and noticed his distinctive car he had completed his mission without being observed by a single witness. He thought he would probably be alright, the courting couple would have been too engrossed in their carnal pursuits to have seen him and it was unlikely they had paid any attention to his old motor. He slipped off his latex gloves and popped them into his pocket. He would dispose of them in a litter bin the next time he went shopping. The Morris Minor's engine purred quietly as Mr Spurgeon drove sedately through the deserted side streets towards his garage. He was too excited to sleep immediately he got home so he planned to have a glass of scotch before retiring to his bed. After all he had something to celebrate. His third successful mission!

Chapter 15

Miller stamped across the field like an unstoppable force of nature. It was three o'clock in the morning and he had been roused from his bed by a call telling him that it looked as if there had been another murder. He was tired, angry and frustrated and God help anyone who dared to cross him.

Jimmy Mears was waiting for him just outside a cordon that had been set up around the wreckage of the burned out caravan.

"The Chief Fire Office attending thinks that this is likely to be arson. It took him a while to come to that because they needed to evacuate a couple of vans that were occupied and wait for the fire to be damped down sufficiently to get close enough to see what had happened."

"So what did happen?"

"It looks as if someone deliberately ignited the gas bottles. Apparently the gas leaked under the caravan and when it went up – it went up. Up in the air and down on its side. The occupant's car went up in flames too and the petrol tank exploded before the firemen got here. It's all a bit confused but they think there are probably two bodies. The remains are badly burned and have been scattered over the whole area so we won't know for sure until forensics get here and do their stuff. The only thing I can tell you with any degree of certainty is that it looks as though he used some sort of barrow to move stuff around. There are wheel marks leading down from the road and back again plus marks going back and forth to the next caravan in the row. It looks as though he nicked their gas and added it to what he already had."

"What have you done so far?"

"I've got a team talking to the people who have been evacuated. When they've been questioned they'll start to knock up the people on the far side of the site. Not that anybody could have slept through the bang when it went up, I heard it and I was asleep in bed at the time. Forensics are on the way and the fire service will remain on site until they are completely sure that there is no further danger. They will have their own specialists here in the morning to ascertain how the explosion occurred."

"Any idea about the victims?"

"The caravan belongs to a bloke called Johnson. He comes here for the fishing most weekends but he keeps himself to himself. He sometimes has a mate stay over but not always the same one. One of the chaps down the field said that he thought Johnson worked for an energy company but he wasn't sure. I'll get someone to find out his registered address through his licence plate. We'll turn his gaff over as soon as we know and we should find something that will tell us where he worked."

"Well done Jimmy, it looks as though you have it all in hand and there is nothing for me to do until the morning. Divert as many bodies as you need from the Bentley and Tomlinson inquiry. I want everyone on this site questioned and a fingertip search of the field for a five hundred metre radius of the locus. When forensics get here, kick 'em up the arse and tell them that this takes priority over anything else and I want a preliminary report in my hand before noon."

He gave an evil little smile and added, "I'll be getting Mr Wildchild out of bed and telling him the body count has probably risen to four. If you listen carefully you'll probably hear another explosion when he blows his top. Seriously Jimmy, you've done well again, no more than I would have expected of course from my apprentice, but pleasing nonetheless. I'll make sure the over-educated git is aware of that when I break the bad news."

"Thanks Guv, I'll see you at the station when this little lot is making some sort of sense."

*****

Miller and Mears were huddled over the desk in Miller's office examining the preliminary forensics report. Miller stood up and gave a cross between a sigh and a tremendous yawn. "It's no good Jimmy we can't both read it, the writing's far too small for my old eyes anyway. You read it out and we'll discuss it as we go."

"Okey-doke Guv, are you sitting comfortably? Then I'll begin."

He quickly scanned through the opening paragraphs that basically gave an alibi to the report's author if anything was incorrect and pointed out that this was a preliminary report that might be superseded by later findings.

"The wheel marks that we thought were made by a sack barrow were made by a sack barrow or something very similar."

"Startlingly bleedin' obvious," Mumbled Miller grumpily.

Mears continued unabashed at his boss's ill temper. "There are marks in the grass made by someone's feet but they are not clear enough to give an indication of weight, height or build. They have found fragments of fabric that indicate some sort of tent may have been erected to give the gas a chance to build up before it went bang. The fabric was soaked in oil. Most likely standard cooking oil but they can't be certain until it's been tested."

He paused and glanced at Miller for permission to continue.

"All clear so far."

"The body count is two not one. Apparently Johnson had a mate staying over, most likely for the fishing but the Fire Officer says they were in the same bed. The bodies were very badly damaged and death would have been instantaneous. The bed the two men were in was next to the wall where the gas bottles were located. And that is about it. The fingertip search of the field is still in progress but nothing of any obvious interest has been found yet apart from bits of caravan and some scraps of fabric that may have come from the tent. There are tyre marks in the layby opposite the entrance to the field but that is what you'd expect. SOCO have taken photographs and casts just in case. There were also a couple of used condoms that appear to be reasonably fresh. I'm not much of a judge of how fresh used condoms are myself but that's what the techies say, so it is possible that someone was having a bunk up while the arsonist was doing his thing."

"Okay. I want that fabric analysed as fast as possible, if we can trace the type and where it was bought we might have a chance of catching chummy before he does any more damage. I'll ask Wildchild to put out an appeal for information, emphasising that we would like the courting couple to come forward and promising them confidentiality if they do. I know this will be manpower heavy but I want as many bodies as you can spare knocking on doors. I want every house on the road to and from the lake spoken to. I don't care if we finish up getting people out of bed at midnight I want to know if anyone saw or heard anything odd or suspicious between the hours of midnight and one o'clock."

"What about his home guv, do we know where he lived?"

"Yeah, Atkins came up trumps again, he lives somewhere on the Bretterton Road and worked for UKgas."

"Have we detailed anyone to search his gaff yet?"

"Not yet, I doubt if there is anything there to tell us much anyway and I wanted to go over forensics with you before I paid Mr Johnson's house a visit. I'll be doing that job myself with a bobby as soon as I've updated Wildchild."

"Are we concentrating on this being the work of the vigilante Guv? We don't know anything about this guy except he was possibly gay. He could have dozens of enemies for all we know and if he worked for the gas company you can count me as a suspect, I got the quarterly bill yesterday and haven't recovered from the shock yet. And the vigilante hasn't claimed this one."

"This has got that mad buggers signature all over it. It's too like the boat bomb to be a coincidence. As to the note he couldn't pin it to something he was blowing up but we might get something in the post tomorrow. And don't call me Guv."

"As you say Guv. I'll get cracking, when and where do you want to meet up."

I'm not sure Jimmy, I'll ring your mobile when I know which way is up."

*****

While Miller and Mears and all their gophers were working themselves into the ground Mr Spurgeon was relaxing. He had had a few hard days and a very late night and felt he deserved to wallow in unaccustomed idleness. He wouldn't even be bothered to cook today, he would treat himself to a nice plate of fish and chips from the only chip shop left anywhere near his home. There had once been four purveyors of that most English of meals in the area but three had sold up and been turned into Chinese or Indian take-aways. They were actually closer to his home than the chip shop but he couldn't possibly eat the foreign muck that they served up. There had been rumours about local cats disappearing and ending up on their menus as chicken and as his father used to say, there's no smoke without fire. No, a nice plate of cod, chips and mushy peas washed down with a bottle of pale ale from the fridge would do him nicely.

He occupied himself until it was time for his evening meal soaking in a nice hot bath, very good for relaxing tired muscles, and then wrapped in a thick bathrobe and oblivious to the hot weather, he sat in his armchair and watched television. That was in itself a rare event, Mr Spurgeon didn't believe in television during the day and hadn't much time for it at night. The pictures were better on the radio. Today though, there was a Randolph Scott western film that he hadn't seen for many years and he had a lot of time for Randolph Scott. He always played upstanding men fighting for justice against terrible odds. He always won through though and good always triumphed over evil in the end. A bit like himself in fact. Except he was older.

The rest of his day went according to plan and he was fast asleep in bed before ten o'clock, sleeping the sleep of the just.

*****

"Rex, how are you this bright and sunny morning?"

Miller's voice was full of false bon homme and grated on the editors slightly hung over nerves. "What do you want Dusty? It had better be good to wake me up at this time on a Monday morning."

"Not much Rex, just checking on an old chum to see if you're keeping well and that Wildchild is looking after you."

"Come off it, you know that arsehole wouldn't give the local rag the time of day."

"I didn't actually, he told me that he was giving all the media a fair shake of the stick. We'll have to do something about it. Tell you what, why don't I pop round to your office this morning for a coffee and a biscuit? I'll even bring the biscuits if your petty cash can't spring for them and we'll have a nice little chat about police/media co-operation."

"You're up to something you old bugger but you know you are welcome to visit anytime you like."

"See you later then, Be good."

Miller turned to Mears, "He knows I'm up to something but he hasn't twigged what. I'll take myself round to his office just before the mail arrives and with any luck I'll be in his office in time to intercept any notes from that sick bugger we're chasing."

"Have I ever told you you're a bit of a sly old fox on the quiet."

"No, but you can start whenever you like. Tell you what, you should have finished briefing the team before I need to walk over the square, why don't you come with me and we can gang up on old Rex? The house to house stuff has brought us nothing except people saying that they heard a bang in the early hours of Saturday. No response either from the courting couple, one of them is probably married and scared that that their other half will find out about their dirty doings in laybys. Forensic say that they are going as fast as the tests they're doing will permit and they may have a result on the tent fabric this afternoon. I'd like you around when that comes in so if there's anything helpful we can action it right off."

Miller was putting on a front. He was actually despondent, the case had ground to a halt and he couldn't think what else could be done. If the fabric didn't help he really would have to tell Wildchild that he needed to bring a profiler in to help. Either a profiler or a clairvoyant to read the runes. He would dance naked with druids around Stonehenge if it would help to crack his last case.

*****

While Miller and Mears were comparing notes Mr Spurgeon was sitting on a bench opposite the railway station observing commuters rushing around like lunatics. Railway station he mused, yes, railway station, not train station as so many modern people said. And people were *passengers* not customers.

He had learnt nothing during his period of observation, not that he had expected to really. He had visited the station before and now had a timetable at home. What he was watching and waiting for was inspiration. How would he tackle this target? So he sat and patiently watched. Confident that something would happen to steer him in the right direction. He wasn't a religious man but he knew deep inside that some greater power was looking after him, not guiding him exactly but making sure that he could carry out his role as the Vigilante.

*****

Miller and Mears meantime had left the police station and were pressing their noses up against a patisserie window and discussing what treats they would take with them to Rex Anderson's office. At the same time, they were watching the postman walking down the side of the Square towards the Star's offices in the reflection in the glass.

"Right, let's move. You're younger and faster than me so you can get the cakes, I'll stroll over and take a seat in Rex's office and you join us with the goodies."

Without giving his colleague a chance to comment Miller strolled off, timing his arrival so that he reached the newspaper's offices a couple of minutes before the day's post was delivered. Miller was a familiar figure and known to be a chum of the editor so was shown straight through to Anderson's office. He politely tapped on the door then shouted, "It's a raid," and threw himself into the room. The editor was startled by his unexpected intruder and spilt a little coffee down his shirt front as he made to leap from his seat.

Miller clutched his chest and howled with laughter at the expression on his old friend's face. "Oh my, who has a guilty conscience then?"

"You utter sod. That has taken five years off my life and doubled my laundry bill. I hope you realise that tonight's headline will be about police brutality. I think we've still got a photo of you somewhere. Probably on the dartboard in the canteen." He added malevolently.

"Oh shut up you tart, mine's coffee with milk and two sugars. Mears will be here in a moment and he'll have the same."

Anderson sighed and picked up the phone to order coffee for his visitors. "I don't see the promised biscuits," He commented wryly.

"Cakes are on their way Rex, Jimmy is in the patisserie making said purchases even as we speak."

They chatted in a desultory way, asking about each other's wives and how their gardens were standing up to the prolonged dry spell until the coffee, Jimmy Mears and the post arrived together.

Anderson greeted Mears. "Hi Jimmy, I'm always glad to see you but I'm surprised you have time for social visits with everything you've got on your plate. It's different for Dusty he's retiring soon and he does bugger all anyway."

"Glad to see you too Rex but this is only partially a social call. Would you mind having a squint at your post? We think matey boy might have sent you another billet doux. Don't touch it if he has, I doubt that there are any dabs but stranger things have happened and we are due a bit of luck."

The editor picked up the paper knife from his desk and began to flick through the pile of envelopes. The letter from Mr Spurgeon was three from the bottom.

"This one looks familiar."

"Hand it over Rex," Mears said eagerly.

"Hold on Jimmy, we don't know it's from the Vigilante yet and we won't until I open it."

They argued good naturedly until they had agreed that Anderson could open the letter as long as he wore a pair of latex gloves when he handled it. If it was from the Vigilante, he would personally photocopy it and hand the original letter and envelope to Mears. They agreed to wait to see the contents before they would discuss if any parts of the letter would need to be redacted.

It was, as expected, from the Vigilante. It began, as had the previous letter to the Star, without salutation.

Nigel Johnson was a boss at a company that is ripping off the public. Pensioners cannot afford to heat their homes or cook a hot meal but he didn't care. Let his death be a warning to all those who seek to exploit the vulnerable. Their fate will be the same. I will continue my mission until we have a fair and equitable society. To prove once more that this letter is not the work of a crank I will tell you something that only I would know. Nigel Johnson was blown up by a child's play house.

The Vigilante

The three men looked at each other as they tried to digest the Vigilante's latest missive.

Anderson was the first to break the silence, "Is that right? Johnson was killed by a kid's *play tent*?" He sounded utterly incredulous.

Miller took charge and said portentously. "A play tent was used during the commission of the crime but I don't want that part published. If you play ball, I'll fill you in with where we are now.

When this mad bugger is locked up I'll give you the inside story before anyone else in the media."

"What about future developments?"

"I'll keep you in the loop as long as I have your solemn word that you won't publish until I give you the OK."

"And what happens if you retire before he's caught?"

Mears spoke up, "I'll take over from the Guv, and we'll have the same deal."

Anderson was satisfied with that and the three men shook hands to bind their agreement then sat back down ready to begin Anderson's briefing.

"Once upon a time……," Began Miller.

*****

The remainder of the week was frustrating for everyone working on the Vigilante case. Asking the same questions of the same people over and over was producing nothing but the same answers as before. The phone lines were reasonably busy but no calls had revealed any new information. Sorting out the genuine callers from the usual crop of confessions from the mad, bad or lonely that plagued every major crime investigation took valuable time. Time that could have been spent on potentially more fruitful lines of investigation. Einstein once said that the definition of madness is to repeat the same actions but expect a different outcome and if the men and women on the front line had been aware of that they would surely have agreed.

Questions about Nigel Johnson's sexual preferences had yielded the information that he was gay but had kept his sex life very much to himself. He had been well liked by his colleagues but they were able to say very little about Johnson's private life. He had no immediate family and no friends had come forward. A team visited the one local pub that hosted a gay night but the photograph of Nigel Johnson had drawn nothing but a blank. The team had now moved on to visit every pub and club in the area flashing the photograph in the hope that someone would recognise the face and be able to offer a lead. Another team had tracked down the secretary of every local angling club but with the same lack of success. It was planned that a team would visit the lake this coming Saturday to talk to any regular weekend anglers who might have some information.

The one stroke of luck was when forensics announced that they had identified the fabric found at the crime scene. It had come from a "Klassic Toddler Tent." It was an expensive toy that sold in fairly limited quantities. Fortunately, each retail outlet would only sell one, two or three during the season. Unfortunately, the numbers of retailers who stocked the play tent stood in the mid hundreds and were nationwide. The assembled teams groaned when Mears passed this information on at the morning briefing session. They knew that they faced days of boring routine enquiries that would probably result in nothing.

"Hold on," Said Mears holding up his hand to quiet down the hubbub that had greeted his news, "DCI Miller has been on to the manufacturers and they are raising a list of all the retail outfits that stock this particular item. It's a big job for them to separate out this information so we won't get it until sometime tomorrow. When we have it we are going to divide the information up into geographical areas and start visiting the shops in and around Clingford Norton first. We'll spread the net wider if we need to but let's hope it doesn't come to that. I know this is a bit of a balls aching job but it's the best lead we have so I don't want any moaning and I certainly don't want anyone taking this lightly. This bugger has killed four people and he'll carry on with his killing spree until we stop him. Any questions."

PC Atkins was braver than most and raised his hand.

"Yes, Atkins?"

"What about the bloke in the caravan with Johnson? Do we know who he is yet?"

"When we find out who he is I promise you will be the first to know," Mears said sarcastically, before continuing, "All we have is a rough idea of his size and age. Around six feet tall and between twenty and forty years of age. The fire and explosion did an extremely thorough job of destroying any evidence. We don't even have any teeth that we could show to local dentists. Our one hope is that someone will report a missing person. We have an on-going appeal for anyone with a friend or relative that went missing in the past few days to contact us. If they do we should be able to do a DNA test and establish his identity. That may or may not be of any use. If he was just a bit of trade that Johnson picked up for a night of fun and frivolity it is unlikely to take us any further forward. Any more questions?"

Mears closed the meeting and headed directly to Miller's office to brief him on the meeting and cadge a cup of coffee before he started to work out new play tent rotas.

*****

The week was almost as frustrating for Mr Spurgeon. The news that he had killed not one but two people in the caravan explosion had set him back on his heels. The shock had left him needing copious draughts of hot sweet tea and a nice sit down. His mother had always advised hot sweet tea for shock, so much better than tranquilisers, tea was comforting. He hadn't wanted to kill an innocent man, only people he had targeted as deserving to be executed were on his list. He had seriously considered hanging up his sword of truth and justice and retiring as the Vigilante. He decided to sleep on it before he came to a firm conclusion but his decision was made for him when he read that day's edition of the Star. It was cleverly done and not spelled out in so many words but the implication was clear. Mr Johnson's friend was a bit more than a friend. Apparently they had been in the same bed when the gas had exploded. That made Mr Spurgeon feel a bit better about killing the man. After all he was a pervert, so didn't count as an innocent person whose life had been accidentally extinguished. His crusade could continue unimpeded by twinges of conscience.

*****

Mr Spurgeon was in a quandary, the dreadful British Rail employee Mick Jones had now moved to the top of his list, but he was making little progress. He needed to observe his movements but he couldn't hang around the railway station without drawing attention to himself and had resorted to walking past the station at odd times to see if he could learn something about his latest target. It was the evening of day three when his luck changed. Mick Jones had obviously finished his shift and was just walking out of the station when Mr Spurgeon rounded the corner. Mr Spurgeon crossed his fingers that he would catch a bus or walk home, so that he could follow him to his destination. If he knew where he lived, he might be able to work out a plan that didn't involve the railway station. His luck was in, Jones walked straight past the small staff car park and proceeded to stroll down the narrow little road that led to the canal.

That was an odd way to go home Mr Spurgeon mused, there were no houses in that direction and the tow path ended at a tunnel after about a mile. Perhaps he was simply taking the evening air after being in a stuffy booking office all day? He couldn't blame him for that, today had been very sultry and he had actually removed one of his cardigans in an effort to cool down. He followed Jones at a distance, knowing that they were heading into a dead end and Jones would need to retrace his steps when he had completed whatever he was doing. That might mean he would see Mr Spurgeon face to face and recognise him from the other day. He would need to be very careful.

It really was very pleasant now he was walking along the tow path, the sun was shining on the water, birds were singing and butterflies swooped around the thick bushes that lined the land side of the canal.

There were one or two other walkers enjoying the idyllic evening and Mr Spurgeon resolved that he would take this walk again. The other walkers were heading back into town and Mr Spurgeon was a little surprised at the knowing looks he received when he bade them good evening as they passed. A little puzzled, he continued down the tow path until he was startled to see two men emerging from the bushes just in front of him. One man was tucking his shirt in and the other zipping up his jeans. The younger man winked at Mr Spurgeon as he moved past him and said, "Good luck general."

The penny dropped with a resounding thump. This was one of those places that homosexuals visited for casual sex. He felt the colour rise in his cheeks. That impudent young devil obviously thought he was there for the same disgusting purpose. How utterly awful. He resolved to return to town as quickly as he could and leave these degenerates to their foul activities. As he turned on his heel to depart he noticed that Jones was talking to a younger man a couple of hundred yards from where he was standing. Not wanting to be seen he stepped back and pressed himself up tight against the bushes. He continued watching and saw Jones and the young man glance swiftly around and then move into the undergrowth. He resolved to stay where he was for the time being and await developments.

After ten minutes or so he decided that he would walk further down to see exactly what Jones and his companion were up to. He forced himself to walk slowly, strolling down the tow path as if he had all the time in the world. He slowed even further as he approached the place where the two men had entered the bushes. He could now hear grunting and the slap of flesh on flesh emerging from the dense bushes. He stopped and peered through the branches. The sight that greeted his eyes filled him with a sort of horrified fascination. Just as drivers slow down at the site of an accident to gawp at the damaged cars and injured people, he knew he shouldn't look but felt compelled to observe what was happening. Jones had removed his trousers and was bent over, his hands gripping his knees to maintain his balance as the younger man stood behind him and penetrated him. The young man was thrusting with tremendous force and Jones was moaning loudly with pain or pleasure, or both.

    Mr Spurgeon forced himself to look away from the disgusting spectacle and walked rapidly towards the dead end, entering the bushes himself a few yards later. He was standing in a small clearing that was obviously well used by homosexuals. Used tissues and condoms were scattered over the ground and a pair of what he took to be ladies panties were hanging from a branch. This was too awful to think about. Mr Spurgeon felt anger rising within him, Jones wasn't just an unpleasant and rude man he was a queer. His scout master had had similar inclinations. His wandering hands had groped all the boys in the troop. He only stopped his nefarious activities when the young Master Spurgeon had sunk his sheath knife through the back of his hand as it travelled up his thigh. Mister Spurgeon had no time for perverts, his target's fate had been sealed before this revelation but was now his demise was doubly certain.

    He picked up a half brick that was lying amongst the detritus on the ground and hefted it in his hand. It felt comfortably heavy. He waited until their perverted antics had come to a conclusion then watched as the younger man sped off down the tow path leaving Jones to try to tidy himself up before he emerged from the bushes.

Jones was in no hurry and sat on a tree stump smoking a cigarette, probably waiting to see if anyone else turns up to join him in his deviant practices surmised Mr Spurgeon, and he too settled down to wait.

Jones gave up after half an hour or so and walked slowly from the shrubbery turning back towards the direction of town. The tow path was deserted. No people, no barges, even the birds had stopped singing. Mr Spurgeon moved swiftly and silently until he was only a step behind Jones. He raised his arm and brought the brick crashing down onto the unsuspecting head of his latest target. Jones slumped silently to the ground and Mr Spurgeon, after a quick glance around to check that he wasn't being observed, rolled his body over the edge of the path and into the canal. The sound of the body entering the water was surprisingly loud and Mr Spurgeon once again checked that he was alone. Satisfied that he was, he walked back towards the town, pausing only to throw the half brick into the dark water of the canal. He was humming as he walked, another job completed satisfactorily. The chances of being spotted were remote and the body might not be found for a few days which would give people's memories a chance to fade if they had happened to notice him emerging from a gay meeting place. He would go home, feed himself and Lady Mae and then compose another letter to the Star.

Chapter 16

Mr Spurgeon sat at the kitchen table. He had eaten a pork pie salad, drunk a bottle of pale ale and fed Lady Mae. The washing up was done, plates and cutlery put away and now he began to compose his letter to the Star.

Mick Jones was a thoroughly unpleasant man who exemplified all that is wrong with modern customer service. He was rude and unhelpful and as an employee of British Rail he has been made an example of to demonstrate that ordinary people will no longer put up with late trains, overpriced fares and shoddy service.

I killed him with a blunt instrument and put him in the water. I won't tell you where but when his body is discovered you will know that it was the work of the Vigilante.

I will continue to execute people who typify the appalling standards we have to endure, those who exploit the vulnerable and rip off merchants in general. I will not stop until they have received my message and modify their behaviour accordingly.

Sincerely

The Vigilante

Mr Spurgeon read what he had written a couple of time to be sure that he had said what he wanted to say. Content that he had, he folded the letter, addressed the envelope, placed a stamp in the top right hand corner and left the house to post his letter in the box on the corner, having decided that there was no way his letter could be traced back to a particular post box.

*****

"DCI Miller, there's a woman on the phone says she will only speak to you. Says she has information about the Johnson case. She sounds genuine. Shall I transfer the call to you?" The young constable sounded excited and Miller decided to take the call, more in an effort to maintain the young man's enthusiasm than because he believed that the call could be genuine.

"Put her through." He sighed, trying and failing to sound as though his interest had been piqued.

"Hello, DCI Miller speaking."

"I was in the car that was parked in the layby the night of the explosion." The soft female voice stated baldly.

She sounded cool, calm and collected, Miller felt a frisson of hope that at last he might have a decent lead.

"Go on." He encouraged.

"My bloke is married and doesn't want his wife to know he was with me. If I tell you what I know he won't have to be involved, will he?"

"That depends on what you know. We might have to have a word with him but the chances of him having to give evidence are remote. We will need to confirm that what you tell us is correct but we can cross that bridge when we come to it. Why don't you just tell me exactly what you know? You could start with your name."

"You can call me Mary, it's not my name but it will do for now. She paused, obviously collecting her thoughts. "When we arrived at the layby I had my head in my feller's lap," She cleared her throat, obviously embarrassed by what she had revealed to the policeman. "So I didn't see the car that was parked in front of us."

"That's understandable, do go on."

"We had moved onto the back seat, I was sitting and my man was sort of kneeling in the foot well in front of me. I could see over his shoulder but all he could see was me. I thought I saw a man crossing the road and going up to the car in front but I wasn't sure until he moved again and I could see him looking into the car at me and my feller."

"What did you do?"

"Nothing," She gave a little laugh, "I quite liked the idea of being watched while we did it, sort of like casual dogging if you know what I mean."

Miller knew. There were a number of dogging spots in the area that were popular on a Saturday night with a certain type.

"What can you tell me about this person?"

"I couldn't see his face, it was far too dark. All I could see was the outline of a figure. I'd say he was about medium height and slim."

"Could you tell his ethnicity?"

"He could have been any colour, there was only a little bit of moonlight and not enough to make out his features at all."

"What happened next?"

"He only watched us for a few seconds then got into his car and drove off."

"Could you tell the colour or make of the car?"

"No, he drove off without putting his headlights on and his interior light didn't come on when he opened the door. All I can say is the car wasn't white. It was definitely a dark colour and it was old fashioned."

"What do you mean old fashioned?"

"It wasn't a modern car, the shape was wrong and it was really slow when it pulled off. I couldn't see any details but I think it might have been something from the fifties or sixties."

"Mary you have been very, very helpful. I'm going to need you to make a formal statement. We can do that here at the station or I can visit you at your home but it is really important that we get your information on paper."

"What about my chap?"

"I don't think we need to worry about him for now and you can be kept out of it too - for the moment. I have to tell you though that it is possible that you might need to give evidence when we catch this so-and-so."

The telephone went silent as Mary digested what Miller had said. He quickly added, "This man has killed four people and we think he will continue killing until we stop him. You can help us Mary, please don't hang up."

Her voice came at last, soft and subdued. "I'll do whatever you need me to do as long as you keep my bloke out of it as much as you can."

"I will Mary, and that's a promise."

Mary agreed to come to the station that evening on her way home from work to make a formal statement and Miller was left feeling more hopeful when he put down the receiver than he had since this whole Vigilante thing started. They had a lead, not much of one but a lead nonetheless.

*****

Mr Spurgeon was angry. Very angry indeed. He reread the article on the front page of the Star, unable to take in what he had just read.

Care Home Ordered to Close

A routine inspection of the Merrivale Rest Home by Social Services has uncovered a catalogue of health and safety breaches and alleged mistreatment of its elderly residents the Star can reveal.

The kitchens were found to be infested with cockroaches and signs of rodent activity were abundant. Fridges were not maintained at the correct temperature and raw meat was mixed with dairy products. Some items were found to be several days past their sell by date. Work surfaces were dirty and wall tiles and the floor caked with grease. The boiler supplying hot water was broken, there was no soap for hand washing and the towels were heavily soiled.

The fire alarm had not been serviced for a number of years and insufficient and unsuitable fire extinguishers scattered throughout the building seemingly at random. The communal areas were dirty and smelled strongly of urine. Carpets were dirty and worn with holes that constituted a serious trip hazard. Resident's rooms were dirty and bed linen soiled.

Some of the frailest and most confused residents displayed bruises and were apparently frightened of the staff.

The Star has tried to contact the rest home owner, Mr Reginald Sims, aged 44, on several occasions to ask him to comment on these very serious allegations of neglect and cruelty but without success. Ms Vanda Wicklow, Social Services Director for the county has given the Star a short statement.

"We seldom order the closure of a home without giving the owners a chance to put right any failings found during an inspection. On this occasion the home was in such a poor condition that we had no choice but to order immediate closure and the transfer of the residents to other homes in the area. The allegations of mistreatment are being actively investigated by my department in conjunction with the police. I would like to take this opportunity to assure the residents and their relatives as well as the general

public that we are taking this matter extremely seriously and will pursue this investigation with all due diligence. Unfortunately owing to cuts in our funding we can only inspect homes as a result of a complaint as we have insufficient staff to monitor homes on a regular basis."

The Star will continue to try to get a statement from Mr Sims and his staff. Anyone with information about the Merrivale Rest Home should contact The Star, Social Services or the Police.

Mr Spurgeon threw the paper down, intense anger flooding his brain as he tried to take in what he had just read. It was hard to accept that such conditions would be allowed to go on for so long in the twenty-first century. Something should be done, and he was the man to do it! The Vigilante had just found his next target and of all the worthless individuals he had sent to perdition this one was the most deserving. This one should suffer. Not for Reginald Sims a quick and painless death in an explosion or the swift exit caused by a blunt object connecting with his skull, this man deserved to linger in agony before his sojourn on this earth was ended. This target's removal would take time and careful planning.

*****

Miller replaced the receiver and swore under his breath. He had just had an up-date from Cope about the paedophile case and it was bad news. Bad news in the sense that nothing had been uncovered that would help him nail the vigilante. The plus side was that more and more evidence was being uncovered that would see the remaining English members of the paedophile gang go down for a very long time. The Met had passed on good news from the States too, several successful raids on homes and offices meant that quite a few perverts would be banged up for very long sentences. That was one thing you could say about the Yanks, when they found someone guilty of a crime they were given a severe punishment, none of the light touch of the English judicial system. No suspended sentences or community service orders for them. At least Cope's case was going the right way and Miller took a little comfort in the fact that he had played a small part in getting these sickos off the street.

He left his office and walked through the large open plan office where paperwork was completed and telephone calls were fielded. He approached the young constable who had brought the news of Mary's call. The officer looked apprehensive as Miller neared his desk. If he had asked the DCI to talk to someone who turned out to be a nutter he would be in for a rather large bollocking.

"Good decision to pass that call to me. It looks as if we may have a solid lead at last. Well done."

The young man's cheeks coloured slightly at the unexpected praise. "Thank you sir, glad it was the real thing."

"You're welcome son. Just keep it up. There is one more thing you can do for me, find Inspector Mears and ask him to pop into my office."

Miller turned and walked back towards his office, confident that the constable would hotfoot it to Jimmy Mears in no time flat.

*****

Mr Spurgeon's mood was not improved when he went to make himself a calming cup of tea and found that the milk was off. He donned his overcoat and flat cap, the weather in England was treacherous and although he was only going to the corner shop he was taking no chances.

The shop was buzzing when he entered. A gaggle of women were crowded around the till all talking at once about the rest home. One large lady with a face like a dyspeptic bulldog and wearing a floral print frock that would have been better as a sofa cover was particularly vocal.

"My Mandy knows all about it. She left that place without giving her notice because of how Sims was. She says he was a right tarter, wouldn't take no criticism off anybody. When she tried to tell him that the place needed cleaning he told her to mind her own business or get another job. Well, she weren't having that were she? She told him to stick his job where the sun don't shine and put her coat on. Them poor old souls didn't do nothing to deserve what they had to put up with did they? And him living it up in that big house of his. Course he could afford them electric gates and suchlike 'cos he never spent any money on the home. Time was only respectable people lived down Atherton Avenue now it don't matter as long as you've got money. And as for them old folks being knocked about, well words fail me. I just wish somebody would give Sims a good hiding then he'd know what it felt like, the swine."

She drew breath and looked at her audience expectantly. Her tirade had stilled the tongues of the other women but now they burst forth adding their own opinions of Mr Sims and his so called rest home.

Mr Spurgeon had felt his mood begin to lighten as he listened to the large woman venting her wrath. He had come out for a pint of milk and was returning with all the information he needed to begin work. No need for trips to the library this time, all he had needed was a little bit of luck. Finding a house with electric gates in Atherton Avenue would not be difficult and best of all his target lived within walking distance of his home. Mr Spurgeon returned to his little terraced house whistling quietly to himself. He was too late to prevent what had happened to the old folks in the Merrivale but he could make absolutely certain that Sims was punished for what he had done and would never, ever, do it again.

*****

"I want you in with me when Mary comes in tonight. You can scribe while I talk to her nicely. I don't want to frighten her off, she seems cool enough but it's taken her a while to talk to us and she is very concerned about the man she was with becoming known. I'm not going to push her on that at the moment. From what she said he was too busy having it off with her to have noticed anything happening behind his back. We can always up the pressure later if we feel the need to have his evidence. Besides, once we know who Mary really is it should be quite straightforward to find out about lover-boy from her friends."

"I've been thinking about what she said about the car guy. There's a couple of things. One, should we try to get hold of some photographs of old motors for her to look at? She might recognise an outline. Two, the language this guy uses is quite old fashioned, if you couple that with an old car, are we looking at an older type?"

"I don't know Jimmy. Some of his language is a bit quaint but that could be deliberate. Perhaps it's a young person trying to sound mature? At the moment I don't think we can rule any age group out. As for showing Mary pictures of old cars, that's a great idea. Young Atkins goes to classic car shows doesn't he? Perhaps he will know a website or something."

"I'll ask him guv, he's catching up on paperwork today so I'll ask him on the way back to my office. The info about the play tent should be arriving at any moment so I want to get the lists to the boys and girls so they can get cracking as soon as it lands on my desk."

"We've got a few minutes before you need to go. Stick the kettle on and I'll break open a packet of custard creams. When I've had a reinvigorating cup of coffee I'd better brief Wildchild with the news about Mary, but before I do that I want to run something past you. Bentley was a paedophile, Johnson was gay. God knows what Tomlinson was, probably a big butch lesbian. Could there be a hidden motive? Does chummy have a down on people with an alternative sexuality?"

"I don't know guv, at the moment I don't know what he is, apart from the man who's wrecking my home life and I don't suppose that's his motive. I hate to say it but we don't have enough bodies to form a definite pattern other than the one he admits to – taking out worthless members of society. What about Wildchild? Is he still going on about getting a profiler in?"

"Only every bloody time I see him. Now we have a witness that might be a big help I'm hoping he'll wind his beak in and let us get on with things without him constantly offering unwanted and useless advice."

"I thought you quite favoured bringing in a profiler guv?"

"I'm not totally against it. If we hit a brick wall and can see no way to progress the case I will happily bring in an outsider but I really want to catch this sod myself. Then I can retire a happy man."

*****

There was no mistaking the residence of Reginald Sims. The large and ostentatious electric gates would have revealed which house belonged to his target but the crowd gathered outside his house confirmed that he had found the right place. A TV crew from the regional television station were busily doing vox pop interviews with the few locals who had stopped by to look at the house of the man in the news. A reporter from the Star was also present as were stringers for a couple of national newspapers. There was an entry phone attached to one of the gateposts and the reporters were taking it in turns to shout into it, asking Mr Sims to come out and give them an interview. No answer was the stern reply.

Mr Sturgeon sidled over and joined the fringe of the group. Not wanting to be remembered, he tried to look inconspicuous by listening to what people were saying but making no attempt to add his two pennyworth to the general condemnation of Sims and all his works. As he listened he studied the house and grounds, not yet knowing how he would tackle this target, he wanted to gain as much information as he could and this was an opportunity to stare at the Sims residence without raising suspicion.

The house was large, probably built at the turn of the twentieth century, it stood a good thirty yards back from the gates. The grounds were mostly given over to lawn with some island beds of annuals. Mature shrubs were planted against the wall that surrounded the property. Twin turrets adorned the front corners, separated by a tiled roof that topped the dark red brick façade. Six bedrooms and servant's quarters in the attic, he thought. Downstairs there would be at least three reception rooms and possibly as many as five. The kitchen was likely to be in the basement. Next to the house stood a triple garage. No cars were visible, not that he could have read a licence plate at this distance anyway so he couldn't have identified a car without its owner being present. Come to that he had yet to discover what Sims looked like and wasn't sure how to find out. He wasn't concerned about that, he was sure that the local paper would find a photograph somewhere and would splash it over the front page. Big stories were rare in Clingford Norton and he had been the lead story almost every day since he had started off his crusade by executing Darren Bentley, but the Sims story would run and run due to the human interest angle. Both local and national politicians would try to get some favourable coverage too and would keep the story alive. The local MP Sir Hector Melrose would certainly be issuing a press statement, seeking favour with the electorate in the hope of gaining their votes at the next general election. That man couldn't see a bandwagon without jumping on it.

Despite listening to as many conversations as he could, Mr Spurgeon garnered little useful information. Most of the comments he heard regarded what the speaker would like to do to Sims given half a chance. He did however, discover that Mrs Sims and the two Sims children had been seen driving away from the house shortly after the news about the Merrivale had broken. He was pleased about that, he had no wish to harm innocent parties and with the Sims family out of the way he had a clear run. The problem was he didn't know in which direction he should be heading. He walked slowly home, wracking his brain in a vain attempt to come up with a plan of campaign. More than anything he wanted Sims to suffer but how to kill him in a way that guaranteed he would linger in agony and have time to reflect on his sins?

*****

Miller and Mears were sitting in interview room one. They had greeted Mary cordially with no trace of reproach for taking so long to contact them. She was pretty in a cheap sort of way and certainly had a good figure. Mears could see immediately why a man would risk his marriage for a bonk in a layby. They were sitting around the table drinking coffee and nibbling on the ever present biscuits – lemon puffs this time, and taking things slowly and gently.

The preliminaries over, Miller started the tape recorder after checking that Mary had no objection to its use. Making use of the tape meant that he and Miller could concentrate on Mary and not have to constantly scribble and ask her to slow down or repeat what she had said. The tape would be transcribed and turned into a formal statement for Mary to sign at another time.

"Can we start off with the basics? Your real name and address."

"My name is Anenome Fairbright and please no jokes about the name, I get enough of that at work. Just call me Ann. I live at 93 Field Street."

"Thank you Ann. Would you like to tell Mr Mears what you told me this afternoon. Take your time, start at the very beginning and just work your way through until the car left the layby. We won't interrupt unless something crops up that we need clarifying. There is no rush so try to make sure that you don't miss something out."

"I have been having an affair with a work colleague for about six months. I am single but he is married, so we can only meet occasionally when he can get away. On the night of the explosion his wife was staying with her sister so he told her he was having a night out with the lads and would be late back in case she tried to ring him. We can't go to his house or mine as we both have nosy neighbours who know all of us and wouldn't hesitate to tell his wife if they thought he was up to something."

"And your boyfriend's name?" Probed Mears gently.

"John Ashton."

"And his address?" Seeing her reaction to his question Mears rapidly added, "Just for the record. We have no intention of interviewing him at this time."

"88 Field Street."

Now the penny dropped. No wonder they couldn't use their houses, they lived opposite one another.

"Thank you Ann, please continue."

"We went for a couple of drinks and an Indian meal. I suppose we left the restaurant at just about midnight and drove to the layby. We got there about half past twelve. We were in the back of the car having sex when I saw a man standing near the car. It was very dark so I couldn't make out his face, just an impression of his figure. I was looking over John's shoulder and he was looking into the car trying to see what we were doing. I didn't say anything to

John as he would probably have got out of the car and hit the man. Besides I quite liked the idea of being watched, it was a bit kinky. Anyway he soon went back to his car and drove off. I thought at the time that he was going because it was too dark to see us. I thought he was just out dogging, saw us and chanced his luck it was only later that we realised he might have had something to do with blowing up the caravan."

"Can you describe the man?"

"As I told Mr Miller earlier, medium height and slim. I couldn't see his face at all so that's the best I can do."

"How did he move?"

"What do you mean?"

"Did he walk like a young man? Did he have a limp? Anything you can add really."

"I could only make out a shape in the dark. I got the impression he was tired from the way he moved but that's all I can say."

"That's fine Ann, you're doing really well and helping us a lot. Now what can you tell us about the car."

"I think it was old from the outline of it but his interior light didn't come on when he entered the car and he didn't switch his headlights on when he drove off, so it's the same story, I simply couldn't see well enough."

"What we would like you to do now is to have a look at some photographs of old cars and tell us if anything you see rings a bell."

Mears placed a coffee table book entitled Classic Cars of the Fifties and Sixties in front of Ann Fairbright. Atkins had actually had it in his desk to browse through while he ate his lunch and had been only too pleased to lend it to his boss.

"I'm not sure I can help with this, I really only have a vague idea of the shape and size of the car."

"Just do your best, if you can't be certain we won't hold it against you but if you have even an inkling as to the car type it will help us tremendously."

Ann reluctantly opened the book and began to turn the pages, glancing at the photographs of the elderly vehicles before moving on to the next page.

Mears and Miller left the woman to it and went outside to discuss what they had heard.

"It's not much guv. All we know for sure is that the Vigilante isn't a fat dwarf."

"I know Jimmy but if she can give us a clue as to the make and model of the car that will help. How many bangers are there on the roads that are fifty or sixty years old? It would make tracking this guy down so much easier."

"That is if this joker is the Vigilante and not just some peeping tom pervert who gets his kicks watching other people have sex."

"That is a possibility but we know chummy must have arrived in a vehicle to transport his equipment. We know that the time frame matches up and this guy's behaviour is at least suspicious. I reckon this was definitely the man we want. Let's hope that Ann can point us in the right direction."

The two men re-entered the interview room and found Ann Fairbright smiling.

"I've found a four cars that might be the one. Most of them are too angular, this one was sort of rounded as far as I could tell."

She opened the book at the first bookmark. Mears was pleased that she had used scraps of paper to mark the pages rather than turning them down. The first picture was of a Wolsey 1500. The second an early Austin Cambridge, the type that preceded the one with American style fins at the back. The third was a Morris Minor and the fourth a Morris Oxford.

"I hope that helps but I can't promise that it was definitely one of these cars. I'm only saying that it might be."

"That's understood Ann. You have been a great help and I want to thank you for coming forward." Miller once again took control.

"I would have come sooner but John........." She tailed off, not wanting to complete the sentence.

"Don't worry Ann you're here now and that's the main thing. There's just one thing that has occurred to me that I'd like to clear up. You said you left the restaurant at midnight and arrived at the layby at half twelve?"

"That's right."

"Half an hour for a short journey when the roads are quiet is a long time. Are you sure you have the timings right?"

"I'm sure. We went to another place before we went to the layby but it was quite busy there and John couldn't concentrate on what we were doing. He's so wary of being spotted by someone we know he gets really nervous and can't do his stuff, if you know what I mean, In the end we gave up and moved to the layby."

"Thanks Ann, that explains it nicely. Now can we fix you up with a lift home?"

"No thanks, I'll enjoy the walk and it's not too far. I think I'll pick up a Chinese on the way home and give cooking a miss tonight."

The two detectives wished her goodnight and headed back to Miller's office.

"The problem is that some of the cars she identified were rebadged and sold with only minor modifications. I'm sure the Wolsey was also a Riley and the Austin was a Morris. The only one that wasn't sold under a different name was the Morris Minor. That will be the easiest to trace but also there are likely to be more of them about, they're a sort of cult like VW Campers. Speaking of VW's I should think a Beetle would fit her description and that would throw a spanner in the works. They're still making those buggers in Brazil or Mexico or somewhere and there are thousands of them about." Mears wasn't sure whether to be upbeat or gloomy.

"We could do worse than give young Atkins a chance to take a bit of responsibility. He knows about cars of that era and other than him there are only old codgers like me who actually grew up with these motors on practically every street."

"One thing I can do Guv, is to ask traffic to keep an eye open for cars of this vintage and keep a note. Then if anything else happens and one has been seen in the area?"

"Good idea Jimmy. I'll leave that to you, let's call it a day and go home for some grub and some well earned kip and don't keep calling me Guv."

*****

The following morning Rex Anderson was in journalist's heaven. He had not one major story but two. He was giving over the front page to the Merrivale scandal again. The Vigilante had monopolised the front page to the exclusion of almost all other news and he was pleased to have something different to present to the reading public. The Vigilante would undoubtedly regain pole position but that story had quieted down a little since the Johnson killing and he could only rehash the facts so many times before his readers lost interest and he started losing readers.

He was turning over in his mind how to force Reginald Sims to break his silence when the post arrived. He quickly scanned through the envelopes to see if the Vigilante had dropped him another note. He didn't expect to find such a letter as he had only received correspondence from the Vigilante after a killing but to his surprise nestling among the mundane was another note that looked identical to the others. He took a breath before sliding the envelope out of the pack with the tip of his paper knife. He slipped on a pair of latex gloves that he had purchased expressly for this purpose and slit open the envelope before easing out the single sheet of paper that it contained. He opened the folded sheet and read:

Mick Jones was a thoroughly unpleasant man who exemplified all that is wrong with modern customer service. He was rude and unhelpful and as an employee of British Rail he has been made an example of to demonstrate that ordinary people will no longer put up with late trains, overpriced fares and shoddy service.

I killed him with a blunt instrument and put him in the water. I won't tell you where but when his body is discovered you will know that it was the work of the Vigilante.

I will continue to execute people who typify the appalling standards we have to endure, those who exploit the vulnerable and rip off merchants in general. I will not stop until they have received my message and modify their behaviour accordingly.

Sincerely

The Vigilante

Anderson picked up the phone and dialled Miller's number.

Chapter 17

Miller finished reading the letter through the poly-pocket that Anderson had placed it in and looked up at his old friend and sparring partner.

"Oh bugger." He uttered with feeling.

He passed the letter to Mears who read it quickly then placed it on the desk.

"What's your take on this Rex?" Miller said, shifting in his seat until his ample frame was ensconced comfortably and his crossed arms rested on his corpulent stomach.

"As a journalist I look at that and see front page headlines. As a citizen I am horrified. What happens if this mad sod takes a dislike to what we write about him? Or he decides that the police are incompetent and starts to bump off bobbies?"

"I need you to sit on this Rex. We don't know for sure that this guy is dead, the Vigilante may be playing mind games. What about his family, should they just read that Mick Jones has been murdered when they pick up a copy of the Star? This needs to be checked. Does this Mick Jones actually exist? If he does exist is he missing? Until we answer those questions all we have is a letter from a bloke who is round the twist making unsubstantiated claims."

"You're right I can't publish until we know for sure that this Jones character is dead. When we do I'll splash it all over the front page. The only thing that could knock this off the front page is the Queen being assassinated."

"Don't even think that, the last thing we want to do is to give chummy any more ideas."

The obese detective hurried his old friend from the room as quickly as courtesy would allow and turned to his stick thin colleague.

"What do you reckon Jimmy?"

"The first thing I noticed was that he mentioned British Rail. It hasn't been called that since Adam was a lad. If you couple that with Ann Fairbright saying the man she saw moved as if he was tired and my notion that this could be an older person might well be correct."

"A good point, well made. Let's see what young Atkins turns up. How was he when you gave him the cars to look at?"

"Like a dog with two dicks Guv, I really thought he was going to hug me when I gave him his book back and told him he was in charge of tracing chummy's car."

"That lad wants to get on and he's done well on this case so far. He deserves his chance to prove that he's up to snuff. If he does well enough it will help his prospects no end."

"So what do we do about Mick Jones?"

"First thing is to send a team to the railway station to check if Jones does actually work there. If he is there, I want him brought in for questioning, there may be some link with the Vigilante that he isn't even aware of. If he's missing they can get his address and pay him a visit. If there's no-one at home, we'll need to get a search warrant and turn his gaff over."

"Fair enough but I think you should have a word with a friendly magistrate and get them lined up to sign the warrant as soon as we need it."

"Now you're thinking DI Mears. You may find that your acting rank becomes permanent if you keep it up."

"Thanks Guv, you're a proper toff and no mistake." Mears responded in a mock cockney accent.

*****

DS Sharon Bristow rapped sharply on the window of the apparently deserted ticket office. A voice came faintly from a distance. "With you in just a moment."

Bristow turned to her teammate DC Colin Farmer and raised her eyebrows.

"At least someone's home." He said in response to her unspoken criticism.

After much more than a moment a short plump figure emerged from the side of the ticket office. "Sorry to keep you waiting but we are a bit short handed today. Now what can I do for you?"

Bristow held out her warrant card to be inspected. "DS Bristow and DC Farmer, we'd like a word with Mick Jones if he is available."

"Can't help you there I'm afraid. Mick hasn't been in for a couple of days and he's not answering his phone."

"Did he call in sick?"

"No, he was fine when he left here. Probably got himself shacked up with one of his young men and too busy shagging to think about coming in to work."

"I'd like his address please." Bristow said, studiously ignoring his comment about the missing man's sex life. There would be time to investigate that if he really was off the radar.

The ticket office clerk gave the information willingly enough and Bristow rang the information through to Miller who told her to skip going to Jones' house first and go straight to the home of a co-operative magistrate who would have the warrant ready to collect when she arrived.

*****

"It looks as though the letter was accurate. Jones hasn't been to work and can't be raised by phone so I've told Bristow to get the warrant and go straight to his house. If we leave now we can just about get there before she arrives."

As the two detectives walked side by side from the station the faint sound of the Cuckoo Waltz being whistled could be heard emitting from an open window on the first floor. Miller looked at Mears and chuckled, "Cheeky bugger. Do they really think we don't know what they call us behind our backs. Call themselves coppers, they couldn't find their own arse with both hands."

"I wonder what they'll call me when you retire Guv, Laurel without Hardy won't work will it?"

"I'm sure they'll come up with something suitable and not very flattering. They're just like school kids, must have a nickname for the teachers."

They arrived at Jones' house and were parked up and waiting when Bristow and Farmer arrived.

"Got the warrant?" Miller snapped.

"Yes sir."

"OK, we'll try ringing the bell first and if that doesn't work DI Mears can practice his lock picking."

DS Bristow rang the bell and hammered on the front door with her fist. There was no response to the racket she was creating, although it was loud enough to rouse even the deepest sleeper. After giving anyone inside enough time to get to the door Mears inserted a plastic credit card into the side of the Yale lock and wriggled it about. The door sprang open almost instantly and Mears turned to Miller and said, "That took longer than usual, I forgot to say open sesame."

Miller ignored Mears and bellowed into the hallway, "Police, if there is anyone here show yourself now."

Receiving no response, he gave instructions to his officers. "Bristow and Farmer take the downstairs. I want a proper search, canisters in the kitchen opened, cereal boxes emptied and the fridge and freezer contents examined. Then move into the lounge. I want anything you find that is even vaguely suspicious or odd brought to my attention. Got it?"

"Got it sir." The officers chorused.

"OK Jimmy, you and me upstairs."

"Blimey guv, you know I'm not like that."

"Stop buggering about, no wonder they call us Laurel and Hardy when you're always taking the piss."

The sight that greeted them in the bedroom rendered them both speechless. A four poster king sized bed was covered in a leopard skin print duvet. The side curtains and tester were of the same material. Handcuffs and manacles were attached to the four posts ready for use as required. A large painting of a naked Adonis being buggered by a satyr hung over the mantelpiece of a blocked off fireplace. Statues of naked boys and men were liberally scattered on all available surfaces. A television with a fifty inch screen and DVD player was mounted to the wall opposite the foot of the bed. A large wardrobe and two bedside cabinets comprised the only furniture. The room was neat and tidy, no worn clothing strewn on the floor and everywhere was dust free.

"You do the wardrobe and I'll look in the bedside cabinets," Said Miller when he had regained his equilibrium.

The cabinets contained only condoms, lubricant and a very large vibrator that made Miller's eye's water at the thought of what it would feel like.

Mears search had revealed only an impressive collection of gay porn, majoring in bondage and sado-masochism plus a collection on whips, ropes and assorted ironmongery the purpose of which Mears was happily ignorant of.

They moved into the second bedroom. This was obviously where Jones normally slept. The master bedroom being used for sexual entertaining. A pile of dirty clothing was in one corner and was home to more than one pair of well worn socks judging from the aroma that permeated the room.

"Jees Guv, how could anybody sleep in here, it's enough to gas you."

Miller nodded and threw open the window, letting in a light breeze that did nothing to dissipate the smell of cheesy feet. As he stepped back from the window his mobile rang. He listened intently to what was being said, only saying the odd word until the end of the call. "DI Mears and I are on the way to the scene."

He turned to Mears who was gazing expectantly at his boss. "They've just fished a body out of the canal. It was only a few hundred yards from the railway station. It's male and it answers Jones' description. Looks like we've got another Vigilante murder on our plate."

The two men hurried down the stairs, pausing only to tell Bristow that she was now in charge and to complete the house search then make it secure. Miller added as he left the house, "SOCO will no doubt be having a look at this place and will not be very happy if the place has been turned over or a bunch of squatters have moved in, so get crime scene tape over the garden gate, windows and doors before you leave."

"What's happened sir?" Bristow enquired.

"A body has been found and they think it is Jones."

With that he hurried down the path to join Mears in the unmarked pool car. "Blues and twos Jimmy, we need to get a shift on."

Mears reached under the dashboard and switched on the two tone siren and blue flashing lights that were secreted behind the front grill and floored the accelerator.

*****

While Miller and Mears were racing towards the canal Mr Spurgeon was refining his plan to execute Reginald Sims. He was in the workshop at the bottom of his garden and was sorting through a sack that contained a variety of lengths of electrical cable. There was a variety of thicknesses too and Mr Spurgeon selected the thickest he had, the one that would carry the strongest electrical current without burning out. He measured the length, it was just over seven feet, more than enough for what he had in mind. He pared off the plastic coating to reveal six inches of copper wire at each end, then twisted the wires together to give a smooth finish to the shiny metal and smiled in grim satisfaction at his work.

His plan was simple and had arrived almost fully formed as he stood amongst the crowd outside the Sims residence. The electric gates were imposingly tall and looked extremely heavy. If it wasn't for the electrical assistance the gates would have been a real struggle to drag open. The box that controlled the gates was situated on the outside, mounted to the stone pillar that supported the gates. It was linked to the entry phone system and must have been placed outside for ease of servicing when Sims was away from home or to make repairs easier if the gates jammed.

He had considered his options very carefully and had come to the conclusion that to make Sims suffer would be impossible. He could think of no method of killing that would guarantee a lingering death and resolved simply to do him in. He had decided to disable the opening mechanism and then link the electricity supply directly to the gates. Sims would have to get out of his car to open the gates and when he touched the live metal he would have several thousand volts surging through his worthless carcase.

He had one little problem to sort out before he could execute his plan – and Mr Sims. How could he ensure that Sims was the one who touched the gates? The reporters all went away at night and locals had rapidly lost interest, but there was no guarantee of when Sims would actually try to leave and his trap could be set for days before his plan succeeded. He had to lure Sims out, but what bait would get him to leave the security of his home.

He left the workshop and walked slowly up the gravel path admiring his small but immaculate lawn and neat, almost regimented, display of bedding plants. His eagle eye spotted a weed that had had the temerity to intrude among the bright scarlet of his pelargoniums and bent to pluck it out. A wave of nausea overwhelmed him as a lightning bolt of pain shooting through his head transfixed him. He staggered and almost lost his balance, flailing his arms in an effort to maintain on his feet before placing his hands on his head in a futile attempt to stem the agony. He stood still for a moment and waited for the pain to subside. Perhaps he had been overdoing it a bit lately. He was no longer young, although he thought he did pretty well for a man of his age and was generally as fit as a flea. He could still do most of the things he could do as a younger man, they just took longer. He hadn't the same strength for sure but it was his stamina that was the main problem. He made his way to the kitchen and put the kettle on to make tea, he glanced at the clock and was surprised to see that he was late for lunch. Perhaps his blood sugar was a bit low and he needed something to eat. He still felt a little odd and decided that a chocolate biscuit with his tea would be as much as he could manage. Lady Mae was rubbing herself against his leg, signalling that she wanted some attention or possibly something to eat. Possibly both. He sat down and scooped her onto his lap, tickling behind her ears. He was rewarded with a loud purr and felt a little better.

*****

"Can't we get the car any closer than this?" Miller asked grumpily as they exited the car.

"Sorry guv, the tow path is the only way in or out unless you count boats. It's not too far now."

Miller grunted in an unconvinced way. "Bloody inconsiderate, disposing of bodies in places with no vehicular access. That's the trouble with murderers today, no thought for anyone else."

Mears maintained a tactful silence, he knew that Miller was feeling the stress of watching the body count rise and making no progress in identifying the culprit.

Black and yellow police tape had been strung across the entrance to the tow path and two constables were guarding the only entrance to the canal. They looked bored with their mundane duty but snapped to full alertness when they spotted their senior officers approaching. Miller acknowledged the two men and asked, "Anything?"

The taller of the constables spoke before his colleague could frame a reply. "All quiet sir. It's very isolated down here and I don't think the local residents have twigged yet. We've only turned away one guy walking his dog, although we have seen a couple of chaps who turned around and disappeared as soon as they saw us. Probably after some cock." He added crudely.

"Thank you for your insight constable. Who is down there?"

"Sargent Smith's in charge sir. SOCO haven't arrived yet."

"Thanks." Miller turned to Mears, "Come on Jimmy, can't hang round here all day chatting."

Mears smiled, he hadn't said a word while the DCI was quizzing the constable. "Yes Guv, as you say."

The two men ducked under the tape and after a few paces rounded the corner. A small knot of people could be seen midway between where they stood and the canal tunnel.

"Here we go again," Miller said heavily, "If the body count gets much higher we could sell the story to Midsummer Murders. Let bloody Barnaby sort it out!"

"Let's hope that the bastard has slipped up this time." Mears responded as they walked rapidly towards the group of police awaiting their arrival.

The corpse of Mick Jones was lying on the towpath, the three policemen keeping a respectful distance from the body. That was due to unwillingness to compromise forensic evidence rather than any finer feelings of wishing to show their respect to the murdered man. Miller and Mears displayed no such regard and walked directly up to the body. In life Jones had been of stocky build and the time in the water had further swollen his body and discoloured his skin. The corpse emitted a foul odour of decay that made Mears cough and Miller curse and hold his breath as he stood over the lifeless thing that had once been a man. The wound on the back of his head was plain to see, a large area had been caved in and white fragments of bone protruded through his thinning, sodden hair.

"Not much doubt about the cause of death Gov." Mears offered.

"No, even if the blow didn't kill him and he drowned while unconscious, the result's much the same."

They peered down at the body in silent concentration, trying to spot any clue that could help them to identify the killer. Finally, Miller broke the silence, "Where the devil is SOCO? Useless shower! We're not going to do any good here staring at a corpse and hoping for inspiration to strike, we need them to find something useful. Find out what's holding them up Jimmy while I have a think."

He turned and noticed a young man sitting on the grass in the shadow of the bushes that lined the towpath. He turned to the nearest constable. "Who is chummy?" He asked, gesturing with his thumb towards the young man.

"Name's Dick Reeves sir. He spotted the body in the water and tried to pull it out. It was too heavy for him to get it over the side of the canal but he kept hold of it while he called 999 on his mobile. He's a bit shaken up but we asked him to stay until you arrived."

"Good lad, I'll have a word with Mr Reeves then you can organise getting him home."

Miller walked over to where Dick Reeves was sitting and plumped himself down beside him. He sighed at the pleasure of getting off his feet and squirmed his ample rump until he was comfortable before addressing his companion on the grass.

"Good morning Mr Reeves. I am Detective Chief Inspector Miller and, if you are feeling up to it, I'd like to ask you a few questions. Just informally for now but we will need a formal statement from you later."

The young man nodded. "Anything I can do to help, just ask away."

Miller paused before he began, his eyes roaming over Dick Reeves in an effort to assess him. Reeves looked to be about twenty-four. A good looking lad with blond hair, a nice tan, white teeth and a toned body. He wore loose shorts and a tight athletic vest that clung to his torso like cling film. No prizes for guessing why he was in a gay cruising site Miller thought.

"You are going to have to be completely honest with me. No holding back of anything. I know what this place is used for and I couldn't care less what you were up to when you found the body but you must tell me everything. Even the slightest detail may match up with what we already know or what may come to light as we investigate. Understand?"

"I understand and I'll tell you everything I know, not that it is a lot."

"Start by telling me why you were down here today."

"This is a gay place and I came down hoping to meet someone for sex."

"And did you?"

"No, I was walking up towards the tunnel, there's a good spot in the bushes there and there's often someone waiting for some action, when I saw this thing floating in the water. I realised it was a body and I thought he had to be dead but I tried to pull him out anyway, just in case he was still alive. I didn't realise who it was until I saw his face."

"You know who it is then."

"Oh yes, that's Mick Jones. He's always down here, bit of a nuisance really. He's not my type but he would never take no for an answer. I suppose he came on to the wrong bloke and he turned nasty."

"Carry on."

"When I couldn't get the body onto the bank I kept hold of his sleeve so he didn't drift away and fished my mobile out. I gave you guys a ring and waited until you got here. Your guys helped me to get him out and since then I've just sat here."

"Fair enough. Are you up to answering a few questions?"

"I'm OK, a bit shaken that's all. I've never seen a dead body before let alone one with a bloody great hole in its head."

A bloody great hole was pushing it a bit thought Miller but a little exaggeration was understandable in the circumstances.

"Tell me about this place and who comes here."

"It's very popular with married guys. They can't go to the gay clubs or have a regular boyfriend so they come here when they fancy a bit of man on man action. There are more bisexuals about than most people think. A lot of gay guys too who just want anonymous sex with no strings attached. It is busier in the evenings after work but there are usually a few guys about during the day so it would be unusual not to be able to hook up with someone whenever you came here. It's much quieter than usual today......" He trailed off, biting his lip as he realised that the sight of several policemen gathered round a corpse would be enough to put the horniest cruiser off his intended purpose.

Miller smiled sympathetically, "Carry on when you're ready."

The young man sniffed and nodded, obviously more effected by finding the body than he was prepared to admit.

"There's a real mix of guys, sixteen years old some of them, any age really up to seventy-odd. White, black, Asian, fat, thin, you name it. Some are regulars, you get to recognise faces when you've seen them a few times. Mick was one of those. He worked at the station, I know that because he often came here in his work clothes when he finished a shift. He was as likely to be here in the daytime as he was in the evening, depending on when he was working. He was a bit kinky, liked being tied up and beaten. He was always trying to get me to go back to his place. He said he had a playroom where he could do what he liked. He wasn't my type though so I never had sex with him, I must be one of the few that didn't though because he was known to take on anybody with a stiffy and most of the guys who come here have probably had him at one time or another."

"Did you see anyone else this morning?"

"Not a soul, the place was as quiet as the grave." The young man made a hiccupping sound as he realised what he had said and reddened with embarrassment.

"Was there anyone who was especially friendly with Mr Jones? Or anyone who he had upset recently?"

"Not that I know of but I only come here for a quickie when I feel horny and you don't go in for conversations in those circumstances. Very often no words are exchanged at all, you just do what you need to do and go."

"Are there any names that you can give me, people who might know more about Mr Jones?"

Mears voice interrupted the conversation. "Sorry guv, just to let you know that SOCO have arrived."

"OK Jimmy, I'll be over in a minute."

Miller turned back to Reeves.

"Names?"

"I only know the full names of two guys who come here. They're both openly gay and I know them from around town. Peter Pattison and Harry Edwards but I don't know where they live or anything. Other than them I know a few guys by their first name but that's it."

"Thank you Mr Reeves you've been very helpful. I appreciate you're being so frank. One of my constables will take you home now. Give him a list of all the names, including the first names of anyone you know that comes here. We'll get a formal statement later in the week when you've recovered a bit from the shock of finding Mr Jones.

The fat detective heaved himself to his feet and brushed the leaves from his trousers before moving off to put a rocket up the collective backsides of the forensics team.

Chapter 18

Mr Spurgeon was feeling much more chipper. He had spent the past couple of hours mulling over how to get Sims out of his house and now he thought he had the answer. Sims was a greedy, selfish type who had happily exploited the vulnerable people in his care. He had broken rules and the law in his pursuit of bigger profits not to mention affronting common decency. It was likely that his finances wouldn't stand close examination. After all, if he could treat the people in his care with such cavalier disregard for their welfare it was likely that his accounts were suspect too. The Inland Revenue could perhaps be used to lure him out.

He walked through to his kitchen and dropped some potatoes into the sink. Sausage and mash tonight he decided, nothing like good plain English cooking. He couldn't understand the modern generation's obsession with foreign food. He had never tasted Indian or Chinese cuisine but he knew instinctively that he wouldn't like it. Full of garlic and spices, not proper grub at all, and almost guaranteed to give him heartburn. Filthy muck! As he peeled the potatoes he decided that he had to take a risk. It was only a small one but it was a risk nonetheless. He had to buy a mobile phone. He had never owned a mobile and was often heard declaiming his detestation of the infernal devices. When he was a lad only middle class people owned a telephone. Working class people walked down to the box on the corner and inserted four pennies before pressing button A to be connected. Or button B to get their money back if the call failed. Now everyone had a telephone at home and a mobile in their pocket. Times had changed but they hadn't got any better.

He decided that he would take the train down a couple of stops and buy a mobile in a town where he was unlikely to be known or remembered. His was confident that he would be able to operate the device once he had read the instructions and could then move the execution of Reginald Sims forward. He began to whistle softly to himself, he was pleased with his plan and sure that it would succeed. He decided to open a tin of processed peas to accompany the sausage and mash. He liked that meal, it reminded him of Saturdays when he was a youngster. His mother had been a good cook but each day of the week had its set meal. Sunday was roast beef and Yorkshire pudding, Monday cold roast beef, Tuesday pork chops, Wednesday mince, Thursday stew, Friday meat pie and Saturday sausage and mash with processed peas. His mother and father were long gone but their influence still guided him through daily life.

After his evening meal he switched on the television to watch the local news. He was feeling a little full and pleasantly dozy when the news reader announced the finding of a body in the canal. Instantly he was wide awake and taking notice. The item was short and simply said that a body had been found in suspicious circumstances and the police were investigating. Mr Spurgeon relaxed back into the settee, as his eyes began to close he thought he must remember to pick up a copy of the Star tomorrow.

*****

As expected the SOCO team had been unable to tell Miller and Mears anything that they hadn't already observed, but had promised to prioritise processing the body and to report as soon as they could. Mears had set up a search team to go over the towpath and its environs to look for a weapon or anything else of interest. He wasn't hopeful and didn't envy the team the task he had set them. Used French letters and tissues was likely to be the sum total of their trawl through the bushes. Miller left Mears to get on with it and made his way back to the station. He had to brief Wildchild and he wasn't looking forward to the meeting one little bit.

*****

"Come in." Wildchild's voice sounded through the door in response to Miller's knock.

Miller entered the Commander's office feeling like a schoolboy summoned to appear before his headmaster. Not that it showed. Outwardly he was his usual confident self, inside he knew that the vigilante case was no nearer being solved than it had been when he was assigned the task of bringing the murderer to justice.

"Sir." Miller stood in front of Wildchild's desk.

"Sit down man, this may take a while."

"Any chance of a coffee then sir, there was no chance of a drink down by the canal and I'm parched."

Wildchild sighed theatrically but rang through to order a pot of coffee and a plate of biscuits. He knew Miller's propensity for biscuits as did every other serving officer in the station. Miller was famous for his ability to eat biscuits at every opportunity and had been known to munch them during an autopsy until stricter regulations had caused him to stop.

As soon as he had a cup of coffee before him Miller commenced the briefing. Wildchild listened intently, he already knew about the warning letter to the Star so wasn't taken by surprise when the body had been discovered but was horrified to learn of the man's sexual habits.

"The fact that he was a promiscuous homosexual is going to complicate matters. Finding men who are willing to talk is going to be tough, you did well getting Reeves to open up." The DCS added.

"He's a decent enough fellow and was keen to help. We were lucky that he saw the body, if it had been one of the married chaps the chances are they would have buggered off and let the body sink again."

"Can you see any pattern emerging? I know it is early days but can you see any link to the other murders?"

"Other than the startlingly bleedin' obvious, that the vigilante did it, I can't. Mears has pointed out that all but Cllr Tomlinson had some sort of alternative sexual lifestyle, but I think that's a red herring. I think the vigilante is killing for the very reasons he gives in the letters. He obviously has a screw loose, but not loose enough for him to have come to our attention in the past. Jimmy also thinks he could be elderly because of the language he uses but I'm not convinced. He could just be using old fashioned language to muddy the waters. He's a clever bugger and I wouldn't put anything past him. He might be crackers but he has a very original way of thinking, I mean who would imagine using a Wendy house or a rubber boat as a murder weapon? I hate to say it but if forensics don't pick something up I really don't know how we are going to catch this mad bugger. I know that budgets are tight but I think the time is fast approaching when we need to consider bringing in a profiler."

Wildchild leaned back in his chair and smiled his satisfaction. "I'm glad you said that DCI Miller because I have come to the same conclusion. I've been talking to some people at the Met and they have come up with a couple of names. I'm going to see which one is available and ask them to come up for a preliminary chat with a view to bringing them into the investigation."

"Fine with me, the sooner the better as far as I'm concerned. I'm on borrowed time before I retire and I want this done with before I go. Jimmy won't be happy though."

"Why is that?"

"He has worked in a team with a profiler before and it didn't go well. Now he thinks all profilers are quacks, little better than fortune tellers. Don't worry about Jimmy though, he'll be OK, he wants this case done with as much as I do. He also wants to be made up permanently and knows having his name attached to solving this case is his best chance. He won't rock the boat whatever he thinks."

"Good. Now if that is all DCI Miller I want to get on with things. I shall want you and possibly Inspector Mears present when I talk to the profiler so no disappearing tricks."

"As you say sir."

Miller left the commander's office with a mixture of relief and regret. He had desperately wanted catch the vigilante without outside assistance but recognised that unless he had some help the killings were likely to continue and a profiler was a better alternative to handing the case over to the regional crime squad.

*****

Mr Spurgeon was displeased at the service he had received at the railway station. The insolent woman behind the glass of the ticket office window had been intolerably rude and unhelpful. He hoped her attitude would change when the news of Jones' execution and the reasons for it reached her, otherwise he might have to make a further example of a British rail worker. He sat in a dirty carriage and was feeling extremely hot. It was a nice warm day but the heater beneath the seat was blowing out hot air and the window would not open. The sandwich wrappers and discarded food that littered the floor exacerbated his discomfiture. To cap it all the journey which should have taken thirty minutes had already taken just over an hour. When the train finally pulled into his destination station he hurried from the train as though pursued by all the devils in hell. He considered making a complaint to the station staff but decided against it as he didn't want to draw attention to himself. Instead he caught his breath, bit his tongue and walked unhurriedly from the station precincts. It was just too darned hot to rush about.

The twelve year old boy masquerading as a shop assistant in the phone shop patronised him terribly and he struggled to control his temper as he was talked down to. He was sorely tempted to call on God to send a thunderbolt to strike down the acne ridden little weasel but using great self-control managed to resist the impulse. After refusing to buy an all singing, all dancing device that would do everything except make him a cup of tea Mr Spurgeon left the shop with a basic pay as you go mobile phone. The spotty adolescent cretin had fitted the sim card and battery so all Mr Spurgeon had to do was charge up the phone when he got home.

He was back on board the train and on the way home when he had an awful thought. The police would be able to trace him to the shop if he rang Sims. They were sure to examine ingoing and outgoing calls on both Sims' landline and mobile. The idiot who had sold him the phone had made it clear that they sold very few "Granny phones" and would be sure to remember him and give a description. There might even be CCTV evidence. He cursed himself for a silly blighter. He hadn't thought it through properly and had almost made a serious mistake. He would have to use the public phone box in Abbott Avenue and chance being seen. If he wrapped up and called late at night, he stood a good chance of getting away with it. Damn, he had endured this ghastly journey and spent thirty quid on a useless gadget that would be slung into a drawer and forgotten as soon as he arrived home. That would teach him not to rush into things. He had killed Jones on an impulse and been lucky to escape detection and now he was making silly mistakes. He had to take his time and think things through properly. Slow and steady wins the race as his father used to say. That and more haste less speed. That was true, he had wasted a day as well as his money on a fruitless and dangerous expedition. He would crack on with the Sims execution. Apart from the mobile phone error he was confident his plan would work, then he would slow down and plan the next target's demise slowly and carefully.

*****

The next two nights were fine and Mr Spurgeon spent them relaxing in front of the television. There wasn't a huge choice of programmes as he refused to have satellite TV and disliked soap operas and reality programmes, but by flicking through the five channels he did have he managed to keep himself entertained. He had also amused himself by buying a large scrap book and pasting in all the cuttings from the Star that referred to the Vigilante. It was three-quarters full and quite thick by the time he had finished. He had enjoyed re-reading the articles as he cut them out of the papers he had been saving for recycling. He felt proud of what he had achieved over the past weeks and felt energised to continue his good work. He had also composed a note accepting responsibility for the death of Reginald Sims. It was much shorter than his previous missives but it would do.

I don't need to tell you why this piece of worthless scum has been executed. I only need to tell you that this was my work.

The Vigilante

On the third night it was raining and that was what he had been waiting for. His plan might work without the rain but the rain assured its success. He waited until almost midnight, then wrapped the electric cable around his waist, donned his mackintosh and slipped the few tools he would need into his coat pocket. He had plenty of change and Reginald Sims telephone number written on a scrap of paper in his wallet. That had been surprisingly easy to obtain. He had just looked in the phone book and there it was. The idiot wasn't even ex-directory. He had rehearsed his little speech and was confident that it would make Sims run. Run, straight to his death. He picked up the old fedora hat that he had rescued from his father's wardrobe and pulled it down. It was a little on the large side but so much the better. With his raincoat collar turned up and his hat pulled down there would be little for any witnesses to describe. Nonetheless he took the added precaution of assuming a bad limp as he neared the phone box. Any witnesses would describe a slim man with a limp and that wasn't him!

He glanced around the deserted avenue, peering through the driving rain as he checked for late night dog walkers or returning revellers. All was clear, not even a stray cat in sight. For once the council were being helpful, their policy of switching off alternate lampposts meant that he could stay in the deepest shadows as he moved silently towards his target. Most houses were dark, the occupants in bed sleeping the sleep of the hard working who had to get up in the morning. He slipped into the telephone box, grateful to get out of the driving rain and withdrew the slip of paper from his wallet. He cleared his throat and fumbled for some change. This was it. The game was on.

The phone rang in his ear and continued to ring for what seemed to Mr Spurgeon a very long time. At last the receiver was picked up and a very grumpy voice barked, "Yes, what is it? If you're the press you can bugger off."

"Listen carefully. I will not repeat myself. I am going to give you some information that will prevent you from going to prison for a very long time and allow you to keep your money. Do you understand?" The voice that emitted from Mr Spurgeon was not his own, he had deepened it and spoke with the trace of an Irish accent.

"Yes." The voice sounded uncertain but Sims spoke clearly enough.

"If I give you this information I want your word that you will pay me two thousand pounds in cash."

"How do I know you are genuine or that the information is something I don't already know?"

Mr Spurgeon gave a hollow laugh. "I can assure you that you are not aware of what I am about to tell you. Now do you agree or do I hang up now and let you go to the dogs."

Sims hesitated for a moment then spoke in a rush. "OK, I'll pay you but only if the information is useful."

"Very well. I work for the Inland Revenue. There is a combined police and Inland Revenue force that is going to raid your house at five o'clock in the morning. They will seize any records or cash that you have in the house and arrest you for fraud and tax evasion. You have got the rest of the night to hide whatever there is to hide."

"How do I pay you?"

"Don't worry, I'll be in touch when things have calmed down. Don't try to do me down, I wouldn't like that and you wouldn't like the consequences."

Mr Spurgeon hung up the receiver and calmly slipped from the call box. He limped down the road towards the Sims residence. There was no hurry. He only needed five minutes to rig the gates and Sims would take longer than that to assemble the stuff he wouldn't want the authorities to see.

The rain was still falling heavily and Mr Spurgeon could feel wetness penetrating his mackintosh as he moved along. His old bones ached as he moved, his knees were really giving him gyp as they always did when it was damp. He didn't mind, soon he would be back in the warmth of his home and Sims would be roasting in hell.

He pulled on his heavy duty rubber gloves then levered open the control panel with a large screw driver. Quickly he disabled the switch that operated the gates and connected the cable to the mains electricity supply, then stepping nimbly to one side, he twisted the bare copper wires around the side bar of the gate. He smiled as he noticed the large puddle that had formed under the gates. Now he was certain that Sims would fry. He decided to stay for a while and see his plan through to completion. He moved stealthily to stand in the shadow of a tree on the other side of the road and waited for the rat to desert the sinking ship. He was fairly sure that Sims would run, taking whatever cash he had stashed away with him, leaving the Irishman who had tipped him off high and dry. That didn't matter. Whether he ran or just left the house to hide his ill-gotten gains and intended to return, he would be killed when he tried to open the gates manually.

He didn't have long to wait. After just a few minutes the headlights of a vehicle could be seen driving a little too fast down the drive. It looked as if the car would collide with the gates as the driver expected them to open as he approached but he braked heavily when they remained resolutely shut and the car drew to a halt just short of the gates. Sims backed the car up enough to allow the gates to open then dashed for the gate, hurrying to get on with his journey and to get out of the pelting rain. The panic stricken man grasped the gate with both hands to pull open the heavy portal. There was a bright blue flash and he convulsed as the electricity tore through his body. Soundlessly he slumped against the gates, his hands still holding tight to the metal in a death grip that he could not release. Mr Spurgeon's old eyes could not make out any detail through the rain but he could smell the odour of burning flesh and knew his task had been completed successfully.

Mr Spurgeon walked over to the control box and disconnected the deadly cable. After all he didn't want any innocent parties being injured. He moved across to gaze down at the mortal remains of Reginald Sims. He felt no remorse, just satisfaction at a job well done. Reaching down he slipped a note into his victim's top pocket. Task accomplished. He walked home as briskly as his phony limp would allow and only resumed his normal gait when he reached the end of his street. He would have a nice hot cup of tea and a warm by the fire before he went to bed. Perhaps a celebratory glass of scotch too, he deserved it.

Chapter 19

Miller broke the news about the profiler with more care than he usually gave to a subordinate's feelings. He knew that Mears was unhappy at the prospect of a profiler joining the investigation and needed to keep his junior partner on side. Happily, for them both Mears greeted the news with what seemed to Miller to be relief.

"At this stage any help would be gratefully received. We are stretched so thin trying to investigate all these murders simultaneously that we are failing dismally to make any progress on any of them. Anyway we don't have to accept everything they say as gospel."

"Wildchild wants you in with us when we have a chat with the prospective profiler so you'll have a chance to shove in your two pennyworth. My advice is to say as little as possible. Wildchild has made up his mind to bring someone in so don't bugger up your career prospects by throwing a spanner in the works."

"Don't worry Guv, I'll behave. I'll even help as much as I can and if that doesn't tell you how desperate I am I don't know what will."

"Come on then Jimmy, let's grab a coffee and you can bring me up to speed."

*****

"It boils down to this. We simply don't have enough bodies on the ground to do the job. We're simultaneously investigating several murders and we don't have the manpower to do it properly. We're cutting corners, prioritising what we do and probably missing valuable information because we haven't got round to talking to someone. The boys and girls at the sharp end are working their socks off, doing overtime without moaning about it, never taking a day off but they can't keep going like this forever. Even with the extra bodies that Wildchild has scrounged from other divisions we are desperately undermanned."

"I know Jimmy and I've told Wildchild exactly that, he reckons that unless the Home Office come up with extra cash to cover what we're currently spending the force will be technically bankrupt at the end of the year. To be fair I think he understands exactly what the situation is but without the money he's snookered. He says the Chief Constable has asked for an urgent meeting with the Home Secretary to discuss our difficulties but we've had to accept deep cuts to our budget due to their bloody austerity policy this year and trying to get some of it back from that hard faced cow in Whitehall will be a conjuring trick that Paul Daniels would envy. Our best hope of sorting this lot out is the profiler. Even then I'm concerned that Wildblood will go for the cheapest rather than the best."

Miller dunked his fruit shortcake biscuit in his coffee and slid the soggy result into his mouth but not before a sodden piece of biscuit had separated from the whole and dropped onto his waistcoat. "Damn, these wretched things are unfit for dunking purposes. I should have stuck with ginger nuts."

Mears gave a weary smile as he watched Miller trying unsuccessfully to remove the detritus from the badly stretched fabric of his waistcoat.

*****

Miller and Mears rose rapidly from their seats as the Commander entered the small conference room. Not to show respect for their senior colleague but because he was accompanied by a very attractive woman and they didn't want to appear ill mannered.

"Gentlemen, may I introduce Dr Sandra Patterson, Dr Patterson this is DCI Miller and acting DI Mears."

Miller and Mears grinned and said they were pleased to meet the profiler. Miller certainly was, he was very taken by Dr Patterson although his interest was far from purely professional. Her startlingly blue eyes regarded him with a hint of amusement. She was probably used to being ogled by men old enough to be her father Miller thought, still, she was worth looking at. An attractive face that was just imperfect enough to stop short of being mundanely pretty. Dark hair cut into a bob that suited her heart shaped face. Add in long shapely legs and breasts that looked firm enough for her to dispense with a bra when she wasn't working and she was definitely worth a second look.

With the introductions over Wildchild took charge and suggested that Miller gave an overview of the Vigilante case while Dr Patterson chimed in with any questions that wouldn't wait until the briefing was over.

Miller did as the senior officer suggested and was pleased that the profiler for the most part sat silently listening and making notes throughout his presentation. When she did interrupt with a question it was to seek clarification. This wasn't a woman who liked the sound of her own voice. That would suit Wildchild because he loved the sound of his.

Miller wound up by saying, "Any comments Dr Patterson?"

"I would need to review all the case notes and visit the scenes of crime before I could draw any firm conclusions that would enable me to make any sensible contribution so all I can give you is a preliminary reaction to what I've heard this afternoon. First impressions if you like."

Miller was about to respond but Wildchild was quicker off the mark. "That is all we could expect Dr Patterson, please share your thoughts."

"OK, as long as it is clear that none of this is set in stone."

"Crystal." Responded Miller.

"I've been given an outline and I am responding in kind. Most serial killers are between thirty and fifty years old. They are usually sexually motivated and kill women in the vast majority of cases. They are almost exclusively male with a basic education. There are obvious exceptions such as Myra Hindley and Rose West. They may have a history of cruelty to animals or sexual offending. Petty crime and arson are not rare. Your serial killer is outside the norm in that he kills predominantly men and there appears to be no sexual angle other than, possibly, the sexual proclivities of the victims. There is a conundrum in that he could be attacking his victims because of their sexual preferences or his notes could be exactly what he says they are – indictments of their perceived crimes. A justification of his actions if you will. So there is a stark choice, is this Vigilante telling the truth or is he disguising his real motive? If we can discover that we are one step further towards catching him. I say him because I am ninety per-cent certain that the killer is a male, I'll be able to get closer to one hundred per-cent as I study the case in depth. You'll have to forgive me gentlemen but I don't make guesses based on an overview of a case," She nodded deferentially to Miller, "However senior or talented the presenter. The FBI have never used the term 'Profiler,' they use 'Analyst', an altogether better description as the profile of the killer is developed by analysing the evidence before extrapolating a theory. There is no voodoo in what I do, I use empirical data collated over many years and form a conclusion based on probability."

"Like I do when I visit the bookies and place a bet on the Derby." Mears interrupted.

"Yes Inspector Mears, if you analyse every horse in the race taking into account it's past form, it's jockey, the course conditions, the weather and all the other elements that could affect the outcome of the race. If you interview the jockeys, the trainers and the owners, have a chat with the stable boys about the animal's diet……..," She tailed off, "I'm sure you get the idea." She smiles sweetly at Mears but there was a hint of steel in her eyes.

Mears raised his hands in surrender. "You win Doc."

"Thank you Inspector Mears but please don't call me Doc, Sandra will do nicely."

Wildchild intervened before this went any further, "Miller? Anything you want to ask *Dr* Patterson?" He emphasised her title and glared at Mears who responded with an insouciant grin.

"I don't think so, except to ask Sandra," he winked at Mears on Wildchild's blindside, "About her experience of working a serial killer case."

The analyst and commander exchanged a rapid glance. Miller had obviously asked something they would sooner have remained unasked.

"This will be my first actual case. I have worked extensively on the behavioural psychology of serial killers at the university where I lecture in criminology. I feel totally confident that I can help to catch the Vigilante by bringing a different perspective to the case. Different, not better." She emphasised her last statement and attempted to look cool as the two detectives took in the fact that clever or not she was a complete rookie in the real world of catching bad guys.

Miller broke the silence. "We all have to start somewhere, and we can use all the help we can get. If we don't catch the bugger soon he'll have offed half the population of Clingford Norton." He turned to Mears. "What do you say Jimmy?"

"I'm with you Guv."

Miller angled his gaze to Wildchild. "We'll have no problems working with Dr Patterson if you can sort out the finance etc." He rose from his chair, "If that will be all sir, we'll make tracks. If we can catch the bugger in the next few hours, we'll save you a bit of cash."

Wildchild gave his assent and Miller and Mears departed with a cheery wave to Sandra Patterson and a barely civil nod to their commander.

They reconvened in Miller's office. As usual coffee was the first priority, then they sat and Miller reluctantly offered Mears a custard cream.

"Well Jimmy, she can't make things any worse than they are now. Bugger all leads and none likely to appear by the look of it."

Mears had just popped a whole biscuit into his mouth and sprayed crumbs as he mumbled his agreement. "You know how I feel about profilers, but I'd sup with the devil if I thought it would get us any closer to closing the case."

"She doesn't look like the devil though does she?" Miller said archly. "I thought your eyeballs would drop onto the table when she walked in."

"I don't think I was the only one guv, you were a bit slack jawed yourself and God knows what Wildchild was like when he first saw her. He was sniffing round her like a Jack Russell scenting a bitch on heat."

"I'd make sure you save that sort of remark for when we're alone Jimmy. Wildchild can put a spoke in your promotion wheel if you upset him too much."

"As you say Guv."

They were settling down to chat through exactly what impact Dr Patterson would have on the case when a sharp rap on the door sounded and Constable Atkins poked his head into the room. "Sorry to interrupt you sir, but I think this is important."

"Come in Atkins, you're making the room untidy. Spit it out."

"The company who made the play house have finally supplied us with a full list of the shops who stock it and there are only twelve within a twenty mile radius of Clingford Norton."

"Well done lad, bring me the list then get yourself a wad and a cuppa while I talk to Inspector Mears about what we do next."

The young constable exited the room sharply, completely failing to disguise the look of pleasure on his face at being praised by Miller. He returned moments later carrying the long sheet of fax paper as though it were the most precious thing in the world. He handed the information to Miller and returned to his desk, hoping that he would be given the task of visiting some of the stores on the list.

Miller stared down at the paper. "Why these daft buggers couldn't e-mail this is beyond me but at least they have broken it down as we asked."

"I know Atkins said twelve close by but how many altogether?"

"I dunno, looks to be approaching a couple of hundred. Some of those are in Scotland and other God forsaken parts of the country so I suppose there's about a hundred to chase initially before we have to look at venturing into uncharted territory."

"That's do-able Guv."

"It had better be. This might mean we won't need Dr Patterson at all if we get a shift on. And don't call me Guv."

"This play tent thing is expensive and it is odds on that the purchases were made with a card of some sort. The problem is going to be getting the stores to divulge their customer's details. They might cite the data protection Act and refuse to co-operate without a court order."

"If they prove difficult tell them to stick the Data Protection Act up their arse, mention the possibility of a snap VAT inspection, customers being given parking tickets, the Fire Service wanting to inspect the premises and anything else we can come up with," Miller snarled, "If that doesn't work we'll get Wildchild to do something useful for a change. He can use a friendly judge to get a court order."

"What do you think about using Atkins?"

"He's a promising lad but if someone has to throw their weight about he may not be ideal. We want a bit of a bruiser for this. How does this grab you? Atkins can ring the companies and tell them a police officer will be visiting them shortly. He can be officious on the phone and they can't see that he is still a bit green. He mustn't divulge what we want, just that we are coming, that should put them nicely on edge. Then we want three teams of two. Use the most experienced and physically imposing officers we have. Then all we do is pray that it works."

"Mears nodded enthusiastically. "It shall be done. I suggest that we go home and relax for a couple of hours. Watch some crap TV, have something to eat and grab an early night. The boys and girls are in at seven and it will be nice to be able to give them some good news for a change."

"This is going to take a while. The shops can only give credit card numbers and the name on the card, we've got to chase the banks for the addresses. I suspect it won't be as easy to lean on them for some speedy co-operation and we may need to use someone senior to Wildchild to get them to supply the info."

*****

Miller licked the last of the custard from his spoon, sat back in his chair and sighed with pleasure. Steak, chips and mushrooms followed by spotted dick and custard. That was proper grub to give a man after a hard day's work. "That was smashing Elsie, absolutely first class. That Herman Bloomingtail can bugger about with snail porridge and liver and onion flavoured ice cream but give me proper English grub every time. And you're sexier that that Lawson bird." He added lecherously, receiving a smile of appreciation from his long suffering better half.

"You work too hard, I'll be glad when you retire and we can start to enjoy life a bit."

"It won't be long now. We can start to do all the things we've talked about. Maybe take that cruise round the Med."

"I can't wait."

Maybe you can't, thought Miller, but I can. He'd been so busy working the Vigilante case that thoughts of retirement only popped into his head occasionally and usually involved him sitting on a river bank with a fishing rod in his hand. Now the big day was imminent the prospect of all that free time loomed over him like a threat. He couldn't go fishing every day, the garden was small and Elsie kept it tidy so that was a non-runner. How on earth would he fill his days? He wasn't one to get involved in clubs and was too old and fat for sport to be an option. He would need a hobby of some sort, something that would hold his interest. That was the problem. After forty years spent sorting out crime what would stretch his mind enough to stop him climbing the walls with boredom?

Elsie interrupted his reverie, "Perhaps you should write your memoirs? That would keep you occupied and stop you getting under my feet."

It was as though she could read his mind. That's what happened when you had been married all these years. She was a good wife. Loving and supportive enough to put up with him being dragged back into the station at inconvenient times, even the odd cancelled holiday when he couldn't or wouldn't leave a case for someone else to take over. She was still attractive too, past sixty but still with a trim figure and a face that had only a few lines. She had weathered the years much better than he had that was for sure.

"That's not a bad idea," He responded. I've handled a few interesting cases over the years and this Vigilante case would be the icing on the cake. I could probably get it serialised in one of the Sunday papers, you know the sort of thing. Ace 'tec tells all, the inside story of the hunt for the Vigilante blah blah blah."

He cheered up at the thought that he could keep himself occupied, the cash would be handy too. After forty years on the force he had an excellent pension to come and they had never been big spenders so there was a decent amount tucked away for a rainy day. Shame they couldn't have had kids, when they had gone they had no-one to leave anything to except perhaps the local dogs home. He pushed his chair back from the dining table and made for his spot on the settee. Eastenders was about to start and Elsie would be glued to the goggle box for the next half an hour. He didn't get the attraction of watching such a miserable programme, why would anybody want to spend their leisure time being depressed? He settled back and closed his eyes, at least it gave him the chance to grab half an hours shut eye.

*****

He awoke, bleary eyed and cursing, the ringing of the telephone rousing him from his well earned slumber. "Miller," He growled, then listened intently for a few seconds. "On my way. I'll meet you there."

Elsie had stirred when the phone rang but had almost instantly returned to sleep. She was used to the phone ringing in the early hours and had long ago learned the art of dropping off again. Miller slipped from under the duvet and headed for the bathroom. The bloody Vigilante was getting beyond a joke.

*****

Miller drew up outside the Sims residence. Jimmy Mears was already there and had taken charge of the crime scene. Two constable secured the area, not that there was anyone about at five o'clock in the morning but they would be needed later when the rest of the world woke up. Mears had had the area from the verge cordoned off and to Millers amazement the duty pathologist was kneeling by what appeared to be the body of Reginal Sims. SOCO were also present apparently doing a fingertip search of the surrounding area. Mears was giving instructions on his mobile phone with his back turned towards the senior officer. Miller walked around him so that Mears could see he had arrived.

"Got that?" Mears said, then ended the call. "Morning Guv, lovely day for a murder."

"What goes on Jimmy? Why am I the last one here?"

"A young chap on his way home from his girlfriend's place spotted the body and called it in. I knew you were knackered so I left calling you until forensics were here. There was nothing for you to do except wait for them so I thought you might appreciate an extra couple of hour's kip."

"Thanks, good call. What do we know? Is it Sims?"

"Yeah, one of the constables knows him and says it is definitely Sims."

"Well, we don't need to ask why he's been singled out by this bloody vigilante. No chance of an accident I suppose?"

"No Guv, it's definitely murder and definitely the Vigilante, there was a note tucked into his jacket."

"Better have a shufti then." Miller held out his hand and Mears placed a polypocket onto his open palm.

I don't need to tell you why this scum has been executed. I only need to tell you that this was my work.

The Vigilante

"That's very much to the point," Miller stated wearily. "But for once I find it hard to disagree, this couldn't have happened to a more deserving bloke. Anything useful so far?"

Mears rubbed his hand over his face as though he could wipe away the fatigue he felt. "He wired up the electric gates so that as soon as chummy touched them he received a fatal shock. Last night's rain left a nice puddle for him to stand in and ensured that he was nicely earthed so death must have been pretty well instantaneous."

"I wonder if the bugger waited for the rain or if the puddle was just luck?"

"Our experience of this character tells me it was planned."

"You're probably right Jimmy, but I'll make sure to ask the bugger when I've got him in an interview room."

"The more often he strikes the more chance there is he'll make a mistake. I reckon I'll be in that interview room with you."

"Has anyone been up to the house?"

"I went up as soon as the SOCO boys would let me past the gates. There's no-one in, or they're not answering the door. I've made a couple of calls and it appears that Sims was married but his wife took the two kids and disappeared when the shit hit the fan. I've detailed a couple of uniforms to try to find out where she might have gone."

"We can't do much here, we'll have a shufti inside the car as soon as SOCO have finished with it, let's walk up to the house and have a look around his gaff."

Chapter 20

Mr Spurgeon had overslept and had woken up with a muzzy head and a feeling of being somehow disconnected. He hadn't experienced many hangovers in his orderly life but he'd had a couple when he was a young man. This felt very much like that, the beginning of a headache was making itself known and he wondered why he felt so rough after only having a couple of small celebratory glasses of scotch. Perhaps he had picked up a bug? He hoped not, he was seldom ill and hated being incapacitated.

He visited the bathroom, used the lavatory and splashed cold water onto his face. He ran his false teeth under the tap and slipped them back into his mouth. He didn't feel any better. He made his way to the kitchen, fed Lady Mae and put the kettle on. He would give breakfast a miss but a cup of tea was absolutely essential.

He switched the wireless on and perked up when the sound of a tuba filled the room. Hancock's Half Hour, that would cheer him up. It didn't matter how many times he listened to an episode he still chuckled at Hancock. This episode was "The New Secretary" that was a good one, Hattie Jacques made her debut and gave Hancock a hard time. He poured his tea and settled down to enjoy a programme that was over fifty years old. Tony Hancock was much nicer than modern comics, no swearing or sex, just good old fashioned fun. He was starting to feel a little better, perhaps he was going to be alright.

*****

Mears and Miller walked side by side up the drive. Neither said anything, each lost in their own thoughts. As they neared the house Miller broke the silence. "I don't suppose you've told Wildblood?"

"No Guv, didn't see the point of waking him at sparrow's fart just to get a bollocking. I thought that you would want to tell him when we've had a chance to see how the land lies."

"Thanks Jimmy, that was very considerate." Miller replied dryly.

After fruitlessly banging on the door and ringing the bell Mears worked a little magic on the lock and the detectives entered the house. Mears called out that they were the police and asked anyone present to show themselves. No reply.

"OK Jimmy, let's split up and check each room, I want to know if anyone or any *body* is here. You take upstairs I'll work back from the kitchen. Shout if you find anything of interest"

Miller passed rapidly through the large kitchen, there was nothing of interest to a policeman in that sterile and underused room. It looked as though no-one had ever cooked a meal or washed a pot in its pristine environs. Either that or someone had an obsessive compulsive disorder for cleaning. The fat detective passed through the hall and reception rooms finding nothing of interest until he located what was obviously Reginald Sims study. What should have been a pleasant working environment looked as if it had been visited by the chaos fairy. Desk drawers were open, as was the single filing cabinet. Papers were strewn haphazardly over the desk and some had fallen to the thickly carpeted floor.

Miller seated himself behind the desk and systematically searched the drawers, then did the same to the filing cabinet, finally casting a glance over the scattered papers. Nothing. Nothing that indicated a possible lead. He hadn't really expected to find anything substantial. If Sims was doing a runner the stuff he was after would probably be in the car. He was ready to call it a day when Mears called from upstairs. "Better come and take a look at this guv."

Miller climbed the stairs, begrudging every step. He was tired and ascending stairs left him breathless these days. Mears was standing in a doorway at the end of the landing beckoning him. "What you got Jimmy."

"A wall safe that I can't open, a few sex toys and a shotgun."

The sex toys were piled on top of a bedside cabinet. Miller glanced at them, grinned and said, "At least this one's no more kinky than your average pervert. The shotgun was laid on the bed, Miller picked it up and examined it. "Nice gun, not super special like a Purdy but nice. Make a note to see if he had a licence for this Jimmy. Where was it by the way?"

"Propped up in the back of the wardrobe."

"Should be kept in a secure cabinet, particularly as he had kids. I wonder if this is a new acquisition that he picked up in case some of the relatives of the care home residents got a bit frisky?"

"Possible Guv, or he might have taken it from its cabinet to have it handy if trouble did break out. There's a lot of people who would have loved to give Sims a good hiding."

"Yes and I doubt that we'll get a lot of co-operation from Joe Public, after this they're more likely to want to pin a medal on the Vigilante's chest and buy him a beer than they are to give us information to help catch the sod."

Miller told Mears about the study and suggested that he have a team attend the house to search it properly immediately after the seven o'clock briefing. He glanced at his watch, "Speaking of briefing, we'd better get a shift on or they'll start without us."

The two detectives paused at the gates to scan the vehicle Sims had been using to flee. SOCO had given it a thorough search and had found a substantial amount of paperwork and a large quantity of cash in the boot. Miller instructed them to get the documents to the station and get them looked at as a matter of urgency then hotfooted it to his car with Mears at his heels.

*****

Miller called Wildchild from the car as Mears drove to the station. The commander was far from happy. He had been enjoying a breakfast boiled egg and soldiers and thinking about Sandra Patterson when his mobile rang. His wife, a hatchet faced woman who had long ago fallen out of love with her husband, looked down her nose at the untoward interruption and he had felt obliged to leave the breakfast table to take the call in the garden. As he talked to Miller he noticed that blackfly had infested his favourite tea rose and his already black mood turned stygian. Once he had finished cursing Miller, the Vigilante, Rex Anderson, the electricity board, society in general and the Vigilante again, he calmed down enough to issue instructions. "Dr Patterson is due to meet me at nine o'clock. Make sure your briefing is over by then and take her straight to the locus. Make sure that nothing is moved, including the body, until she has seen the situation for herself." He ended the call without saying goodbye.

"That went well." He said dryly.

"I could hear, I don't know why he bothered with a phone he could have just opened a window and yelled. Still at least we get to see the lovely Sandra."

"I'm more interested in what she has to say than what she looks like."

The rest of the journey was made in silence, both men lost in their own thoughts.

*****

The briefing went well. The news of the list of stores that sold the play house was well received, as was the news of Dr Patterson joining the team. The Sims murder elicited a mixed response. Anger that the Vigilante had killed again compounded with the knowledge that he might have slipped up and left a clue, all topped off with feelings of secret pleasure that the scumbag Sims had got what he deserved.

Miller guessed that Sandra Patterson would be early, wanting to make a good impression on her first day so he left Mears to it and ambled over to Wildchild's office, with luck he could kidnap the Doctor and escape before Wildchild arrived. He took a seat in the waiting area and put his feet up on the highly polished coffee table, pushing the slim pile of glossy magazines to one side. He began to go over the case from day one when Darren Bentley had been killed. He had got as far as Janet Thompson when a lightbulb went off in his head. What about the blackmail? Had that been chased? He didn't remember being given any feedback. Had it slipped through the net? It wouldn't be surprising if it had, Jimmy and the team were as knackered as he was and tired people made mistakes. He made a mental note to ask Mears if he had heard anything from Cope and was just regaining his train of thought when the door opened and Sandra Patterson entered. She was dressed in a dark blue business suit that had her brand new shiny police ID card attached to a lapel. She carried a large briefcase that already looked heavy in one hand and pile of books under her arm.

"Good Morning Dr Patterson," He greeted her, "All set to start work?"

"Good Morning, please call me Sandra and yes, I'm raring to go."

"Call me Dusty when we are on our own or with Jimmy Mears, in front of the team it will have to be DCI Miller I'm afraid, and I'll call you Dr Patterson, Sandra."

"Has something happened? I expected just to be meeting DCS Wildchild this morning to review the case."

"You could say that, the Vigilante has claimed another victim during the night and I'm here to take you to the scene so you can gather your impressions before it all gets tidied away."

Dr Patterson took the news with little sign of concern. "Perhaps we ought to go then?"

"We'll go via my office so that you can drop off your stuff. Jimmy is briefing the team but if he has finished we'll collect him and head over together."

Jimmy Mears had just finished the briefing session and allocating tasks to individuals and was wondering if he had time to filch a coffee from Miller's office when the portly detective arrived with the profiler. Greetings were swiftly exchanged, coffee offered and to Jimmy's surprise refused, and in a matter of minutes they had pulled up in the road outside the Sims house. A large tent had been erected over the gates, its purpose both to preserve the locus and also to prevent the general public and journalists from viewing the crime scene. The two officers who had secured the scene were now off duty but had been replaced by four new faces. Across the road from the house a motley band of on-lookers has congregated. Talking eagerly to one another and staring at the tent with hungry eyes.

Miller glanced at the crowd. "Vultures," He spat, "Got nothing better to do than stand around staring at a tent. What they think they'll see I don't know." He called over to a constable, "Move that lot on please."

"Sir."

The constable was a tough looking fellow named Grimes. Miller knew him well, he was known as Grim down at the nick and seldom had an appellation been more suitable. He had been promoted to detective constable three times and had always managed to do something to get himself put back in uniform. Ideal for this particular job.

Miller spoke quietly to Sandra. "Look, I'm not being sexist by saying this and I don't know how many corpses you've seen, but this one is not a pretty sight and you need to prepare yourself for what you are about to see. To be blunt he looks as though he'd been barbecued. You can probably detect the smell of cooked meat in the air out here and it's going to be a lot stronger inside the tent. You know about contaminating the crime scene so if you feel sick you must get out as fast as you can. No-one will think the worst of you if you find it too much. Now are you up for this?"

The profiler gazed steadily into his eyes and smiled. "Thanks for your concern Dusty but I think I'll be fine. Let's go in and find out."

The corpse was covered by a thin plastic sheet, not out of respect for the dead man but merely to preserve any evidence from contamination or from being blown away by the wind penetrating the tent. Miller made to pull the sheet away but Sandra Patterson stopped him with a word. "Don't. I'd like to look around the scene before I view the body if that's OK?"

"Of course Dr Patterson, however you want to play it."

Miller accompanied Patterson as she slowly walked the scene. It didn't take long. A look at the sabotaged control box, the gates and the drive up to the house and the first part of the job was done. "I'm ready now," the profiler said in a low voice. Miller escorted her back to the corpse and without pause bent and pulled back the sheet that hid the badly burnt body.

The face that was revealed wore a rictus of agony, the lips pulled back from its teeth in a grim parody of a smile. The hands were charred, white bone exposed in places where the flesh had been burned away by the elemental force that had surged through the fleeing businessman's body. The clothes that Sims was wearing had suffered too, both trousers and shirt had ignited only to be extinguished by the rain and the puddle into which Sims had fallen.

Patterson's face muscles tightened as she gazed upon the human wreckage that had once been a man. Visibly moved by the sight she straightened slightly as she fought to maintain control of her gag reflex. Her eyes flicked over the corpse, taking in every visible detail. Finally, and with an obvious effort, she gulped, "I think I've seen enough."

Miller swiftly restored the sheet to its original position. "I'm sorry you had to see that."

Patterson stepped swiftly from the tent as she replied, "All part of the job DCI Miller, I'd like to say I've seen worse but I don't think I have. It's suddenly very real, no longer a paper exercise, some sort of mind game that I need to play against the killer. I suddenly feel very motivated to do everything I can to help you catch the Vigilante."

"That's good because we need all the help we can get. What do you want to do now?"

"I'd like to take a look around the house. Try to get some sort of idea of the victim's character. I don't know if that will help but I want to build up as complete a picture as I can. Then back to the station. My priority is to review the first murder. Something triggered off this killing spree and if I can find out what started him off it should help."

"Good luck with that," Miller said lugubriously, "Bentley was a paedophile, it would be easier to list up the people who didn't want him dead than the people who did."

"I doubt it will be easy, if the solution was obvious I wouldn't have been called in." Suddenly aware that her words implied that Miller and his team could only handle simple problems she hastened to explain, "I didn't mean………"

"That's OK Sandra, no offence taken." The fat detective sighed, "You're right, if I could have sorted it out you would be back at the university doing whatever Dons do. But you're not, and I'm glad you're here to help, if you can take us one step closer to closing this case I will be eternally grateful." He paused for a moment, "Anyway, I have to get back to the station so I'll leave Jimmy to look after you," He turned to Mears who was already nodding, "You OK with that?"

"Yes Guv, no problem. We'll see you back at the nick."

Miller exited the tent on the side that abutted the road and was dismayed to see that far from being moved on the crowd had grown, worse still there were several journalists present who were doing a vox pop with the locals. Lurid quotes from the townspeople would undoubtedly adorn the front page of not just the Star but of red top nationals too. He had almost made it to his car when a loud cry pierced the air. "Mr Miller, is it Sims? Is it the Vigilante again? How many more before you get him?"

Other reporters joined in the shouts and almost immediately a cacophony of questions was hurled at the increasingly angry detective. He hurried the last few steps to his car, threw himself behind the wheel and was moving swiftly away from the scene before the journalists had a chance to mob the car. Even Wildchild will be better than this he thought morosely as he headed back to the station.

*****

Mr Spurgeon entered the convenience store and saw that it was once again crowded with gossiping women. He moved across the aisle to a rack of magazines and pretended to be browsing the glossy reading matter. He wasn't. He was listening avidly to what was being said.

"Serves the so and so right," The obese woman with a penchant for tight fitting floral garments was once more in full flow, "Couldn't have happened to a nicer bloke. Police, don't talk to me about police, Sims would have got away with a slap on the wrist if it wasn't for the Vigilante," She paused to suck in air like a demented hoover before continuing triumphantly, "They should give that bloke a bloody medal, the way them poor folks suffered in that 'ome, it shouldn't be allowed, and where were the police when them old dears was being knocked about? Drinking tea at the station I shouldn't wonder, it took the Vigilante to sort Sims out good and proper, he won't be taking no more advantage now will he? I 'ope he gets away with it, the coppers needn't come askin' me for any help, cos' they won't get it!" Having run out of breath she looked around her small audience for signs of anyone daring to disagree with her. She caught Mr Spurgeon's eye but he quickly dropped his gaze and, picking up a copy of a gardening magazine made his way through the assembled ladies to the till.

"What about the others though?" An over made-up woman dared to ask in a faltering voice.

"Far as I can see they were all out of the same mould as Sims, parasites and perverts. I reckon if the Vigilante did 'em in, they got what was coming to 'em."

A chorus of assent echoed in Mr Spurgeon's ears as he exited the shop. His cheeks were tinged with pink at hearing the praise for his crusade. Praise that seemed to be quite prevalent if the group of women in the shop were anything to go by. There was a spring in his step as he walked back to his small terraced house, the Star and the police disapproved of his actions but it seemed as though some people appreciated his efforts on their behalf. He was now even more determined than ever to carry on with his crusade.

Chapter 20

Miller pushed open the door to the incident room and strode purposely towards his office. He had scarcely taken half a dozen steps when he was ambushed by a constable who had only recently finished his probationary period.

"Mr Wildchild says he wants you to go straight to his office as soon as you come in sir."

Miller grunted a response that could have been "Sod him," if the unfortunate message bearer had been close enough to hear his venomous mutter. He paused for a moment gathering what little patience he possessed. "Thank you, just what I need to set me up for the day." The constable who had delivered the message nodded and made a rapid exit relieved that the DCI hadn't blown his top. He knew all about the bearers of bad news being shot and he didn't fancy joining the list of casualties.

The DCI slipped out of his raincoat and hung it on a peg at the back of his office door. He quickly scanned his desk for urgent messages and finding there was nothing that wouldn't wait until after he had seen Wildchild, he headed for the Commander's far more salubrious office. He emerged half an hour later. Half an hour that was spent listening to the DCS ranting about the Vigilante and demanding to know why Miller and his team were no closer to catching him. Miller had stood silently during his dressing down until he finally had had enough.

"I am due to retire very shortly, if you think that anyone else can do a better job, I am perfectly willing to stand down. I'm owed God knows how much leave and I could take it immediately, giving the new guy a clear field."

Wildchild instantly backpedalled, "No need for that Miller, look, I'm sorry, I know you and your team are doing the best you can but I'm being battered from above. The Chief Constable has been giving me grief and talking about bringing in the regional crime squad. I told him that they wouldn't do a better job than we are doing and that he should hold fire and give Dr Patterson a chance. I've held him off for now but I'm not sure how long he'll wait before he brings in the big guns."

To Miller's surprise the DCS ended the interview by standing up to shake his hand and assure him once more that he enjoyed the commander's full confidence. Yeah, thought Miller as he walked back to his office. Just like the manager of a football team enjoys the full confidence of the club chairman when the side is poised one spot above the relegation zone.

On entering his office, the portly detective found that the kettle was empty and his biscuit supply amounted to a solitary digestive of dubious provenance. He cursed under his breath, this day was going from bad to worse. He sat at his desk and picked up the phone, paused then slammed it back into its cradle. Blast it, he had been up since the crack of dawn and he was damned if he would do without essential supplies. He moved purposely into the hive of activity that was the general office. Officers were talking animatedly into telephones or typing into computers or shuffling papers. The news that he wasn't in a very good mood had obviously reached the team. He caught the eye of the constable that had given him Wildchild's message and beckoned him over. The young man sped over to him, his face a mixture of eagerness to be given a task by the DCI and concern that he had done something wrong.

Miller handed the officer a ten pound note. "Go to the nearest shop and buy some biscuits. I want a mix, don't get all the same. When you get back I want you to fill my kettle and make me a cup of coffee. If you're quick enough I might spare a biscuit for you."

The constable grinned, relieved that he wasn't going to be hauled over the coals for some minor misdemeanour. "Back in two ticks sir." He said and bolted for the exit.

The DCI returned to his office and once more picked up the phone. A voice answered the phone's summons on the second ring. "Cope."

"Hello Henry."

"Hi Dusty, I'm surprised you've got time to call me. I heard he'd got another one."

"Yeah, a nasty piece of work called Sims. The bloke who ran the care home that was closed down. I've left Jimmy Mears looking after things. He's a good man and whatever the outcome of this case he deserves to be confirmed in his acting rank. How's the paedophile case going?"

"Slowly, we've more or less stitched up things on this side of the pond and the Yanks are making good progress but on the continent it's always manana. They reckon a good lunch and a bottle of wine have priority over banging up kiddy fiddlers. Useless garlic munching bastards."

"Sorry to hear that but at least we're going to put Cadbury and that other arsehole away for a nice long stretch. Still, that isn't why I called. I was wondering if you'd made any progress on the large payments made to Janet Tomlinson. I'm clutching at straws so if you think there could be any possible link………?"

"Funnily enough I think we have just about put that to bed. It's taken a little while but we finally identified JM a couple of days ago. The money was transferred from an account in Jersey and as soon as we had the necessary paperwork sent over they were very happy to co-operate. It seems that the Channel Islands are trying to lose their reputation for being a place to hide dodgy money.

Anyway to cut a long story short the money came from a company registered over there but wholly owned by Jonas Morrison, a local builder who has contracts to build a leisure centre plus lots of smaller bits and pieces. All told the contracts are worth several million pounds. Tomlinson chaired the committee that awarded the contracts and seems to have been amply rewarded for her services. So no apparent connection to your case."

"Why the regular payments, some sort of retainer, do you think?"

"Either that or she thought that one big payment would stand out like a sore thumb, any way we are scheduled to raid brother Morrison's premises in the morning and hopefully we can put that one to bed too."

"I wish to God I could put the Vigilante to bed, then I could retire happy."

"You'll get him, he can't keep going like this without making a mistake and then you'll have him."

"I'd like to think so but I keep thinking about Peter Sutcliffe and how long he was able to keep killing before he was caught and he was barmy, mind you I reckon the Vigilante must be unhinged too, what sort of character would do what he is doing if they were totally sane?"

"One that thinks he has a cause. I think the Vigilante has more in common with suicide bombers than Peter Sutcliffe. The Yorkshire Ripper was seeking sadistic sexual satisfaction from the murders he committed whereas your bloke seems to genuinely think he is doing the right thing."

There was a pause as Miller took in what his colleague had said. "Thanks Henry, I've been missing so much sleep lately, you know how it is, never having a minute to actually sit back and think.

He's had us so much on the back foot that we've just been reacting, as fast as we begin to get top side of one killing he kills again and off we go again on the blasted merry-go-round, interviewing neighbours, chasing possible leads that get us no-where. You've given me food for thought and I thank you."

He rang off just as a carrier bag full of biscuits was placed on his desk. "Thanks lad, now get that kettle filled up and you can get back to doing something less important."

He was sipping coffee and chomping on bourbon cream biscuits when Jimmy Mears and Sandra Patterson returned from the Sims house.

Mears dragged in an additional chair while Miller organised coffee and offered a biscuit to the profiler. "No thanks Dusty, I have to watch my figure and biscuits are on the banned list."

The fat DCI was about to say that if her figure needed watching he would be happy to oblige when Mears caught his eye and raised his eyebrows. Belatedly Miller remembered the training course on diversity he had attended a few months before and substituted an anodyne comment about not wanting to share anyway, for the heavy handed compliment he had intended to make.

"Can I leave you to talk to Sandra Guv, I want to check that the teams chasing the stores that stock play houses are making progress."

'Yeah, you do that, I want to have a chat with Sandra before she toddles off to see Wildchild – and don't call me Guv, we're not the Sweeney and this isn't the east end of London."

"Yes Guv."

"You two get on well don't you." Patterson observed as Jimmy Mears left the room.

"We ought to. We've worked together for a long time. You might say that Jimmy is my protégé, not that he wouldn't have made it without me keeping an eye on him. He's a damned good copper and when I retire I hope he'll be the one to take over from me. Now, tell me what you made of things this morning and then I'll run something past you."

"There wasn't a lot to learn from the house. Signs that his wife and children left in a hurry and he wasn't coping very well on his own. The kitchen looked clean and tidy at first but there were dirty dishes and cups tucked away in the oven and the dish washer was full but hadn't been turned on. The microwave was disgusting, a few empty glasses and a couple of empty whisky bottles behind the sofa in the living room. God knows how he could get the place in such a state in only a short amount of time. As far as the actual murder scene goes I have some preliminary observations. The killer displayed a good working knowledge of electrical circuitry. Not everyone could have disabled the gates and wired them up to carry sufficient electrical charge to kill. He was organised and patient. He took away any bits of wire that he had trimmed while working to remove any signs from the scene that would alert someone to the fact the control box had been interfered with. He also took the time to fix the wire to the gates in such a way as to make the electrical connection very difficult to see for a casual observer and virtually impossible for Sims to see in the driving rain. He came prepared to carry out his plan so must have reconnoitred the site. He did it in full view of the road, showing either a complete disregard for being seen or total confidence that he would escape observation. He must have wired up the gate after he was sure that he wouldn't be observed, probably sometime after midnight. He waited until it rained before committing the crime to ensure the maximum chance of Mr Sims being killed and not just seriously injured."

"Can't argue with any of that, so where does that take us?"

"When I left here yesterday I took some files home and worked on them until the early hours. Based on the notes particularly, I think I can give you a very preliminary view of the Vigilante. The language in his messages leads me to suppose that we are looking for an elderly man or a man who had been brought up by elderly parents in a very sheltered environment. At the moment I favour an elderly man. That is based on the fact that, apart from Mick Jones all the killings were performed in a way that required no physical strength or personal contact. Even Jones was struck from behind. He believes that what he is doing is right but he is seeking approval for his actions, he is likely to have been upset with some of the comments that have been made by the force and the Star newspaper. He is likely to have a conservative view of the world and a strong dislike of change. He is likely to be either a bachelor or a widower, possibly but less likely, he may be an unwilling divorcee. With his conservative outlook he is likely to disapprove of divorce. Almost certainly he lives alone but is likely to have a pet, probably a small dog or a cat. He will be reasonably fit for his age, as demonstrated by his ability to shift heavy gas bottles. The crimes have been committed over a short time frame but have been well executed, demonstrating an ability to plan quickly and well, but most importantly to act on those plans without hesitation." The profiler had been leaning forward in her chair but now sat back and smiled at Miller. "And that DCI Miller is as far as I have got. I must stress that these findings are preliminary and are subject to change as I continue to analyse the case."

"Very interesting Sandra and what you say about the Vigilante being elderly certainly ties up with something Jimmy said about the killer possibly being an old man. The rest of it sounds reasonable too. I'd like you to attend the team briefing in the morning and share your thoughts with the guys on the sharp end."

"Guys?" The analyst queried with a raised eyebrow.

"Sorry, just shorthand, of course I meant the whole team. I suppose I'm a bit of a dinosaur, perhaps just as well I'm going to be put out to grass shortly."

"Now you sound like the Vigilante. I suppose you have an alibi for these crimes?" She enquired mischievously.

She joined in his laughter, bade him goodbye and left him for the more elevated company of Detective Chief Superintendent Wildblood.

*****

Mr Spurgeon was having a lie down. He was tired after his late night and the temporary lift he had gained from the praise the Vigilante had received in the corner shop had receded to leave a mild sense of satisfaction. His head still ached a little but it was almost constant now and he was used to the dull throbbing in his skull. Only when the lightning bolts of pain shot through his head did he consider visiting the doctor's surgery. As soon as the pain disappeared so did his intention, he hated admitting that he was ill and hated even more visiting the health centre that had replaced the surgery a few years ago. He remembered when you simply turned up and sat in the waiting room until you were seen. You knew everyone in the waiting room and being given a number was unnecessary, folks simply took their turn. Now you had to press buttons on a screen to say you were present and sit in the waiting area until an electronic board displayed your name and told you which room to go to.

He was laying on top of the bed covers, too tired to read, he was listening as the wireless played softly on the bedside cabinet. He had removed his slippers but was otherwise fully dressed, he should really have removed his cardigan but he just couldn't be bothered to make the effort. The candlewick bedspread was warm and comforting beneath him, it reminded him of when he was young and his mother had tucked him in and read him bedtime stories. Fairy stories and Enid Blyton's tales of the Faraway Tree and the Wishing Chair had been his favourites until he was able to read for himself and had graduated to the Biggles books of Captain W E Johns. He had read them all, some of them twice or three times. He could remember the librarian in the children's section of the library telling him that his favourite author also wrote a series about a character named Worrals and the thrill of excited anticipation he had felt as he rushed home clutching the precious first book of the Worrals series. Then the profound disappointment of discovering that Worrals was a girl! The book remained unread and was exchanged for a novel about Raffles, the gentleman cracksman. His parents hadn't approved of his choice, after all the man was a criminal however well-bred he was, but he had been enthralled and after he had read all the books in the series he progressed to reading about the Saint, Hercule Poirot and even Miss Marple, although as a female she obviously wasn't as good as the others.

    With an effort Mr Spurgeon dragged his wandering mind back to the present. He had succeeded in all his efforts to bring stern justice to a few villains but there was still a huge number of neer-do-wells that needed the same treatment. When he had started his crusade he had only wanted justice for himself, now he was serving the community. Not that he liked that word, nowadays it was used in all sorts of odd ways. Whoever had heard of the estate agent community or the retail community until recently? A community was a group of people who all lived in the same place. The way the English language was being ill-used made him very cross. Only the other day a young lad operating the check out at the supermarket had handed him his change with a cheery, "There you go." Mr Spurgeon had been tempted to respond with, "Where?" But had managed to resist the impulse as he was sure it would go straight over the youth's head and he couldn't be bothered to explain.

Once more Mr Spurgeon had to concentrate hard to focus on the subject he really needed to think about. What should he do next? Would it be wise to take a break, recharge his batteries and just allow the police to continue to chase shadows or should he continue to bring justice to those that the criminal law could not punish or could not punish adequately and risk being caught. He knew that sooner or later he would make a mistake and find the police on his doorstep. Then it wouldn't just be routine and a convivial glass of whisky with DC Atkins. He would be handcuffed, taken to the police station and charged with several counts of murder.

His reverie was broken by the unwelcome sound of music blasting through his bedroom window, the bass so loud he could feel it reverberating in his chest cavity. It rapidly became louder until it reached maximum intensity before gradually diminishing until only a faint throbbing bass persisted. Inconsiderate pestilential young idiot he thought as his headache worsened in response to the noise. What sort of racket was that? It wasn't music as he knew music. He liked a bit of fifties music and even some from the sixties. He thought the Beatles were a good band until they had apparently lost their minds and discovered drugs and Indian meditation but Frank Sinatra and Elvis Presley were top of his hit parade. The cacophony he had just endured was just noise, electronic static and whistles being blown. How could you call that music? The only place for a whistle was on a football pitch held firmly between the referee's lips as he signalled a foul. His head was really throbbing now and he was out of painkillers. He had meant to pick some up when he was in the corner shop but the gaggle of women in there had sent his purpose flying from his mind. It was no good he would have to return and get some paracetamol, perhaps two packs would be better so he would have a spare pack in hand.

He rose unwillingly from the bed and swopped his slippers for a pair of sturdy brogues and made his way downstairs. He pondered making the sort walk in his shirtsleeves, it was a lovely hot and sunny day but decided instead that keeping his cardigan on would be a sensible precaution in case a breeze sprang up.

As he stepped over his threshold a small red car sped around the corner, music blaring from its open windows as it proceeded far too fast between the cars parked on either side of the narrow street. Mr Spurgeon involuntarily brought his hands up to his ears in a vain attempt to block out the noise that made his head feel as though it might explode.

The driver, having observed Mr Spurgeon's discomfort pulled up alongside him. For a moment Mr Spurgeon was naïve enough to believe that the driver was going to apologise for his thoughtless actions. Instead the burly, tattooed oaf shouted, "What's up Granddad? Don't you like my music? Fucking hard luck." He flicked a V sign at the elderly man before driving off laughing uproariously at his coruscating wit.

Mr Spurgeon was speechless with helpless rage, that young man represented all that was wrong with the youth of today. Selfish, rude and aggressive without a single redeeming feature. He walked slowly towards the shop thinking about how times had changed so much for the worse over the years. In his day people had been brought up to respect their elders, moving to one side on pavements to allow them to pass, giving up seats on buses to let the elderly or women sit down. Nowadays they had to have designated seats for those less able to stand during a journey, something that had been not just unnecessary but unthought-of of in his day.

The shop was cool after being in the bright sunshine and Mr Spurgeon's eyes took a moment to adjust to the change in the light. Prem, the plump and cheerful proprietor of the shop called out, "Hello Mr Spurgeon, did you forget something when you were in earlier?"

"I need some painkillers. I've got an awful headache."

"I'm not surprised, did you hear that dreadful racket Damian Taylor was making driving up and down the road?"

"I had a little headache before but it's ten times worse now."

"Better get used to it, young Taylors a nasty piece of work who does more or less what he likes."

"I don't know him."

"And you don't want to either. His family moved in around the corner in Frogmorton Street a few months ago and they're a rough lot. The council made them move and gave them a nice semi with a front garden. It's already an eyesore with all sorts of rubbish in the garden. The people who live near them are really upset but when they tried to talk to them about tidying the place up and being a bit more considerate all they got was a torrent of abuse. Damian only got out of the nick a couple of days ago and he's already upset a few people."

"What was he inside for?"

"He mugged a pensioner in the park. Did two years for it, so it must have been serious. He is definitely not a nice man. Still the way he carries on he'll be back inside before you know it and we can go back to a quiet life."

Mr Spurgeon sniffed. "Being kept at the taxpayer's expense with all mod cons no doubt."

"You've got it. Makes you sick how we mollycoddle these people. He'll be signing on and getting the dole I expect, not that he'd have much choice, I can't see anybody giving that bugger a job so he's got the perfect excuse to sit on his backside leeching off respectable people who pay their taxes."

"Big family is it?" Mr Spurgeon inquired, trying to sound casual.

"No, just him and his father. Now he is a bad lot, you've only got to look at him and you can see where Damian gets his unpleasantness from. The mother took the two younger kids and buggered off shortly after they moved in. She'd had enough but it's got worse since she left."

"I can't understand why I don't know anything about them. I've lived in this street all my life, I was born in the front bedroom and I've never been anywhere else."

"They lived on the other side of town, I know about them because they lived near where my brother lives. He was over the moon when they moved out but his good luck is our misfortune."

Mr Spurgeon felt it was time to draw this very interesting conversation to a close. He didn't want Prem to think he was taking an unwarranted interest in Mr Damian Taylor. "I'd better get on I suppose, can I have some paracetamol please Prem. Better make it two packets."

"I'm not supposed to sell you more than one box Mr Spurgeon. It's the rules," he added portentously.

"What's that all about then?"

"It's supposed to stop people using the tablets to commit suicide, although what's to stop them buying a packet a day until they have enough to do the job or buying one packet from several different shops I don't know. It's health and safety gone mad Mr Spurgeon."

"I'm not one to break the rules even if I neither understand nor agree with them, I'll take just the one packet then please."

"You're old fashioned Mr Spurgeon, pity there aren't more like you."

"Thank you Prem, I take that as quite a compliment."

So saying Mr Spurgeon left the shop and headed home. His indecisiveness of earlier in the day had gone and his headache had subsided to the normal dull ache. He had a new target and one that would improve the area in which he lived. This afternoon he would give some thought to solving the problem of Damian Taylor.

Chapter 21

"Sit down Jimmy, how are the boys and girls doing chasing down the play house sales?"

"Not too good guv, the stores are, by and large, playing ball. One or two have been a little unwilling to supply credit card details and we had to lean on them a little but most are happy to help and we've been able to do all the out of area stuff by phone. The good news is that all the cards are either Visa or Mastercard which should cut down the chasing. Our problem is with the banks that issue them. We have the names and credit card details but no addresses to go with them. We've asked the banks for the information but they just quote the data protection act and flatly refuse to help. Bloody Jobsworths!" The acting DI spat the last word as though it were the foulest oath he could think of.

"I think I can help you there, I anticipated that we might have a problem with the banks and asked Wildchild to earn his keep. He has been on to his Grand Panjandum or whatever he's called and used the Mason's network to speed things up. They've agreed to collate the information into geographical areas and have it ready to give us as soon as we drop a court order on them. Give me what you've got and I'll pass it to him. He can sort out court orders much faster than I could hope to. A nod, a wink and a funny handshake and he'll have judges falling over themselves to help out."

"Thanks Guv, I was starting to think I'd hit a brick wall. Taking on the banks is a little out of an acting DI's league."

"No worries Jimmy, happy to feel useful. I've got to admit that the bloody Vigilante is doing my head in. No witnesses, no clues that you could call a clue and bodies piling up all over the place. I've got half a mind to postpone my retirement until the bugger's caught. On the other hand, if this lack of progress continues I could still be looking for him when I'm ninety."

"Don't let the team hear you talking like that guv, they went out on a high this morning after meeting Sandra."

"I was going to ask how it went but Wildchild was in early for a change and wanted a little chat. Bloody waste of time but he's the boss so I had to do as the master ordered."

"They were a bit suspicious to start with, I think the fact that she's an attractive woman threw them a bit. I'm not sure what they expected, either a shambolic old professor or a smooth operator straight out of an American TV series I should think, anyway when they saw Sandra they didn't take her seriously at first. That changed as the briefing went on and they could see she really knew her stuff, their mood altered completely and they started work as motivated as I've ever seen them."

"All of them?" Queried Miller drily.

"Apart from the usual suspects, there's always a couple of pessimists and one or two found it hard to accept that we are now looking for an old bloke."

"Yeah and it's usually the same couple. Motivating Blackshaw and Cummins would take more than even the lovely Dr Patterson can offer."

"I don't know about that Guv, I reckon she could motivate me to do all sorts of things."

"Get your mind out of the gutter DI Mears and get that kettle boiling. I want to review Darren Bentley's murder. That's where this nutter started his killing spree and if we can work out his motive for knocking off that creep we'll be a step forward. Something must have triggered him off and we just have to work out what pushed him over the edge."

Mears picked up the kettle and made towards the door. "Sure thing Guv, but I reckon the problem is not finding a motive but whittling down the list of suspects until we find our man" He moved towards the door then stopped and turned on his heel. "Sorry Guv, I almost forgot. Atkins had a brainwave about the old cars. He reckoned that they wouldn't have to pay road tax but would still have to register that the car was on the road with the DVLA at Swansea. He's had a word and they've supplied him with a list of tax exempt vehicles registered in the county. There's an awful lot but he's busy fileting the list down to the sort of cars that match Ann Fairbright's description, then he's going to start chasing the owners. He won't be able to do it on his own so I'll need to sort out some help when I know the number of interviews that need to be done."

"That's good Jimmy, at least we are making some sort of progress. That Atkins is a good lad and could be going places if he keeps it up."

*****

Mr Spurgeon walked slowly down Throgmorton Street, it was easy to identify the house he wanted. The Taylor residence stood out like the proverbial sore thumb amidst the neat and tidy gardens that surrounded it. The picket fence that had once stood proudly on the edge of the property had been knocked down. It looked as if the rusty and battered Ford that sat on what had once been a lawn had been driven straight through the fence to reach its resting place. Various cardboard boxes were scattered about at random, soaked through by rain they rotted where they had been discarded. An old fridge lay at an angle half covering the stone paved path that led to the front door, its door resting on its hinges, its body full of stagnant water. To complete the picture of decay a front window had been broken and a piece of hardboard nailed across the hole. Damian Taylors little red car was parked on the pavement and Mr Spurgeon was forced to walk in the road to get round it. He tutted under his breath, didn't Taylor care that women with prams, people in wheelchairs and the elderly would have to step into the road to get past. He had obviously never read the highway code.

It was far too early at nine o'clock for the Taylors to be up and about, so Mr Spurgeon took his time and tried to remember every little detail of the front of the property. He didn't know yet how he was going to execute Damian Taylor so he needed as much information as he could obtain to assist in the planning process. He was pondering his next steps when a chap of a similar age to his own hailed him from behind a neatly trimmed privet hedge. "It's a disgrace. Brings down the whole street. I saw you looking, couldn't believe your own eyes I should think."

Mr Spurgeon vaguely recognised the man from his infrequent visits to the Conservative Club and responded civilly. "Morning, it is a bit of a mess, I imagine all the neighbours are a bit cheesed off living near that."

"Cheesed off!" The man exploded, "It's driving us up the wall. The cretin who lives there refuses to do anything about the state of the place. We all signed a letter to the council and they've been round and told him to tidy the place up but it's like water off a duck's back. A duck's back." He repeated as though he couldn't believe what he was saying.

Mr Spurgeon didn't want to appear overly interested in the property or its occupants but he couldn't let this opportunity to garner information from a near neighbour pass by. As casually as he could he said, "I suppose it's a big family, that sort always seem to have lots of children."

"No, just one man and now his pig of a son. The mother flew the nest with a couple of kids just after they moved in and left the father on his own. Now the son's living there too." He leaned over the hedge and lowered his voice, "They say he's just been released from prison. Did time for beating up and robbing an old man, the dirty scumbag."

"That's terrible, they should have locked him up and thrown away the key."

"That's too good for scum like that, they should bring back the birch, flog the little shit then put a bullet in the back of his head. People like that never learn, he'll be in and out of prison for the rest of his life and when he isn't inside he'll be sponging off the state, getting handouts from the social and living the life of Riley at our expense." He broke off as he ran out of breath and began to cough.

Mr Spurgeon saw his opportunity to escape and swiftly made his excuses, resuming his slow circular walk back to his own neat and tidy home.

Lady Mae rushed to meet him as he entered the house, rubbing against his leg and meowing loudly. "Now, now Lady Mae, give me a chance to hang my jacket up, I'll feed you in a minute." He bent down and tickled the top of his feline companion's head. "Come on then," He commanded, leading the way into the kitchen, "Let's find you something in the fridge."

Once the cat was settled, munching on some cold chicken and he had made a cup of tea, he adjourned to the sitting room to think.

This situation was a real poser. He couldn't duplicate any of his previous exploits, a petrol bomb couldn't be used so close to a footpath and neighbouring houses, interfering with the steering or brakes of Taylors car was impossible when it was parked out in the open and besides the street was level and he couldn't be sure where a crash would occur. The idea of smashing him on the back of the head with a half brick was repugnant and even if he had the opportunity he doubted he had the stomach for such an action. When he had killed Mick Jones it had been on impulse, his actions driven by his revulsion at what the revolting man had been doing in the bushes. No handy gas bottles or electric gates either. As Holmes would have said, "This is a two pipe problem Watson," or in Mr Spurgeon's case a two teapot problem.

As he sipped his tea Mr Spurgeon mulled over the various methods of execution he could use. If he had a firearm he could certainly shoot the blighter. He still remembered the instruction he had received in the territorials and was sure that he could use a rifle or pistol effectively. The problem was that his eyesight wasn't what it had once been and he was uncertain about his ability to shoot accurately from a distance. A pistol was better for close quarters but could he be sure of hitting his target when he was wound up and his hands were probably shaking. Mr Spurgeon reluctantly dismissed using a firearm and began once more to consider and then discard various methods of sending Damian Taylor to hell. One after another he ruled them out; strangulation (not strong enough), poison (haven't got any and couldn't administer a fatal dose) stabbing (same as using a pistol but it was easier to obtain a knife) and other methods of killing that grew more and more esoteric as the afternoon passed. In the end Mr Spurgeon gave up and adjourned to the kitchen where he prepared his dinner of liver and onions, mashed potatoes and tinned garden peas and once more fed the always hungry cat.

After eating he adjourned to the sitting room. His mind was buzzing and he couldn't settle, he tried the wireless but it couldn't hold his attention. His library book that had seemed so enthralling when he began reading it had lost its ability to hold his attention. In desperation he turned on the television and rapidly flicked through the small number of channels the set could receive. A film had just started on Channel Four, it was typical American rubbish – cops and robbers stuff, but as much as he normally disliked this type of so-called entertainment he found himself being drawn into the flimsy plot. A maverick cop was blowing away bad guys that the law couldn't touch and doing it in increasingly violent ways. Mr

Spurgeon felt a glimmer of empathy for the American cop and watched the film until it ended long after his usual bedtime.

The film had given him the glimmer if an idea. What he needed to do now was to watch Damian Taylor and find out if his movements. If he was regular in his habits it would make his plan much simpler to carry out. He reached for his notebook and began to jot down his thoughts.

1. Obtain a shotgun.
2. Saw off the barrels.
3. Wait in his car for Taylor to come home one night.
4. Shoot Taylor through the window of his car.
5. Drive away before any witnesses saw him.

Quite straightforward really.

The biggest stumbling block was getting hold of the shotgun. His nephew, he knew, had owned one and had spent a few weekends shooting pigeons on a local farm. As with everything that lad did, he rapidly lost interest. The gun was probably safely locked up in the steel gun cupboard that had been installed in the small room his nephew described as his study. If he could somehow get hold of that it would be weeks or even months before it was discovered to be missing and no-one would associate its theft with harmless old Uncle Horace. It was time that Uncle Horace paid a visit to his nephew and he determined to arrange a visit for the coming weekend.

*****

"Bloody Uncle Horace wants to visit us at the weekend." Geoffrey Spurgeon shouted to his wife who was peeling potatoes in the kitchen. "I've put him off for a week but I couldn't just say no."

"Well, it has been a while since we've seen him and he's always quite generous to the kids." Celia Spurgeon called back.

Geoffrey entered the kitchen as he replied, "I know, but he's such an old fart, everything always has to be just so and he's always going on about how everything was better in the old days. He just gets on my wick."

"Better to keep the right side of him. He owns that house and must have a fair bit tucked away. We're his only relatives since your dad died and if you upset him too much he'll leave it all to that bloody cat."

"A good point, well made. I'll put up with him wittering on and keep my thoughts to myself. It's only an afternoon after all, so I'm sure I'll cope."

"Just be sure you do and you'd better have a word with the kids before he comes I don't want them upsetting him either and you know how cheeky young Tom is getting."

"If he does play up I'll nail the little bugger. He won't sit down for a month."

"Keeping him in and docking his pocket money would be more effective. Slapping his backside is a waste of time."

"Fair enough but I'll make sure that any failure to behave will not be tolerated and will result in severe punishment."

"When is Uncle Horace coming exactly?"

"A week on Saturday. He'll be here at three o'clock precisely and will depart after tea."

"It's been ages since he was here, what do you think we should feed him?"

"Oh, I dunno, tinned salmon sandwiches and some fruitcake I should think."

"Well at least that is straightforward."

"Uncle Horace is a very straightforward man."

*****

Mr Spurgeon was standing behind a large bush in the front garden of a certain Mrs Kelly. Prem at the local shop had told him that Mrs Kelly had had enough of the disturbance caused by the Taylors and had gone to stay with her daughter in Brighton indefinitely. According to Prem, Damian had come home every night at around midnight playing music at maximum volume on his car stereo and slamming his car door as loudly as he could. As Mrs Kelly's home was directly opposite the Taylors house she had suffered more than most from her noisy neighbours. Mr Spurgeon was sorry for Mrs Kelly but her departure suited him very well as it allowed him a vantage point that was concealed from anyone more than a yard or so away from the bush. Anyway, if his plan came to fruition she could move back home and once more enjoy the peaceful existence to which she was entitled.

Mr Spurgeon had been observing the house now for almost a week and Prem's information had proved to be correct. Every night at midnight, give or take five minutes, the lout had returned home, playing his music and slamming his car door just as described. His plan now hinged on being able to get his hands on the shotgun. If he could he would just park at the end of the road and wait. As soon as he saw, or more likely, heard Taylor coming home he would drive towards him, pull up alongside Taylors car and fire both barrels through his open car window and drive around the corner to put the Morris safely back in his garage. It meant using the car again but he would only be driving a few hundred yards. He would drive without lights and, as long as he reacted immediately he had fired, he would be round the corner before anyone could see his car. Once again he was grateful for the council cuts that meant only half the streetlamps were illuminated and those that were lit now went off at midnight. There was little chance of any pedestrians being about at that time in the week so he thought he stood an excellent chance of pulling it off as long as he could get the shotgun. It all depended on the shotgun. He had no idea of how to get hold of the weapon so he would have to extemporise when he visited on Saturday.

As usual Damian Taylor carried out his homecoming routine. Mr Spurgeon waited until he had entered the house and then silently slipped out of Mrs Kelly's garden gate and made his way home. He was satisfied that Taylor would continue to follow his pattern of behaviour and resolved to end his midnight vigils. He would be glad to get some early nights and return to his own routine. In bed with a good book no later than ten o'clock was his habit but staying up until past midnight meant he was too tired to read when he finally got to bed.

*****

"Come in Uncle Horace, it's so good to see you, you're looking well." The smile on Celia's face fell just short of sincere.

Mr Spurgeon had taken the bus ride across town and had arrived at his nephew's home at three o'clock, exactly as planned. He had paused to admire Geoffrey's front garden which was vibrant with the bright reds of pelargoniums and roses before walking up the garden path and ringing the bell. The door had swung open almost instantly and he had been greeted by his nephew's wife.

"Hello Celia, it's nice to see you again."

His niece by marriage stepped back from the threshold to allow Mr Spurgeon to enter. As he stepped into the hall he was greeted by two boys of eight and ten years who stood at the bottom of the stairs. "Hello Uncle Horace,' They chorused.

"My my, this is a nice welcome. Hello boys, how are you?"

His grandnephews informed him they were OK and eyed the small package that was clutched beneath Mr Spurgeon's arm.

"Can I take your jacket Uncle Horace it's rather warm today?" Celia inquired.

"I'll keep it on for now dear if you don't mind, my old bones don't seem to get warm these days however hot it is."

"Come on through, I think Geoffrey is putting the kettle on and if he isn't, I will."

Celia ushered Mr Spurgeon through to the sitting room and made him comfortable with an extra cushion when he sat in a large arm chair. Geoffrey entered the room carrying a tray laden with all the accoutrements required for a small tea party. "Hello Uncle Horace, it's good to see you." He placed the tea tray on an occasional table and shook Mr Spurgeon warmly by the hand. Another one faking sincerity and making a fair job of it too. He ought to go into politics thought Mr Spurgeon but he didn't say so, instead he echoed his nephew's sentiments.

The two boys were still eying the package with avaricious glances and Mr Spurgeon decided it was time to hand over the goods.

"Come here Tom, come on Harry, I have a little something for you."

Tom and Harry did as they were bid and stood before Mr Spurgeon's chair awaiting their gifts. Their eyes lit up when Mr Spurgeon handed them both a model aeroplane kit.

"Tom, yours is a Spitfire and Harry, yours is a Hurricane. When you make them you'll find that they look similar so don't get them mixed up. These were the aeroplanes that won the Battle of Britain so make sure you look after them." The boys looked puzzled at his reference to the second world war but thanked him politely for their gifts. Mr Spurgeon smiled as his grandnephews rushed from the room, already arguing which boy had the best plane.

"That was very kind Uncle Horace, I'm sure the boys will enjoy making those models."

"I'm pleased they like them. To be honest I was at a bit of a loss to think what to get them. These days it all seems to be the inter-web and mobile telephones and playing games on computers, then I remembered what I had enjoyed as a boy and I didn't think that lads these days were so much different."

The afternoon passed pleasantly with conversation revolving around Tom and Harry and various, mostly deceased, relatives. The two lads had commandeered the table in the separate dining room and were hard at work assembling their war planes leaving the adults in peace. Every now and then either Celia or Geoffrey would pop their heads through the door and tell them to keep the noise down when the volume of their discussions reached an unacceptable level. Salmon and cucumber sandwiches and home made fresh cream scones had been consumed and the time for Mr Spurgeon to depart was rapidly approaching when he lurched forward in his chair and almost toppled to the floor.

Instantly Geoffrey was on his feet and helping his uncle back into his seat. "Are you alright Uncle Horace?" He asked with genuine solicitude, "You looked as though you were going to pass out."

"Give me a minute, I'll be fine in a minute." Mr Spurgeon gasped, sounding far from alright.

Celia and Geoffrey hovered over him, making reassuring noises until Mr Spurgeon, apparently feeling he was being smothered by kindness, asked if he could have a glass of water and perhaps a few minutes on his own.

"Why not sit in my study for a while, it's on the cool side of the house and there's a fan if it gets too warm."

Mr Spurgeon allowed himself to be ushered into his nephew's study and seated in the large leather office chair behind his desk.

"I'll leave you alone for a little while then I'll come back to check on how your feeling."

Mr Spurgeon simply smiled and nodded his thanks. He was out of his chair and examining the gun cupboard as soon as the door had closed behind his nephew. The cupboard lock looked to be of reasonably good quality but not outstandingly so, just the sort of thing you would find on the post boxes that people fixed to their fences if they had toddlers or dogs loose in the garden and needed to restrict access to the house. He swiftly jotted down the serial number that was engraved above the keyhole, then returned to his seat. So far so good. Now all he needed was to find a key to the front door. He quickly pulled open the right hand side desk drawer. Nestling in the corner was a small bunch of keys. He picked them up and scanned them. This was almost too easy. One key for a mortice lock, one for a Yale and one for the gun cupboard. His mind went into overdrive and he quickly moved across the room and unlocked the gun cupboard. He still intended to get a key cut for the cupboard but he had a back-up in case the key wouldn't work. It was unlikely that Geoffrey would discover that the door was unlocked and if he did he would blame himself for being careless. He returned to his seat, swiftly noted down the Yale and mortice lock key numbers, slipped his notebook away and sipped at his glass of water.

He didn't wait for Geoffrey to return. He made his way slowly along the short passage and entered the sitting room.

"Are you alright Uncle Horace?" Celia and Geoffrey chorused.

"I'm fine thank you, don't know what came over me I'm sure."

"Sit down and I'll get you a nice fresh cup of tea." Said Celia brightly.

"Celia is very kind," Mr Spurgeon said to his nephew when she left the room, "She keeps the house looking nice too and that must take some doing with your lads about the place. Is she still working?" He added casually.

"Yes, she's still full time at office. She keeps talking about going part time but with the economy the way it is it's more sensible for her to keep her hours while we don't know what's around the corner. At least her hours are reasonable, nine to five Monday to Thursday and Friday mornings so she has a sort of extended weekend."

"And your job is secure?" Mr Spurgeon enquired, as a caring uncle should.

"As far as anybody's is these days. We have little blips and had to let a few people go last year but we seem to be weathering the storm better than some."

"There's not much good to say about being old, but being retired with a pension is one of them. I might not have a large income but I know it will always be there every four weeks as regular as clockwork, and of course, I have a small works pension to top up what the government give me."

Celia brought in fresh tea and they chatted amiably until Mr Spurgeon announced it was time he was going. Geoffrey immediately said he would run his uncle back. Mr Spurgeon protested but was not allowed to decline a lift home. Celia summoned the boys and affectionate farewells and repeated expressions of appreciation for the gifts were spoken as Geoffrey and Mr Spurgeon left the house. Uncle and nephew continued to chat amiably enough until they reached Mr Spurgeon's little house.

"We mustn't leave it so long. You must visit more often, you know where we are, just give me a ring and I'll come and pick you up."

Mr Spurgeon thanked Geoffrey for bringing him home and promised to keep in touch. Geoffrey waited in the car until his uncle had opened his front door then accelerated away with a sigh of relief that his duty had been done. Meanwhile his uncle was thinking how smoothly the operation had gone and congratulating himself of his acting ability. Perhaps not up to the standards of the Old Vic but good enough to fool Geoffrey and Celia.

*****

Mr Spurgeon thought that there was little chance of him being linked to the theft of Geoffrey's shotgun but nonetheless decided to play safe. The following day he caught the bus into town and a connecting service to a town twenty miles away. He had rarely visited the place before, there was no need to when it offered nothing that wasn't available in Clingford Norton. He was confident that there was little or no danger of either being recognised or remembered when he entered the old fashioned hardware shop. He made an excuse about needing a set of keys for his cleaner and handed over eight pounds to pay for his new keys. He considered the fee to be extortionate for two tiny pieces of metal but kept his opinion to himself, he didn't want to do anything that would make him stick in the memory. Within thirty minutes of arriving in the town he was sitting on a bus heading back to Clingford Norton.

Now he had just one small problem to solve before he could take possession of the shotgun. How would he get it home? He had to take it during the day when Geoffrey, Celia and the boys were out, their house wasn't overlooked but it would be unfortunate if a neighbour saw him leaving the house with a shotgun shaped parcel or if he was seen with it on the journey home. What was the name of that fellow who used to be on the wireless with Robert Robinson? He had invented the concept of lateral thinking. Edward de Bono! He thought triumphantly, I have to think laterally. He tried coming at the problem from all sorts of angles until finally a lightbulb went off in his head. If he sawed off the shotgun barrels before he left Geoffrey's house rather than when he got home the weapon would fit in the bottom of a decent sized bag, he could place a few lightweight purchases on top of the gun to hide it from view and catch the bus home without a care in the world.

He called at his home, had an early bite of lunch, fed the cat, located a sturdy canvas shopping bag and his hacksaw and was soon back on a bus heading towards Geoffrey's house.

*****

He glanced up and down the lane, in the distance he could see vague shapes that were probably a mother pushing a pram. His old eyes certainly weren't as good as they had once been, perhaps he needed distance glasses to go with the little pair of readers he had bought off the shelf at Superdrug. That would mean a visit to an optician's, a group of people he put in the same class as doctors. It occurred to him that perhaps his headaches were connected to his deteriorating vision and made up his mind that he would make an appointment to see someone as soon as possible.

He walked quickly up the garden path, not taking the time to admire the flowers on this occasion. He had the front door key ready in his hand and thrust it into the lock the instant he reached the front door. The key grated and refused to turn. Mr Spurgeon caught his breath and an image of the key cutter being blown to kingdom come appeared in his head. He shoved harder at the key and it seemed to move forward a fraction. He twisted the key and pushed. The door swung open and he stepped inside. The key jammed when he made to withdraw it from the lock and he twisted and pulled it several times to no avail. When, after what seemed like a very long time but had probably only been a very few seconds, the key finally jerked free he breathed a huge sigh of relief and swiftly closed the front door behind him.

He paused for a moment, breathing heavily. He had subconsciously been holding his breath and now his lungs demanded oxygen. As soon as he had regained control, he made his way to Geoffrey's study and placed his shopping bag onto the desk. He swung around and moved over to the gun cabinet, he pulled the handle down and forward and the door glided smoothly open. Thank goodness, the unlocked door had not been discovered. Clipped to the rear of the cupboard was a fine looking weapon. Geoffrey might not be using it much these days but he had certainly looked after his gun. Both the wooden stock and the twin barrels gleamed in the shaded light of the cabinet. Stacked neatly in the bottom of the cupboard were three boxes of twelve bore cartridges. Wonderful, now he had everything he needed.

Mr Spurgeon reached in and grasped the gun by the barrels and pulled it free from its retaining clip. It wasn't as heavy as he had anticipated and he swung the weapon up to his shoulder in an easy movement. He sighted along the barrels then lowered the gun and examined the engraved metal plate attached to the stock. Webley and Scott was etched into the metal. Mr Spurgeon knew little about guns but he could tell that this was a fine example of the gunsmith's art. He sighed with regret, it would be a shame to destroy it, but he comforted himself with the thought that it would be for a good cause.

He placed the gun on Geoffrey's desk and delved into his shopping bag. Under the bags of potato crisps he had bought earlier at Prem's shop he found his hacksaw. He piled the packets of crisps on one side of the desk, removed the hacksaw and placed the shopping bag directly under where he intended to saw off the barrels. He removed a plastic refuse sack from his pocket and lined the shopping bag so that the metal swarf produced from sawing the barrels would be safely deposited in the sack. There was little point in staging a theft that would not be discovered for a long time if he left a pile of evidence of his wrongdoing on the carpet. He shifted the gun so that the barrels protruded over the side of the desk and positioned his left hand to steady the gun as he offered the blade of the hacksaw to the shiny metal. The gun moved as he tried the first cut and the saw blade skimmed over the barrels leaving a light scratch on the metal's surface. This wasn't going to be easy. After a couple more futile attempts Mr Spurgeon modified his plan. He placed his shopping bag alongside the gun and gauged the minimum amount of barrel he needed to remove to reduce the gun's length in order that it would fit into the bag. With most of the gun now on the desk, sawing through the barrels was easier. Easier, not easy. The stock still shifted in response to the pressure the hacksaw put onto the barrels but less often and less frequently. The effort of putting all his weight onto the stock while operating the hacksaw was hard work and Mr Spurgeon began to sweat. He wasn't about to take a break though, he wanted to tidy up and be out of Geoffrey's house as fast as possible. He persevered and, although the stock slipped more than once on the desk's polished surface, at last the barrels succumbed to the saw and fell with a dull thud into the plastic lined shopping bag below.

He lifted the bag onto the desk and tied off the top of the plastic liner to prevent the swarf from contaminating the shopping bag. Perhaps he was being over scrupulous but better safe than sorry as his father used to say. Next he removed the three boxes of cartridges from the gun cabinet and placed them in the bag. He followed them with the shortened shotgun, then topped off his haul with the packets of crisps. Returning to the gun cabinet he took out the key he had had cut and locked the cupboard door. He stood by the door scanning the room, searching for any traces of his visit. Finding none he closed the study door and exited the house.

He walked quickly, but not so fast as to look suspicious, up the garden path and turned in the direction of his bus stop. There was no-one about to see him leave his nephew's home and he felt a great sense of satisfaction at a job well done. Mission accomplished.

The strain of his morning activities had left Mr Spurgeon feeling washed out. Being the Vigilante was very tiring and he resolved to do just one more little job and then rest. He would have an early night with his book and perhaps a mug of cocoa so that he was fit for tomorrow night.

Lady Mae fussed around him as he entered the house, rubbing against his legs and getting under his feet. He walked through to the kitchen and placed his bag by the back door. He tore open a sachet of cat food that was alleged to contain tuna but probably didn't, or a mere trace of the huge fish at best. Lady Mae began to meow plaintively, demanding her food instantly and he placed her bowl onto the kitchen floor with a few affectionate words that the cat ignored as she greedily wolfed down the food.

Mr Spurgeon hefted the shopping bag and made his way down to his workshop. It was a matter of moments before he had the stock of the shotgun held securely in the vice mounted to his work bench. A short energetic burst of activity later and he was looking down at a much shorter weapon. In the film he had watched one of the bad guys had also sawn off the stock to make a weapon not much larger than an overgrown pistol, but Mr Spurgeon refrained from following his example. He, though not exactly frail, wasn't all that strong and he was concerned that by shortening the stock he would lose control of the powerful weapon. He freed the gun from the vice and examined his work. The cut across the barrel was neat and a brisk rub around with a file was all that was needed to finish the job to his satisfaction. Next he placed the sawn off shotgun and the three boxes of cartridges under his bench and covered them with some off cuts of wood. He looked at the pieces of barrel that he had removed and wondered if they might come in handy but discarded the thought almost as soon as it had crossed his mind. He was something of a magpie and hated to throw away nuts, bolts, screws, left over bits of wood or anything that he thought might one day come in useful, but keeping the barrels would be very silly. Direct evidence of what he had done if the police ever came visiting. It wouldn't take a forensic scientist to put two and two together, the greenest bobby would arrest him as soon as the barrels were found. They would need to be disposed of somewhere that couldn't be linked back to him. He would have to think about that little problem. Tomorrow he would place the loaded gun in his car and think about where he could hide it after executing Taylor, so that it was safely tucked away but handy for the next time he needed to clean up the streets of Clingford Norton. He was too tired to do anything more that day and badly needed a rest. The cartridges could stay where they were, if he needed more than two shots the game would be up anyway.

Chapter 22

"We've finally finished interviewing everyone on the play house list who lives within a twenty mile radius of Clingford Norton. It's taken forever to get through them but everyone who has been visited was able to show us a Klassic Toddler Tent so we could rule them out immediately. How do you want us to extend the search Guv?"

Miller reflected for a moment. "Time for Wildchild to do his stuff again. I'll get him to ring his opposite numbers in the various forces involved and ask them to visit the people on their patch."

"That should be straightforward with most of them because we're talking about penny numbers but there's a lot that the Met would have to cover and they might not be too happy to help out their poor provincial colleagues."

"How many are there exactly? Do you remember?"

"Off the top of my head, fifty-three."

"That is a lot of interviews scattered all over the smoke." He thought for a moment. "I'll ask Wildchild if we can second a couple of lads to help out. The danger is that they might say send half a dozen and you can do them all. Wildchild can be a wily bugger though and he'll probably talk to one of the funny handshake brigade again."

"If we do need to send a couple of lads, they'll need digs. You know what these things are like, they'll have sat nav for getting around but a lot of the people they'll need to see will be out during the day and will need a follow up evening visit. I'd want to send single men, most of the married chaps have seen very little of their families since this case kicked off and I don't want to be blamed for any divorces."

"Quite right. Tell you what, send young Atkins and the lad who's just finished his probation. It'll be what our new style senior management call a developmental intervention to aid career progression." He paused then added under his breath, "Idiots!"

"I should ask for volunteers really Guv."

"Yes, you should and I've just volunteered Atkins and whatsisname."

"Perkins Guv."

"Call me Guv one more time and I'll bloody send you." Miller snarled in mock anger.

"I think I'd appreciate the rest Guv, you and I are doing more hours than anyone else on the team and they're all bloody exhausted."

"All we can do is keep pressing on. This toddler tent thing is our best," He paused and corrected himself, "No, only substantial lead. If the bloody banks had been more co-operative we could have either caught the bugger by now or eliminated the toddler tent purchasers as suspects and moved on to other areas of inquiry." He added bitterly.

"I'll put the kettle on guv, Sandra's due in any moment and she's very partial to one of your biscuits with a cup of coffee."

"That's what happens when you get to my age. The young ones prefer a custard cream to a night of torrid passion with an experienced and skilful lover like myself and the old ones who do fancy me can't get up the stairs."

Mears stared at Miller's corpulent figure, his belly was straining against his shirt, forcing the buttons apart and revealing flabby white flesh. As much as he liked his boss he found it impossible to see him as a star bedroom performer. Diplomatically he said nothing. He was just stirring the coffee when there was a tap at the door and Sandra Patterson's head appeared, "Alright to come in?" She enquired, although as she was half way through the door it was more or less a rhetorical question.

"Come in Sandra, Jimmy is just making you a coffee and I'm in charge of the biscuits."

"I thought it was time I made a contribution to your biscuit barrel so I brought some in to top up your supply." With that she delved into her capacious handbag and produced a packet of milk chocolate digestive biscuits and another one of Jaffa cakes.

"Just what the doctor ordered Dr Patterson." Laughed Miller as he stretched out and ripped open the Jaffa cakes. He slipped a whole one into his mouth and then remembering his manners offered the biscuits around. To his disappointment both Mears and Patterson took advantage of his courtesy by swiping a couple of the moreish treats and then dipping in for more.

They discussed the progress that had been made since the last time they had met but there was little to say. Dr Patterson had continued to study all the paperwork relating to the Vigilante and had visited the scenes of each murder but had found nothing that significantly changed her preliminary findings. Mears updated her with their plans for the Toddler Tent enquiries and then the discussion just petered out.

"As far as I can see if the tent doesn't lead anywhere the only way we'll get the bugger is if he kills again and slips up." Miller said gloomily.

"I wish I could argue with you Guv, but I think you're right. Let's hope if he does do another one in that it's a swine like Sims, then we won't feel too bad about not catching him before."

"What about your retirement Dusty? Is it still on?" Sandra asked.

"Wildchild has asked me to stay on, He doesn't want to bring in another DCI to replace me at this stage and politically he can't let Jimmy, who is only an acting DI, take charge of such a high profile case. I've said I'll stay until we get him or until it becomes obvious that we're not going to get him, at which point I shall slink off with my tail between my legs for a good long sulk."

*****

"I don't believe it!" Sargent Dave Braithwaite yelled across the squad room. "I've only got to drop everything and help the bloody turnips find a Wendy house."

Cat calls and derisory comments flew around the room and Braithwaite rapidly wished he'd kept his mouth shut. "I don't know why your laughing, one of you lot has got to team up with me – and I get to choose who it is!"

The noise in the squad room subsided a little but this was the best laugh they'd had in years and the chuckles rumbled on. Dave Braithwaite, the man who thought he was on a fast track to the Assistant Commissioner's office had been given a job that would have been more suited to the greenest constable in the station. Couldn't have happened to a more deserving bloke was the general consensus. If ever an uppity so-and-so needed taking down a peg or two it was Dave Braithwaite.

"And the DI said that as the section house was full, would I kindly sort out some digs for 'em. What am a bleedin' travel agent?"

The squad room once more erupted with raucous laughter and a voice from the back of the room called, "You going to tuck them in too Sarge?"

"I recognise your voice Detective Constable Willis. As you have the welfare of our country cousins so close to your heart, you can assist me in tucking them in. More than that, you can fill their bloody hot water bottles and take them a glass of water if they wake up in the night. Come over here and I'll brief you."

The laughter gradually faded away and the room returned to the normal buzz of a busy office except that occasionally a chuckle would break the sound of honest toil as another joke was made at Braithwaite's expense.

Willis made his way over to Braithwaite, he was thirty years old with a rugby players build and a face like a bag of spanners. He was always at the front when trouble kicked off and thrived on the adrenaline that a good ruck sent coursing through his veins. If he hadn't been a copper, he would have made a good football hooligan. His high pitched voice always surprised people the first time they heard him speak and a few dared to take the micky but no-one did it twice. "Do I really have to do this Dave?" He wheedled.

"Too bloody right you do, why should I have all the shit that flies round this nick? I'm a great believer in sharing the misery equally. Sit down and I'll put you in the picture."

Willis took a seat and listened while Braithwaite outlined the tasks they had to perform. When he had finished his explanation he said, "So how do we play it?"

Willis shrugged. "Get on with It and get it done with as fast as possible I should think."

"Wrong. I want you on the blower sorting out some digs for the turnips. We are definitely not talking about the Ritz, find somewhere that is just above doss house level. That way the turnips will want to get back to some sheep shagging as fast as they can. We are going to take our time and make sure that the country cousins do most of the work. It's only right," He added, "It's their bloody case."

*****

Mr Spurgeon had enjoyed his day of rest. He had pottered about in the garden, deadheading a few annuals and pulling out the odd weed. Strangely he felt very relaxed about what was going to happen that night. This would be the first time that he killed someone in cold blood face to face. He had killed Jones in a fit of righteous anger and would not have attacked the man in that way if he had meticulously planned the execution. When he thought killing Damian Taylor all he felt was a frisson of excitement at the prospect of ridding the area of a confounded nuisance. His evening meal was beefburgers and chips, something that took no time at all to prepare. He would have preferred a nice pork chop but his false teeth were not up to the job and bits of meat got stuck under his plate. There might have traces of horse meat in them but at least beefburgers were easy to chew. After dinner and washing up he listened to the wireless for a while then read his book until it was time to put his plan into action. Just enough time to compose a note to leave with the body.

This is Damian Taylor. He has just been released from prison for beating and robbing a senior citizen. Since he has been free he has made his neighbours life a living hell. The police either couldn't or wouldn't do anything to put a stop to his antics so I have taken action. I will continue to act as long as worthless types like Taylor contaminate the lives of ordinary law abiding people. Let this act as a warning to others of the same ilk.

Sincerely

The Vigilante

He scanned what he had written and was satisfied with his missive, no alterations needed. He waited until twenty minutes to midnight before leaving the house. That gave him adequate time to walk to his garage and take up his position at the end of Throgmorton Street. He didn't want to be too early and attract attention to himself by sitting in his car for too long, but he daren't be late and find his target already in the house. As he walked down the dark street he kept a weather eye open for anyone who might notice and remember him, he was taking a big chance operating as close to home as he was but this job had to be done. The shopping bag containing the sawn off shotgun swung gently to and fro as he walked, it's weight strangely reassuring.

He had oiled the garage door again earlier in the day, there was probably no need but he was a belt and braces type of fellow. The up and over door moved almost silently, coming to rest with a soft clang of metal on metal. He climbed into the car and put the shopping bag on the front passenger seat. He pulled out the choke, turned the ignition key and listened with pride as the old car burst into life. Like him, his car was old but still useful in times of need. He drove away without stopping to close the garage door. There was a remote chance that someone would see the open door but he was prepared to accept that risk. It was more important that he get the car out of sight as swiftly as possible after he had accomplished his mission.

He parked the car at the top of Throgmorton Street looking down towards where Taylor would turn the corner. He was confident that he could put his car into position before Taylor could exit the vehicle. He had left the engine running and had removed the shotgun from his bag and placed it across his lap. Next he pulled on a pair of thin latex gloves, his fondness for detective fiction gave him the knowledge that the residue from a fired weapon would be easily identifiable if a simple swab was rubbed over the skin of his hands. He wound his window down and released his seatbelt. All he had to do was pick up the gun and fire.

He heard Taylor's car before he saw it and was moving slowly down the street as the little red vehicle turned into the street. Coolly, he timed the cars arrival perfectly, drawing up so closely to Taylor's car that he could not open the door. Taylor looked at him with an expression of fury on his face. His window was down, as it habitually was, so that he could share his taste in music with his long suffering neighbours. "What's your fucking game Granddad?" He shouted, "Shift that heap of tin before I beat you senseless, you stupid old git."

"Good evening Mr Taylor." Mr Spurgeon responded politely, "I don't know if you remember me but you were awfully rude to me the other day. Anyway, that doesn't matter. I'm here with a noise abatement notice from your neighbours."

Taylor was gawping, trying to comprehend Mr Spurgeon's words when the old gentleman swung up the shotgun and fired both barrels into his face. Mr Spurgeon felt a tremendous kick from the weapon as it discharged its cartridges and couldn't prevent the heel of the stock striking him hard in the chest. Simultaneously, Taylor's head exploded and a fountain of blood, bone and brain matter painted the interior of his vehicle. Mr Spurgeon was distressed to note that some of blood had splattered his face. That was most disconcerting and completely unexpected. For a long moment he was frozen, stunned by the enormity of what he had done, then, getting a grip on his emotions, he dropped the shotgun onto the front passenger seat, tossed the prepared note onto Taylor's lap and slammed the car into first gear, driving as fast as a Morris Minor can go to the end of the street. Once he was round the corner he slowed down to a more sedate pace. His garage was close by and he didn't want to attract attention by driving like a lunatic. He was out of sight and he didn't believe he had been seen, certainly he had not noticed any lights going on in the houses around the Taylor residence. Once the car was safely garaged and he was back at home he could relax.

He drove smoothly into the garage and applied the handbrake. He replaced the shotgun in the shopping bag and, not wanting to risk switching on the overhead sixty-watt light bulb, he dipped into his pocket for his torch. He flashed it quickly over the driver's side and was horrified to see that Taylor's blood and brains decorated the rear side window and the roof of his little car. He had known that he had Taylor's blood on his face but now he realised the inside of the car must be contaminated too. Mr Spurgeon was sufficiently provoked to swear, "Damn the man," he muttered, "He's nearly as much trouble dead as was when he was alive. I shall have to give the old girl a very thorough clean tomorrow."

He kept his head down as he walked back to his home. If anyone had seen his face in its current blood splattered state, they would definitely remember him when the police came calling. He heard the faint sound of a police siren approaching as he turned his key in the lock. I should think the police are grateful to me with all the overtime payments they're getting he thought as he entered the sitting room and poured himself a small glass of whisky prior to a much needed visit to the bathroom for a late night bath.

Chapter 23

Atkins was finding the car journey down to London something of a trial. Steve Perkins was a pleasant enough bloke but he had all the charisma of a plastic bucket. He came across as being on the thick side too, although he couldn't be as dense as he appeared or he would never have managed to pass the police entrance exam. Perhaps he has a relative with a bit of pull thought Atkins, that would explain things. How he was going to cope with being partnered with Perkins he didn't know. It was bad enough being trapped in this car with him but he would be working with him all day and then sharing the same digs. At least the Met were taking on some of the work so his ordeal might not last too long. It would be wonderful if they managed to find someone who had bought a Toddler Tent and didn't have it in their possession. It might even be the first house they called at, now that really would get him in DCI Miller's good books and on the fast track to promotion.

He had thought he had cracked the case when he had visited a house on the outskirts of Clingford Norton checking on people who had purchased a play house and the door had been answered by an elderly man. There was no sign of a play house in the garden and for a heart stopping moment Atkins thought he had nailed the Vigilante. His sense of elation had disappeared when the old timer had informed him that he had purchased the tent for his Granddaughter who lived in the next county. The old guy was very co-operative and offered to accompany Atkins to his son's house. That was fortunate for Atkins as he would otherwise have had to call for assistance from the station as he couldn't leave the old fellow unsupervised in case he was the Vigilante and did a runner. They had arrived at the son's house to find that no-one was in and had waited for two hours for the lady of the house to return from a shopping trip. Atkins couldn't even take a look over the fence to see if the tent was in the back garden as the outside area was partially hidden from the road by a tall screen of leylandii trees and an entire estate of Wendy houses could have remained unseen behind the thick foliage. At least the old fellow had been content to sit in the car and chatter aimlessly while they waited for someone to return to the house. The ambitious constable had listened with half an ear as the day disappeared and he fretted at the delay. Once the daughter-in-law had returned it was a matter of only a few minutes for the tent to be shown to Atkins. With many apologies for the trouble he had put the old gentleman to and a word of thanks to the daughter-in-law he had driven the old fellow back to his home in Clingford Norton, cursing that he had used up the best part of a day on a fruitless mission.

At least the old fellow had been able to have a stab at a decent conversation. Unlike Perkins who wittered on about his girlfriend and how much he would miss her or the events in Eastenders, which he apparently recorded assiduously so that he didn't miss a single episode when he was on back shift. Fancy a grown man watching Misery-on-Thames. Sad bastard! The station had been buzzing when they had picked up the pool car. The Vigilante had apparently been busy again. Had blown some bloke's head off, you'd think that Perkins would want to talk about that not his lover or a bloody soap opera. He had taken the initiative and rung DI Mears on his mobile to ask if he still wanted them to go to London or would he need them to help with the latest killing. Mears had told him that what they were doing was vital to the case and to get a shift on. At least Perkins had taken charge of the paperwork, one thing less for him to think about. Not that there was a lot of it, just two duplicate lists of names and addresses to check out. One for the Met officers and one for them. Perkins was saying something about his fantastic sex life and how he was going to miss getting his leg over but Atkins was, mercifully, able to screen it out and concentrate on guiding the pool car through the ever increasing stream of traffic that clogged the motorway leading into the capital city.

*****

"What have we got so far Jimmy?" Miller asked in a weary tone as he looked up from his desk.

"Just what we needed guv, let's hope the bastard has left us something to go on this time. The deceased is Damian Taylor, a nasty piece of work if ever there was one. Fresh out of the nick after doing two years for mugging a pensioner. According to the neighbours he was a royal pain in the arse and they're glad to see the back of him. It appears that the Vigilante blew his head off with a shotgun that he poked through the open car window. Death would have been instantaneous. Taylors blood and brains are decorating the inside of the car, never seen anything like it, you can't see through the windscreen, it looks as though it's been painted black. His blood must have come up like a bloody fountain. One thing is certain, whoever did this must have got blood on his clothes. The usual note was left on Taylor's lap. It was saturated in blood and has had to go to forensics, but as far as I could tell it was the usual self-justifying stuff."

"What about door to door, anything there."

"The near neighbours all say they heard the shot but they thought it was Taylor making more row than usual. Fireworks or whatever. No-one went to their window to see what was going on, not wanting Taylor to see them at the curtains and kick off. I'm not altogether sure that if they had seen something that they would tell us anyway. By and large they're delighted that the Vigilante has rid them of a very dangerous and thoroughly nasty thug, I'm told that more than one person said they'd like to shake the Vigilante's hand."

"Not very promising then. No question about the cause of death or identification of the body?"

"None. There's little left of his head, so no question of facial identification but he was driving Damian Taylor's car and was parked outside Damian Taylors house. We'll get his father to look at the body later, there might be a tattoo or a scar that he'll recognise. Dental records won't help, there are no teeth to look at, so if the father can't make a definite identification it will be down to DNA."

"So we have, if Dr Patterson is correct, an elderly man wandering the streets at midnight. He's armed with a shotgun and leaves the scene with blood on his clothes. Someone must have seen something, it's beyond belief that he could walk about the town, even after dark like that and not be seen by someone."

"I've got a team on it already guv. We're checking every CCTV camera in the area and also in the town centre. Traffic have also been asked to check their cameras for anything that might be useful. We've got people in white suits doing a fingertip search of the street and gardens around the Taylor house. I'm not very optimistic that we'll come up with anything apart from crisp packets and empty take-away boxes but it has to be done. I've also detailed a team to contact every laundrette and dry cleaning establishment in the town asking them to contact us if anyone shows up with blood stained clothing."

"OK then Jimmy, one question. If Taylor has only just got out of chokey how did the Vigilante come to know about him?"

"You think he's got to be local or have contacts in the area?"

"That would seem reasonable to me."

"Have you got a street map of the area Guv?"

"Put the kettle on Jimmy while I sort one out. I think chummy has just made his first big mistake."

*****

Mr Spurgeon had drunk his whisky and scrubbed himself mercilessly in the bath. His skin was bright pink from the combination of the very hot water and the vigorous use of a loofah as he slipped on his blue striped Winceyette pyjamas. As hard as he had scrubbed he still felt contaminated with that awful man's body fluids. He knew what went on in prison, the same vile activities that Mick Jones had enjoyed and he was worried that the blood might give him AIDS or some other horrible sexually transmitted disease.

The adrenaline rush that had accompanied the execution had receded and left him feeling very tired. He had a lot to think about but he couldn't stay awake another minute. He closed his eyes and fell into a deep untroubled sleep.

In the morning he had slept late and it had taken all his considerable willpower to drag himself from under the blankets. His head throbbed and he could tell his headache would be a bad one and last all day. He performed his ablutions then went downstairs to be greeted by a disgruntled Lady Mae. He petted and fussed her, almost losing his balance as he squeezed the cat food from the pouch into the bowl on the tiled floor. He sat down until his head stopped swimming then made himself a cup of tea. He didn't fancy breakfast although he knew it was the most important meal of the day. His mother had said that so many times as she urged him to eat breakfast cereal and toast before he went to school. She had been gone these many years but he still missed her wise advice. His father too had been mentor and guide, always ready with a few words that would cut to the heart of the matter with the skill of a surgeon's scalpel. He shook his head, this wouldn't do at all, he had no time to sit going over the past What was it the fellow had said about the past being a foreign country? If it was, it was a pleasant place to visit but he didn't want to live there. What he had to do now was to go and have a look at his car in the daylight.

*****

Atkins looked around the interview room. Bare painted walls and a table and chairs that were bolted to the floor. He could have been back in the nick in Clingford Norton instead of sitting in a London police station waiting for his colleagues from the Met to join them. He was feeling cheesed off already. Perkins was still chuntering on about bugger all and the Met men were half an hour late for their appointed rendezvous. Atkins wanted to get on with things, he had been noticed by Miller and wanted to use this opportunity to impress the gaffer with his energy and efficiency and he couldn't do that while he was twiddling his thumbs waiting for the Met to show up.

He had just decided he had had enough and would simply leave half of the printed out list with the desk Sargent with a note explaining what was required when the door swung open and two men breezed into the room.

"Apologies for lateness gentlemen, but this is the Met and something came up. I'm DS Braithwaite and this is DC Willis."

Atkins took an instant dislike to the brash detective but stifled his animosity and introduced himself and Perkins. The four men sat around the table while Atkins explained what needed to be done and gave a brief outline of the Vigilante case. He ended by saying, "So this man has killed six, no seven people in the past few weeks," He corrected himself. "His latest was last night and he will definitely kill again unless we can stop him. This play house is the lead that could result in his arrest, so you see how important it is. We are very grateful for your help and would appreciate it if these checks could be done as quickly as possible."

Braithwaite grinned insincerely at him. "You can rely on the Met. We'll do everything we can to make your visit to us as short as possible. I think it would help if we organised your list into geographical areas so that we don't have to drive from one side of the city to the other only to finish up a couple of streets from where we started. How about giving us the list, we can pick out half a dozen addresses that are not too far from the nick that you boys can chase up. In the mean-time Willis and I will check the remaining addresses against a street plan and organise them into a usable document that we can work with tomorrow."

"That sounds good to me," Atkins commented, "That will save a lot of time in the long run."

"I'll show you to the canteen and you can grab something to eat while we sort out a few addresses for you, you might not get another chance today."

"That's very decent of you, I'd be glad to get outside a bacon sandwich and a cup of tea."

Braithwaite showed them to the canteen and told them to stay where they were until he returned with the short list. Atkins and Perkins collected tea and bacon sandwiches and found an unoccupied table in a corner of the large canteen. Atkins bit into his sandwich and made a soft noise of appreciation before saying, "You didn't say a word downstairs, come over all shy with the big city coppers did you?"

"No. I took one look at Braithwaite and his pet gorilla and decided I would trust them as far as I could throw them. Braithwaite is a smarmy bastard and I reckon he'll bear watching. If there's any kudos attached to this operation he'll try to nick them for the greater glory of the Met but mostly for himself."

Atkins was surprised at this display of acuity, perhaps Perkins wasn't as daft as he had thought. He'd formed a similar impression himself but had hoped his judgement was awry. With Perkins backing up his gut instinct, he was now convinced he had been right. He couldn't trust the Met boys an inch. That was all he needed, having been entrusted with a vital task by Miller he wanted to concentrate on the job in hand not continuously watch his back.

As a good friend had once told him, we're all walking a tightrope and the last thing you need is some silly bugger jumping up and down on the other end of the rope.

It was a good hour before Willis returned with a list of six names and addresses. "DS Braithwaite asked me to deliver this, he's continuing to work on the big spread sheet. He wants us to meet up again at eight in the morning to compare notes if that's OK with you guys."

Atkins readily agreed and made a swift exit with Perkins following close behind. In fact, Braithwaite was standing in a small room outside the canteen waiting for the provincial policemen to depart. As soon as they had passed the door he joined Willis in the canteen.

"Go alright?"

"Like clockwork, they were out of here like a rat up a drainpipe and we won't see them until eight in the morning."

"Excellent. I fancy an all day breakfast, how about you?"

"Why not Dave, sorting that spreadsheet should only take an hour, so we have plenty of time."

Chapter 24

Mr Spurgeon gazed at his blood splattered car with disbelief and revulsion. It looked so much worse now that it was properly illuminated. He had had to close the garage door to prevent the car being observed by anyone using the other garages in the small block, but the artificial light was enough to show that he had a hard task on his hands. He had taken the time to bag up the clothes he had been wearing the previous night and had dumped the sack in a corner of the garage when he arrived. He had to get rid of them, that was a high priority, and had considered burning them, but he knew a bonfire would attract the attention of his neighbours. With the execution having taken place so close to his home he could ill afford to draw attention to himself by doing something out of character. A small bonfire to get rid of a few weeds would have passed without notice but burning clothes would have had one of his neighbours looking down from a bedroom window to see what he was up to. He also knew that the police forensics people would almost certainly find something in the ashes if they looked, a button or zip or fragment of cloth perhaps. That's what happened on CSI Miami and other cop shows on television anyway, besides he was risk averse. Unnecessary risk averse at any rate. The clothes would have to remain in the bin bag for now. He needed to get rid of them but not as urgently as he needed to put his car back into good order. How he would dispose of the soiled garments he didn't know but he would give that little problem some thought when he had a few moments and his head wasn't aching quite so much.

The main problem though was the car, the clothes presented a much more straightforward problem. He washed his vehicle religiously every Sunday morning and if he changed his routine someone might notice. He couldn't afford to draw attention to himself, he needed, in modern parlance, to remain under the radar. He couldn't chance anyone seeing him cleaning the car so had to clean it inside the garage. That would be difficult. It was a small car but the garage was also small and he would have a tight squeeze wiping down the outside of the vehicle. Fortunately, there was no blood that he could see on the nearside of the car, it was mainly the roof and driver's side that had been affected. He would have to wipe the car down, removing all the visible blood then give it a proper wash on Sunday as usual. After he had wiped down the outside he would tackle the inside. It was lucky that the seats were leatherette and would be easy to clean. The carpets too were removable and he could take them home and do a proper job if he couldn't get the blood out in the garage. That was all possible but his biggest concern was the roof lining. There was a long streak of spattered blood above the driver's seat that was going to challenge his cleaning skills and the assertions of the TV advertisements that claimed their bottles of whatever it was could remove almost any stain.

Mr Spurgeon kept a supply of cleaning products on a shelf at the rear of the garage and had brought a bottle of carpet cleaner with him from the house. It was an old brand that had been under the sink for quite a while and he found himself humming the advertising jingle that had been a constant presence on commercial television when he was younger. "One thousand and one cleans a big big carpet for less than half a crown." He smiled to himself, you had to be knocking on a bit to have even heard of half a crown. These kids with their decimal coinage didn't know what proper money was and would never experience the pleasure that the feel of a good solid coin in a small hot hand engendered. The new coins were like Micky Mouse money and he was surprised that Her Majesty had permitted their introduction. His headache was slowly disappearing and, taking that as a sign to get cracking, Mr Spurgeon took his bucket to the standpipe the owners of the garages had installed for the use of their tenants, carefully closing the up and over door when he left and when he returned to the garage.

*****

Atkins was driving with Perkins sitting beside him clutching the list. He'd had to tell Perkins to pipe down so that he could concentrate on listening to the sat nav and his verbose colleague was sulking. Atkins didn't care. He wasn't used to driving in such heavy traffic and needed to give his full attention to guiding the car. A glance at the sat nav would indicate which turning to take but the voice of the sat nav told him which lane to get into. That was really helpful when the cars ahead obscured any road markings. Tomorrow Perkins could drive, then he'd see how tricky driving in London was for a stranger to the city. This trip wasn't going well, a late start on the first day and a pair of chancers from the Met to work with was far from ideal, still it was early days and perhaps it would all come good in the end.

*****

"They've taken Taylor's car to that warehouse we used for storing what was left of Darren Bentley's motor. Do you want to come and have a look at it?" Jimmy Mears asked Miller.

As you didn't bother to come and see it at the scene Miller thought, conscious that Jimmy might think he had let him and the team down by not visiting the crime scene. "Why not. I'm sorry I couldn't get up there this morning to see it in situ but I was closeted with Wildchild and the Assistant Chief Constable. If I look a bit shell-shocked it's because I am. The bastards are going to hang me out to dry if I don't get this case closed pronto. Typical bean counters, no idea of what it's like to handle a multiple murder case. They've spent their careers counting bloody paperclips and obstructing proper bobbies, their biggest collar was probably nicking an old lady for shoplifting a tin of corned beef from Tesco. One minute it's please stay on Dusty, we can't afford to lose you Dusty, the next it's implied threats that I might have to go under a cloud before the case is over unless I get it sorted. What am I supposed to do? Wave a bloody magic wand. Bastards!"

Mears had not been offered coffee and a biscuit when he had entered Miller's office, which demonstrated more than mere words, how shaken and angry the older man was after his interview with the top brass. As they walked down the stairs Mears expressed his contempt for their senior officers and they were soon laughing as each tried to outdo the other with far-fetched comments about the ACC's sexual habits and Wildchild's brown nosing incompetence. "He likes to blow winos while he's wearing stockings and suspenders," "He couldn't find his own arse with both hands and a torch," were two of the milder examples of the policemen's wit.

They entered the overflow storage warehouse to see that a large polythene tent had been erected to one side to act as a temporary sterile area. They could see movements through the opaque material and called out, "Anyone home? It's Miller and Mears."

"Put on a suit, gloves and booties and come and join the party." A cheerful voice boomed out. "You'll see the stuff in a box near the entrance."

Mears had to help Miller to into his suit as his large stomach distorted the paper suit so much that the zip seized up, but before too long the detectives had entered the tent and were greeted by the pathologist.

"Glad you stopped by, I was about to ring you with a preliminary report but now you'll be able to see for yourselves."

The two detectives peered through the open car doors. The interior looked as if it had been sprayed with black paint where virtually the entire blood supply of Damian Taylor had spurted from his severed jugular vein before drying on the seats, carpet and roof lining of the car. The coppery smell of blood mixed with the strong odour of excrement and urine hung in the air and despite his extensive experience in dealing with the aftermath of violence Miller was glad to withdraw his head from the vehicle and draw in some slightly fresher air.

"What have you got George?"

"It's exactly what it appears to be. The guy had his head blown off with a shotgun fired at close range. What I can tell you is that either the shooter just stuck the gun through the window and hoped he'd hit the target, or he was bending at the knees to see into the car or, and this seems to be the most likely scenario, the shooter was in a car that drew up next to Taylor's and he fired through both windows. If he was in a car he was either sitting in the passenger seat and fired across the body of his driver because a shot gun would be very difficult to use from the driving seat or he used a sawn off weapon."

"So what you're saying is, the Vigilante was in a car and fired a sawn off shotgun?"

"If you insist. That is certainly the most likely situation."

"Any idea of what sort of shotgun."

"My best guess would be a twelve bore but that really is only a guess at this stage. Does it really matter? If you find someone with a sawn off shotgun in Clingford Norton, I'd lay odds you've got your man."

"Thanks George, anything else of interest?"

"A small bag of grass in the glove box that I'd say was for personal use and what looks to be the proceeds of a burglary in the boot. It's all been bagged up but you can take a look if you like. It's small time stuff, a few oddments of jewellery, a nice carriage clock and a couple of porcelain figurines that might be worth a couple of bob."

"We'll pass for now George. I'll get one of the lads at the station to look through a list of stolen property and see what turns up. It shouldn't take long, the thieving bugger who was driving this car had only been out of the nick a very short time."

Mears had been listening with great interest but now joined in the conversation. "I don't suppose the angle of the shot can tell you the height of the car window it was fired from?"

"I'm afraid not Jimmy, these buggers on the telly with their laser lights and bits of string exist in a world of fantasy as far as this force is concerned. I can see where you're coming from, identify the height and if you can't identify the model you can at least reduce the number of suspect vehicles. All I can say is that I'm one hundred percent certain that it was both barrels and not just one. I'd say your best bet is CCTV and eyewitnesses that actually saw the vehicle."

*****

Mr Spurgeon had washed down the bodywork of the Morris Minor as best he could. He wasn't entirely satisfied but he thought he had done a good enough job to pass all but the closest inspection. On Sunday he would wash it properly. It was the interior that was the problem. The mats had come up well and the seats had presented no difficulty at all, a simple wipe with a damp cloth moistened with kitchen spray had easily done the job, the same with the dashboard and steering wheel. It was the roof lining that was the problem. The more he tried to rub the stain away the further it spread. He had even visited the corner shop to purchase an aerosol of carpet stain remover when his one thousand and one had failed him, but even the modern equivalent had proved ineffective. The only thing left was to make a paste out of the stain removing powder that you put in the washing machine and apply it to the roof lining. Leave it overnight and hope for the best. He had learned one lesson from his latest exploit. If he used the shot gun in that way again he would cover the seats in polythene and wear a pair of those disposable overalls that they sold in DIY stores.

*****

Perkins shook hands with the man at the door and returned to the car where Atkins was waiting. "Time's getting on and it's been a long day. I know there's still two more visits to do but I think we should call it a day and get back to the digs. A reasonably early night and we'll be as fresh as a daisy in the morning."

It was early evening and the sun was still bright in the sky. "I could do with a pint in a beer garden. I don't fancy being shut up inside on such a nice evening. What do you say, I could call Mears while we sup a nice refreshing beer?" Atkins said.

"Sounds like a plan, but do they have beer gardens in London?"

"They must do, or maybe a roof garden, anyway let's give it a go."

Perkins spotted a suitable pub shortly before they arrived back at their digs and Atkins pulled into the tiny carpark, taking the last available space. He was getting on a bit better with Perkins now, having come to realise that his constant inane chatter had been due to nerves. Now that they were actually doing the job he had settled down and was working well. He couldn't quite forget though that this man was a fan of Eastenders and that was close to unforgivable as far as Atkins was concerned. They walked into a bar that seemed strangely dark after the bright sunshine. An agreeable barman passed the time of day about the weather as he pulled their pints and Perkins paid what seemed to him to be an astronomical price for a couple of beers but was quite reasonable for London. They strolled out of the bar and found a free picnic table in a corner of the sadly neglected garden. Atkins took a pull of his pint and looked around. No-one was within earshot so he called DI Mears on his mobile, he watched the phone hunting for a signal for a few moments before he gained a connection. Must be in a dead spot he thought as a voice said "Mears."

"It's Atkins sir, is this a good time to report in."

"I don't think they'll ever be a good time in the foreseeable future. I'm up to my armpits in corpses, at least that's what it seems like."

"How is the investigation going sir?" Atkins asked politely.

"One dead bastard and on-one arrested sums it up nicely. Your turn."

Atkins brought him up to date with what had been achieved and made sure that he included his views on the two Met officers who were supposed to be helping. Mears advised him not to take any bullshit, wished him luck and rang off.

'How did it go?" Perkins asked when he put his mobile away. "I could only hear your side."

"DI Mears sounds all in but he said we were doing OK but not to take any bullshit from the Met."

"Sounds fair enough. Let's get this beer down us and go hunting for some grub, I'm starving."

*****

Atkins was just slipping under the duvet when his mobile rang. He snatched it up from the bedside cabinet thinking it could be Mears.

"Atkins." He rapped.

"Braithwaite here. Got a bit of a problem. Been called to a meeting with the Commander so we won't be able to meet you until noon."

Atkins could here loud music and the clink of glasses in the background. Braithwaite was slurring his words. He was obviously as drunk as a skunk. "That's not good enough." He started to say but was cut short when Braithwaite said, "Tough titty," and ended the call.

The young constable was speechless with rage at the drunken arrogance of the man. How dare he be so obstructive, and to such an important case. Well, DI Mears had said not to take any bullshit and by God he wouldn't. When he saw Braithwaite he would read him the riot act about inter-force co-operation.

He pulled his trousers on and went to the room that Perkins occupied just down the corridor. He tapped lightly on the door and called softly, "Perkins, you awake?"

A sleepy voice replied, "Yeah, what is it."

"There's been a change of plan. You can set your alarm an hour later than we planned, we're going to pick up the two left over from today before we go to the station."

"Cheers mate, thanks for letting me know."

Atkins returned to his room and lay down but sleep was a long time coming. He spent the time waiting for the sandman to arrive plotting DS Braithwaite's downfall.

The following morning Atkins and Perkins reported into the police station and were once more ushered into an interview room to await the arrival of Braithwaite and Willis. Once more they were kept waiting and when the two Met officers eventually appeared Atkins was seething with anger.

"Morning gents ready to go to work?" Braithwaite said jauntily.

"We have been ready for the past forty-five minutes and I have had enough of this bullshit. Let's get this clear, you are assisting us not the other way around and when we agree to meet at a certain time I expect you to be here. This is a multiple murder inquiry and I will not put up with your bloody stupid games." Atkins had risen from his chair and his face was a few scant inches from Braithwaite's as he spat the words.

"Now listen Constable."

"Don't you bloody Constable me *Sargent*," Atkins interrupted emphasising the rank, "I don't know how you do things in the Met but we hicks from the sticks are a damn sight more professional than you lot if this is how you carry on. We've got probationers that would be more efficient than you two. Pin back your ears and listen. You are working for us because my DCS is chums with your DCS, they go back to Hendon and they're both in the funny handshake brigade. One word from me and you'll be taken off this case and replaced by a professional. I'm not saying you'd end up on traffic duty but it wouldn't do your career opportunities a lot of good would it?"

Braithwaite breathed out slowly, obviously trying to control his temper. He sat down and said through clenched teeth, "I'm going to forget what you just said. Let's just get on with it, but when you look at those addresses you might find you lot are not as perfect as you make out."

Atkins ignored the jibe and controlled his urge to smile in triumph, it would do no good to rub salt in the wound. He knew he had won and more importantly, so did Braithwaite.

Willis who had remained silent throughout the short exchange produced some folded sheets of paper and passed a reorganised list to each of the men. All four men sat perusing the list when Atkins gave a shout that would have awakened the dead. "Jesus Christ all bloody mighty we've got the bastard."

Shrugging off questions from the others he dived into his pocket for his mobile phone and called Mears.

"Mears."

"Atkins sir. I think we've found him."

There was a stunned silence as the portentous words sank into the DI's overtired brain. He snapped alert. "Tell me." He commanded.

"There's an address here that's in Clingford Norton. The bank just grouped the addresses by where the sale was made not by where the card owners live. No-one at the station spotted that a local address was included with the London one's and it just slipped through the net. The Met boys were sorting the list into usable order yesterday so this is the first I have seen the list or it would have been spotted sooner. There's more sir. The name of the purchaser is Horace Spurgeon and I interviewed him in connection with Darren Bentley. He's an old chap with a definite grudge against the bank. It's got to be him." Atkins read out Mr Spurgeon's address.

"Good work son, thank the Met for their help and report back to the station."

"Yes sir."

Atkins ended the call and looked up into the eyes of three very surprised men. "Come on Perkins we're wanted back home." He turned to Braithwaite, "My boss says thank you for your help, personally I wouldn't have bothered." With that, he swept out of the station, DC Perkins following in his wake, filled with awe at his partner's bellicose attitude.

Chapter 25

Miller's office door was thrown open unceremoniously and a breathless Mears gasped, "Come on Guv, we're going to arrest the Vigilante. No time to explain now, I'll tell you in the car."

Miller's adrenaline had gone through the roof at the news and he raced down the stairs in hot pursuit of his junior colleague. He hadn't moved as fast as this for years but he didn't slow down until he reached the squad car that was parked in front of the station with its engine running and blue lights flashing. He threw himself in the backseat next to Mears and between gasps for precious oxygen said, "What the devil's happened?"

"Young Atkins has come up with the goods." Mears went on to explain the situation while Miller nodded, smiled and cursed at various points in the story.

"So we've had this information for a while but no-one cottoned on."

"A few days, that's all. No-one looked at the London addresses, we were concentrating on this area as being the most likely first."

"We only believe that this Spurgeon character is our man. There may be an explanation as to why he bought a play house in London. Perhaps he's got Grandchildren down there."

"He was also one of the first people questioned about Darren Bentley but we discounted him as being too old at the time. That is a coincidence too far. I think this is it."

"If it is, he is armed. What about the armed response unit, I don't fancy starting my retirement with by head blown off like Taylor?"

"They're on their way and will have caught up with us by the time we get there."

"How do you want to play it?"

"He has only ever attacked people that he thought were wrongdoers in one way or another. I know he has a slate loose but I don't think he'll cause us any trouble. I think we should just knock on his door and ask if we can come in, he's not likely to answer the door clutching a sawn off shotgun. If it goes pear shaped the guys with the guns will be ready to their stuff but I brought them as a reserve and I sincerely hope that we won't need them."

"This is my last case Jimmy, I'm about to retire. In all the American cop films the guy who's about to retire always gets killed in the final reel. Miraculously they always find the strength to make a pretty little speech before they join the choir invisible but believe me you wouldn't want to hear what I would say to you in those circumstances. You are going to be taking over from me so we'll do it your way, but if I get killed I'll never forgive to you."

*****

Mr Spurgeon was in the sitting room listening to Ed Reardon's Week on the wireless. It was one of the few modern comedies that he cared for. Reardon reminded him in some ways of Tony Hancock, constantly fighting a losing battle with life in general and the powers that be in particular. He wasn't an especially nice person and was certainly dishonest but he always made Mr Spurgeon laugh at the scrapes he got into. Lady Mae was on his lap and his head was beginning to nod as he stroked her. His head had begun to ache again and he was tired. He had a large purple bruise on his chest where the shotgun's recoil had made violent contact with him and he worried that he might have cracked a rib. Old bones don't respond well to being subjected to hard blows with a blunt instrument. A late night and some hard work on the Morris had taken their toll and he thought he would have an afternoon nap and definitely an early night.

A ring at the doorbell roused him and he grumbled to himself as he went to open the door. Two chaps who vaguely resembled Laurel and Hardy stood looking at him. Oh Lord, Jehovah's Witnesses. I'll tell them I'm more of a Jehovah's bystander he thought with a rare flash of humour.

"Mr Spurgeon? Mr Horace Spurgeon? I am Detective Inspector Mears and this in my colleague Detective Chief Inspector Miller, may we come in?"

Mr Spurgeon was badly shocked by the unexpected arrival of the police but he managed to disguise his concern with a tight smile. "By all means gentlemen, I'm always happy to help the police, come in and welcome."

Miller signalled to the two firearms officers stationed at either side of the door to stand down as he and Mears entered the house and followed the old man through into his sitting room. Lady Mae was seated in Mr Spurgeon's chair and he picked her up and invited the policemen to sit down. He sat with his cat on his lap and smiled as he said, "Now what can I do for you?"

"Just a few routine questions Mr Spurgeon," Miller paused for a long moment, then continued, "You could start by telling us why you purchased a Klassic Toddler Tent in London a short time ago."

Oh dear, oh dear thought Mr Spurgeon, it looks as if the game is up. His mind went blank, he couldn't think of a single reason why he would have purchased the play house, let alone why it wasn't still in his possession. He sat silently thinking, all they had to do was search the house and garage and it was all over. The shotgun and bloodstained clothes would give him away instantly and traces of Darren Taylor were still undoubtedly all over the Morris. They only had to look in his garage and they would find enough evidence to end his crusade. He didn't mind too much, he was tired and now the prospect of ending his work as the Vigilante had arrived he found it surprisingly welcome. Perhaps someone else would pick up his fallen sword of justice and take up the battle? His fight against the forces of darkness was certainly over now. He had standards and it wouldn't be gentlemanly to lie to the police

His head had dropped a little when he had heard the policeman's words but now he raised it again to look DCI Miller straight in the eye. "If you promise to take care of my cat, her name is Lady Mae by the way and she likes a little chicken or tinned salmon, sometimes pouched cat food for a change but not tinned or dried stuff, I'll tell you everything you want to know."

Epilogue

Dusty Miller was staring at his float as it stubbornly refused to move. He had been sitting on the riverbank for more than two hours and had yet to have a bite. Not even a nibble, he reflected unhappily as he jerked his line in a pointless attempt to raise interest in a passing fish. He carefully placed his rod on the rest he had inserted into the bank and reached for his flask of coffee.

"Just like old times Guv, I bet you've got some biscuits to go with that coffee."

He looked up to see his old partner in crime smiling down at him. "Hello Jimmy, it's good to see you. I dare say that this flask will stretch to two, and I might even spare you a biscuit if you tell me how you found me out here in the wilderness."

Not quite the wilderness thought Mears, the main road was only fifty yards away and there was a large layby where fishermen would leave their vehicles while they drowned a few worms. "I'm a detective Guv if you remember, finding people is my business. Besides I rang your home and Elsie told me exactly where you would be."

"Pull up my tackle box and sit down. I'll sort out the coffee while you tell me why a newly made up DCI is pursuing an innocent old fellow who is trying to enjoy his retirement, and for the last time don't call me Guv, I'm a civilian now, thank God."

Mears sat down, the tackle box was a little low and his knees stuck up a little too much for comfort. It was better than sitting on the grass but not as good as sitting in a comfortable folding chair like his erstwhile boss. He waited until Miller had poured two cups of coffee and offered him a ginger nut before he spoke again.

"It was quiet at the station so I thought I'd play truant for a few minutes and bring you up to speed with how things are going."

"Great stuff. Make my day and tell me that Wildchild has caught the clap."

"Nothing as good as that, but mostly positive."

"Pity he's not, HIV for preference. Go on then, I'm all ears."

"Cope tells me that the paedophile case has been put to bed. The Crown Prosecution Service are going for the maximum sentence they can get for Cadbury and Smedley, he was the chap from Winchester if you remember Guv. The Yanks have tied up their end and our continental neighbours have finally got their fingers out, so all looks set fair for some very nasty people to be off the streets for a good long time. Morrison has confessed to bribing Janet Tomlinson but only after a forensic accountant went through his books, so Cope's side of the Vigilante case is done with until the actual trials take place and that could be months yet."

"That is good news and it gladdens my old heart to hear it but I suspect that is not why you have come to see me." Miller looked at Mears expectantly.

"Haven't lost your nose for the truth have you Guv."

"I can still smell a rat, when I need to, mind you I've only been retired a few weeks so I haven't quite gone senile."

"Here's something else that will make you smile. With my promotion confirmed there was a vacancy for a new DS. Atkins is now acting Detective Sargent Atkins and reports directly to me. He is as pleased as a dog with two dicks."

"Now that really does please me. He did very well and I thought he had the potential to come good. When Perkins told me how he had ripped into that Met bloke for pissing him about I knew he was the genuine article. Tell him well done from me when you see him."

"Just one more thing Guv. You won't be called on to give evidence against Horace Spurgeon."

"That's good, so you'll be the chief witness for the prosecution then."

"No Guv, Horace Surgeon died in his cell during the night so there won't be a trial. It's too early to be certain of the cause of death but the doctor reckons it was some sort of stroke. Apparently he'd been complaining about headaches so maybe a brain tumour or something. Definitely natural causes anyway."

"I don't know if I'm glad or sorry. One side of me wanted to see him punished for what he did, the other thinks that he was a crazy old man who needed to be looked after in a secure hospital. There was something about his old fashioned view of the world that chimed with me. I suppose that's a sign that I'm getting on in years myself."

"I've been wondering if his head problem might have had some influence over his actions. You know, changed his personality, after all he waited until he was in his seventies before he started knocking people off."

"Probably not, there's too many excuses made by the sandals and macramé handbag brigade for just being bad, but we'll never know now, so he'll go down in the history books as a psychopath alongside Sutcliffe and other assorted nutters. Still, whether he was ill or just bad, the main thing is we caught him and got him off the streets."

They sat in silence sipping the last cold drops of their coffee and nibbling at Miller's biscuits until Miller said, "I don't suppose the bloke who was in the caravan with Nigel Johnson has been identified?"

"Nothing there yet and after this length of time I doubt if we will ever know. Just a bit of trade in the wrong place at the wrong time."

After a moment or two, during which both men considered the sadness of someone who had lived a life that included no family or friends to miss him or mourn his passing. Mears broke their introspection by saying in an attempt to break the suddenly sombre mood, "How's the cat settling in?"

"Lady Mae is fine and Elsie loves her to bits. Says that at last she's got someone to talk to that actually listens to what she says. Spurgeon loved that cat and was far more concerned about what would happen to her than he was about his own fate. Anyway, Elsie had been going on about getting a dog for a while and I didn't fancy having to take a pooch out for walks in all weathers, let alone having to pick up its shit, so I thought the cat might keep her happy and save me the trouble of taking her to the RSPCA. Spurgeon was really grateful that she was going to a good home and thanked me with genuine appreciation."

Mears grinned, his boss didn't fool him for one moment. His tough exterior had always hidden a soft centre and this was just another example of his innate but well disguised kindness.

"He really was a strange character, one minute knocking people off left right and centre without a twinge of conscience and the next he's fretting about his pussycat maybe missing a meal." Mears mused.

"Bit of a split personality perhaps?"

"I don't know what a psychiatrist would make of him but he definitely had two sides to his nature. As far as we can find out he was the most law abiding character in Clingford Norton, wouldn't even drop a sweet wrapper on the pavement let alone commit cold blooded murder. How on earth do you weigh up a bloke like that?"

"I don't know Jimmy and it's too late to ask the man himself. The Vigilante is dead and the case is finally over.

THE END

Author's Note.

I hope you have enjoyed reading about Horace Spurgeon as much as I've enjoyed writing about him. When the time finally came for him to die I felt a strange sense of loss at his passing. If you did enjoy this story, I would be very grateful if you would post a review and tell your friends via facebook or some other modern means of communication. As a first time author your feedback might even encourage me to write a second story.

With grateful thanks that you managed to read this far, sincerely

David Nesbitt

Printed in Great Britain
by Amazon